I0670906

K. Trap Jones

The Sinner

BLOOD BOUND BOOKS

Copyright © 2012 by K. Trap Jones
All rights reserved

ISBN 978-0-9849782-1-2

This book is a work of fiction. Names, characters, business organizations, places, events and incidents either are the product of the author's imagination or are used fictitiously. Any resemblance to actual persons, living or dead, events or locales is entirely coincidental.

Artwork by Stacy Drum

Printed in the United States of America
First Edition

Visit us on the web at:
www.bloodboundbooks.net

For my wife Robyn and my three sons: Chase, Hunter and Ayden.
My whole world begins and ends with you.

preface

A lone farmer, chosen by God to test the boundaries of sin, is isolated in a darkened cave with only a quill, a candle and a stack of parchment paper. His burden is to awaken each day within predetermined encounters involving the seven deadly sins and their associated demons. At the end of each vision, the events will remain within the farmer's mind for a brief period in order for him to transcribe his thoughts. The following are his translated entries within their original narrative formatting.

I

isolation

As I lay dying in my own blood waiting for death to greet me,
  The punishment has ceased, but my wounds
  Serve as remembrance of the turmoil I have endured.

My life's liquid displays like art against the dirt grimed floor
  With small rivers of blood twisting into the black.
  It flows from me as if it is disgusted with my shattered body
  And no longer desires me as its owner.
  Each drip adds to the red current
  And carries me closer to my demise.

Fear of the unknown unites me with this quill.
  I do not know why I have been chosen,
  But this darkened cave filled with shadows is now my
home.
  My fingers are blistered from dragging them
  In the darkness across the rocky walls
  Searching for a path leading outward.
  My eyes no longer shed tears and
  Have become as dry as the dust consumed air.
  My aches from being huddled in this pit
  Reflect the length of my stay here.
  The dryness has murdered any moisture within my mouth.
  My tongue fails to provide my cracked lips with any such
relief.

I am deathly alone with my mind and
  He offers no care for my well being or mental state.

He is against me now; an enemy to my livelihood.
He portrays evilness in the forms of unexplainable sounds
And mysterious movements that lurk within the shadows.
All of which does not assist me with maintaining my sanity.

I do not know how long I have been here,
　Nor do I truly understand my surroundings.
　My last real thought is of my farmland
　And its peaceful memory comforts me.

A task has been presented before me.
　Do not ask me how I know this,
　As I would not be able to supply an answer.
　It is a feeling that is apparent within me,
　An unexplainable knowing of what is real.

I avoided this quill and paper while
　My mind plagued me with the realization of my situation.
　The valley of fear that I find myself in
　Is unforgiving and relentless in its pursuit
　To destroy the essence of what constructs me as a man.

The anger of my dwelling no longer brutalizes me
　So long as I transcribe my thoughts.
　Although, the unrelenting onslaught of pain
　Remains a constant aftermath.

My will is ruined from the bleeding walls I witness.
　My mind is numb from the howling screams I hear.
　My heart is weak from the sheer agony that devours the air.

I am broken; I am no longer whole.
　My captor is well versed in the art of torture
　And has made it known that I face
　Mind altering consequences for not using the tools
provided.
　I cling to this quill as it is the only item I can personify with.
　It has instantly become my friend.

The amount of fear that tears at me
    Is as unavoidable as the pure darkness of this cave.
    It is unyielding and stalks me even when I close my eyes.
    I dare not exit the safe radius of the candle and the
    Protection it provides me as I cannot justify
    The sources of sound residing across the threshold of light.

The flame of the candle flickers yet there is no source of wind.
    The wick burns into the wax, but no excess drips.
    The fire has no care in the world;
    No predictable pattern of movement.
    It dances and is quite soothing to watch.

Although I know that I am physically alone within these
confines,
    My mind observes unexplainable movements
    That fault my rational judgment.
    Shadows. Shadows that move as if alive.
    I crouch closer within the bright circle
    As I believe that they are watching me.

I feel that my evil audience would strike at me if given the
chance.
    I try not to think about my visitors and
    Offer them no traditional welcome to my prison,
    But ignorance has never been a strong trait for me.
    They do not pester me; instead they merely observe.

If I stand and walk in their direction,
    They blend deeper into the darkness
    And only make themselves known
    When I do not share my thoughts.
    I choose not to acknowledge them as to frighten them away.
    Regardless of what they are and their purpose,
    It is quite refreshing to have some companionship.
    From my observation, I have determined
    Eight distinct shadows of various sizes.

Some are more curious and daring than others.
Although I have yet to view any of the forms
Outside of their shadowy boundary,
Some do lurk closer to me than others.

I do not fear them.
They have done nothing for me to be afraid of.
I am, however, curious as to their intentions.
Often times the cave seems vacant,
But at certain times it becomes quite agitated.
Possibly due to my thoughts.
Perhaps they are sent here when God is displeased.
If that were true, silence would be that of acceptance.
I must break from my practice
As my wrist is not accustomed to long periods of writing.

Something wicked lives on the edge
Where the light bonds with the dark.
She thirsts for me to halt my thoughts.
I sense her presence now and smell her hatred for me.
She is my attacker; the one who reaps my spirit
And keeps me humbled and subdued.
Unlike my shadowy friends, she offers me no good will.
My scars and blood loss are evident enough of her strength.
Whereas the shadows embrace my thoughts,
She is content with tearing the flesh from my bones.
With that said, I will write to avoid any further turmoil.

I am neither a writer nor reader of literature,
Which makes me ponder as to why I have been chosen.
The whispers of the shadows speak of a life of sin, but
I cannot translate enough of the sounds to understand
That of which they speak.

I am not a religious person, but I know that God
Has presented me with a task.
How do I know this?
It is apparent within my mind and the thought

Is unavoidable and indestructible, for I have tried.

I often wonder when the task will begin as
    This cave does not provide me
    The same enjoyment that my farm does.
    One can only look upon shadows and dirt
    For so long before insanity forms.
    My patience is scratching at me.
    Questions presented by my mind are increasing,
    Forcing me to argue with myself to be quiet.
    Part of me believes that God has a plan;
    He will inform me when he is ready,
    But my stubborn side believes that he has forgotten about
me.

Have I wronged God in some way
    That his vengeance has been unleashed upon me?
    I do not remember ever wronging God.

    An aura of sin fills the cave now.
    Prophets speak of sin like it is an evil spirit,
    One that will condemn a man's soul.
    Some say it is a traveling nomad
    That corrupts a village by merely treading through it.

I for one do not believe in the tales
    Of a wave of sin flooding the land,
    But alas I have somehow found myself
    In a cave with no exit, so all is possible.
    To my knowledge, sin only lives within the tales.
    My mind informs me that I will live through sin,
    But that cannot be true if indeed sin does not exist.
    Prophets also speak of a choice when approached;
    Virtues that battle the evilness.
    If I am to live through sin within this cave,
    Then I will simply choose the virtue.
    Why would I do otherwise?

I imagine that God is patient,
 That he will get to my task eventually.
 Or has my task already begun?
 Is this cave sin? Is being alone a sin?
 I wish I knew exactly what sin was.
 If I did, my task would be easy to accomplish.

Of all the kings, shepherds and priests,
 Why choose a farmer with little religious experience?
 Would not a prophet who studies sin be more suitable?
 Now I am beginning to think that I am not capable.
 What if I fail God?
 Surely, failing God would be a punishment of death.

The flame of the candle is very mesmerizing.
 I often think that it does its rhythmic patterns
 In order to entrance me, but that would be absurd.

Fear once again draws me back to my friend the quill.
 When writing is the only activity allowable,
 It has altered from a hassle into a blessing
 And is quite enjoyable.
 I have also discovered that during my absence from thought that
 My shadowy visitors become restless.
 They shriek with displeasure and scratch upon the rock walls.
 The eerie sounds startled me as I slept.
 As of now, the sounds are decreasing,
 Calmness is once again filling the cave.

Small memories of my past reinvent themselves
 And graciously allow me to recollect.
 Most are of my farm.
 The images provide me with comfort, but
 Also add to the realization of my confinement.
 It offers me conflict with the sadness and
 Presents me with a dilemma of emotions.

Of all of the livestock that I tended to,
    The goats were my favorite.
    They were always kind and appreciative of my work.
    When I close my eyes, I seek out my farm and it calms me.
    It is my only defense against the isolation;
    The utter darkness of my situation.
    It gives me hope, promise and slows my rapid heart.
    Please do not take that which comforts me.
    Please allow me to keep a portion of my life.

I often consider that my mind has been drained
    In order to provide for approaching events.
    This is no more apparent than with the small act
    Of remembering my own name.
    I have tried, but my mind leads me down a path of
emptiness.
    Once there, it guides me back to present thoughts.
    I hold on to the hope that once my task is complete,
    That my mind will be filled again with my past memories.
    I cannot believe that my visions have been erased for
eternity.
    The mere thought is quite depressing.
    Not even God would be that cruel.

My visitors must be pleased with my ideas.
    They have all vanished from the cave.
    Part of me wants to stop writing
    In order to welcome them to return,
    But I know that they are not my main task.
    Being alone is a sign of acceptance from God.
    An empty cave is a desired acknowledgment.
    It supplies me with great determination,
    But the loneliness is a hardship that is very strong willed.

Constant leaving of my visitors weighs heavy on my heart.
    It drags me deeper into a trench of depression.
    My mind desires the reassurance that I am not alone.

To be deathly alone plays with my emotions.
It sends my thought patterns plunging into an abyss.
I suppose I could stop writing to fetch my friends back,
But that selfish act would displease God.
I thrive on the basis that I know they will return,
But that by itself does not make their departure any easier.
For now, it comforts me that this quill is my only true friend
As I know that it will never abandon me.
Holding it amongst my fingers
Grants me with a supremacy that is indescribable.

I am not a faithful person,
   But that is altering due to my present situation.
   I have seen and heard things within this cave
   That would challenge even the most stubborn being.

Does God exist?
   Something exists as something has entrapped me here.
   I have yet to see God, I doubt I ever will unless
   He has taken the shape of one of my shadowy friends.
   Even then I would not be able to comprehend him.

The cave is becoming restless again.
   The once static shadows are beginning to shift.
   I have displeased God with my previous thoughts
   And my enemy is returning.

She seems more agitated than any time before.
   The safety radius of the candle is slowly decreasing as
   She is overpowering the light.
   It provides no resistance to the dark and is weak in
comparison.
   Darkness has crept up my legs
   And I can no longer see them.
   Violent shrieking and scratching is becoming louder.
   She is here, she has come for me.

The shadows chew at my arm that holds the quill.

My thoughts are decreasing as I witness my hand
Being the only visible item left within the light.
I am sorry. I am sorry for my thoughts.
I have angered her, I have angered God.
I have . . .

II

The day began like any other day.
    There was not much excitement
    Waking up each morning along the city streets.
    My bed was wherever I laid my head the night before.

With the winter season approaching,
    It was beneficial to huddle in groups in order to keep warm.
    The chill in the air was devastating
    Especially in the already shadowed corridors.

I mainly survived by rummaging for food
    And additional clothing to keep warm.
    Many people of my kind
    Sold themselves as servants in order to avoid the streets.
    It was an option all of us had, but
    Some were too proud to venture into that area.

I was propositioned once.
    I accepted, as food was scarce.
    My master at the time fed and clothed me,
    But my personal pride would not allow it to last.

He would whip me violently
    When I disobeyed or showed signs of thinking.
    Instead of fighting back, I crept out of his abode
    The next night and returned to the streets where I was free.

I heard more drastic tales of servants losing their lives,

I considered myself fortunate that I was able to return.
I would rather live freely and poor than rich and confined.
The idea of serving another never appeased me,
But sometimes the starvation became overpowering.

It was not always like that.
    I did not always live on the streets.
    I once had a lovely cottage north of the city in the
mountains.
    It was my own piece of heaven.

The land was beautiful; abundant with vegetation and
    Wildlife that one could survive on for many years.
    That was my fortune, to live off of the land,
    Bother no one and have no one bother me in return.

For quite some time I was able to keep to myself
    Without any threat from the outside.
    There were many settlers on the mountains and
    We each honored personal space.
    There were no fences or boundaries to separate the land.
    It was common courtesy
    That one would not venture too far away
    From their own soil to farm or hunt.

We respected each other by neither expanding our own land
    Nor encroaching upon others.
    We had no laws or regulations
    Written like the cities in order to keep peace.
    We only needed the respect from others in order to survive.

All would change with the approaching battle
    Between the adjacent kingdoms.
    Two ruling kings hated each other so much that they both
    Went on a rampage across the terrain.
    They desired to lay claim
    With their flags on as much land as they could.
    They competed with one another on

Who would control most of the region.

That power struggle reaped across the valleys and mountains,
    Destroying the lives of all in its path.
    The conflict was over territories and
    Never developed into full out warfare.

Occasionally there would be bloodshed
    When groups of guards and scouts
    Came across the same property.
    I believed that the surrounding land
    Was easier to capture than the opposing kingdom.
    Acquirement of massive land amounts
    Translated into more power
    When and if the kingdoms were to fully battle one another.

I was well secluded away in the mountains,
    Enough so that my property remained one of the last.
    I remember the thundering sound of the horses
    Galloping up my mountain path
    Like a black plague creeping across the white snow,
    Contaminating my land with every hoof.
    I merely stood and watched as they approached.
    With their tattered battle flag dancing in the wind,
    They rode upon their shadowed horses.
    Their solid black armor with spikes, chains and weapons
    Probably intimidated most, but I was not impressed.

My ego presented me with only anger
    Knowing that I was about to lose my livelihood.
    I was not going to offer my soul as well.
    The horses were strong in appearance; massive in stature.
    They panted heavily as their warm breath blended with the
cold.
    The travel up the mountainside proved tiresome for them.
    I had intentionally allowed the snowfall to conceal the path.

The atmosphere leading up to their encounter was serene.

The mountain was unusually peaceful and calm.
I knew my life was about to change for the worse.
I knew what they were here for;
I knew they needed to claim my land
To appease the appetite of their greedy king.
Knowing that in advance did not make the ritual any easier,
Instead it provided me with enough reasoning
To conjure up more resentment.

I remember inhaling the mountain air for one last time and
    Smiling as they rode up upon me.
    With each breath I took, the thundering hooves grew louder.
    They were now close enough that I could see the riders.
    Huge, burly men covered in war hardened black armor
    That was scraped and misshaped from previous battles.

As I stood there in my cloth tunic, I did not fear their armor.
    As I stood there armed with only a goblet of tea,
    I did not fear their weapons.
    If it was fear that they demanded,
    Then they would be deeply disappointed.

As they came within the boundaries of my land,
    I could tell the horses did not care for the journey.
    Their mortality was somewhat comforting
    In regards to their barbaric personas.

Their hooves sank deep into the snow and
    Kicked up large amounts as they galloped.
    I imagined them sinking through the ground,
    Unable to move as more snow piled upon them,
    Burying them all alive in a frozen coffin.

Instead, the group halted their movements as they neared me.
    Without hesitation or permission, the lead rider carrying the
flag
    Dismounted and approached me.
    He said a few scripted words and

Stabbed the staff deep within my soil, penetrating my heart.
I knew I was outnumbered, no match for even one of them,
But the insult of claiming my land
Cut me hard within my veins, splitting my emotions.

A frustration built up inside me like boiling lava.
It took the reins of my body and controlled my next actions.
Following my rage instead of my conscience,
I ripped the flag from my land and swung it towards him.

The wooden staff connected with his armored helmet,
Rotated it ever so slightly that he was unable to see out of it.
Unfortunately, my once great powerful frustration
Was not an everlasting experience.
As I stood there with flag in hand,
I watched him readjust his helmet
So that his darkened eyes were once again visible.
The state of silence that occurred at that precise moment
Was more from confusion on the part of the guards.
They were bewildered by a lone peasant in cloth returning
force.
Within moments each of them dismounted
From their horses to join their comrade.
I lowered their flag as a sign of peace,
But I had made my disloyalty well known.
They assaulted me with swiftness and intense brutality,
Of which I had never experienced before.

Blood poured from me and was captured by the snow
Which absorbed my spill and created a red puddle.
Between the beatings and their armored legs,
I witnessed one of them set my cottage ablaze.
No pain they were inflicting upon me
As I laid there on the ground would match the sight
Of my beloved home crumbling beneath the flames.
My eyes rotated upwards in time to see a large war boot
Descending upon my head.

Apparently I had insulted the guards
    So much that I was placed in prison
    Where the beatings would continue.
    As the war between the two kingdoms raged on,
    I was eventually released as they required the prison cells
    For their true enemies.

Although I was free, my situation was not for the better.
    I had no home and no place to go.
    Living on the streets turned out
    To be even more cruel than prison life.

I do not know how I had survived in the beginning.
    I learned quickly and kept to my own.
    I constantly wished I had my mountain cottage again;
    Even contemplated escaping the city,
    But the guards were on defense.
    No one was leaving the city gates.
    I was forced to stay.

I admired the night time; I felt that no one could see or judge
me.
    The day time offered a chance for the wealthy to condemn
me,
    But the dark shielded me from those disgusted expressions.
    I felt that I became alive under the moon, that I ruled the
city
    As the wealthy were tucked away in their houses.
    I was not alone in my feelings, as many of us came out at
night.
    We viewed the fall of the sun as a celebration of life.

On one such night while I walked the city streets,
    I was approached by a wealthy man
    Accompanied by two guards armed with mallets.
    The man accused me of stealing relics from his house.
    I denied his words and stated that I was no thief.

However, the guards wasted no time entrusting the man.
My words meant nothing in comparison.

I was struck by one of the guard's mallets
Across the right side of my face.
The heavy wood of the weapon
Forced me off balance and briefly blurred my vision.

I felt my brain tremble within my skull
And held my head to ease the pain.
The same frustration that I endured
When my land was taken from me conjured up in me again.

I lowered my hands from my head and
Welcomed the shift that occurred within my mind.
I was tired of the guards.
I was tired of the wealthy.
I was tired of the beatings.
I was just, tired.

From my weak kneeling state,
I sensed that the man was about to strike me
With the torch he was carrying.
He needed that power above me.
He needed to show his authority over me.
I allowed it as every strike that I received fed into my anger.

As he raised his torch high in the air
To prove his importance, he laughed.
His weapon of choice descended with weak power.
I grinned in response as the assault did nothing to me
But spark against my cloak.
My disrespectful manner for the beating
Sent the man into an uncontrollable rage,
His onslaught was nothing that I had not encountered
before.
His attacks were minor as I was able to stand while he hit
me.

I sensed his frustration with me.
He gestured to the guards to finish what he could not.

The heavy mallets swung and lowered me down back to the
ground.
    I tried to rise once again, but the guards were well skilled
    In the art of pain and punishment.
    Their weapons were well suited for the task,
    As the unforgiving wood shattered me like a weak branch.

There was no hope for me.
    I laid face down in the street
    With mallets raining down upon me.
    Each attack I absorbed sent me closer to death,
    But I was elated with my sentence.
    I became numb from the pain with my vision
    Fading against the night sky.

Between the armored boots of the guards I saw death in the
form
    Of a grey wolf creeping towards me.
    The pearly white fangs of the beast glistened
    With drooling saliva leaking from the snarled lips.
    It was here to claim my soul and end my suffering.
    I welcomed it wholeheartedly.

The beatings soon subsided and
    Were replaced with the heavy weight
    Of the guards lying upon me.
    The armor slumped down atop of me
    As if the guards fell asleep during their assault.

One by one the guards were lifted from me.
    I felt a hand grab my arm and lift me up.
    I was supported by another peasant
    Who told me that we had to leave.
    In a dazed state I looked for the wolf, but death had
vanished.

I awoke on the ground covered with a blanket.
    I was still sore from the confrontation with the guards,
    But felt much better.
    The place in which I resided
    Was an underground tunnel of sorts beneath the city.
    I could hear people on the streets directly above me.
    The tunnel was dark with the only light coming from the
cracks
    In the ceiling, which allowed moonlight to leak in.

The dwelling was very damp
    With a surplus of water dripping from every crevice.
    I do not know how long I had been there,
    But from the results of my wounds,
    It was long enough to allow me to partially heal.

A voice startled me and asked me how I was feeling.
    Seeing no one, I blindly responded that I was still sore.
    From the shadows a petite woman approached.
    She was strikingly beautiful in her appearance
    And instantly demanded all of my attention.

I thanked her for her hospitality and care that she had given
me.
    She said that I was near death when she happened upon me.
    I asked about the guards; she gave no answer.
    She was more curious as to how I felt emotionally
    Regarding what had occurred.

I responded that I felt anger and hatred
    For what they had done to me.
    She prompted me for more details,
    More specifics about what my thoughts were.

I tried to recollect, but I could not remember.
    She sensed my confusion and said it would come to me in
time.

Her words were comforting and allowed me to fall asleep.
I awoke some time later to the touch of my savior
Rubbing my head with a cool damp rag.
I had not woken up so peacefully since I lived within my
cottage.

I felt completely healed both physically and mentally.
I rose from the bed and stretched my once aching bones.
She asked me how my wounds were.
My response was that I felt wonderful
As if I had bathed in holy water.
She smiled and gestured for me
To follow her as she had something to show me.

I walked closely behind her
While she winded through a series of darkened tunnels.
She soon stopped in front of a lone door which blocked our
path.

I asked her where we were going; she offered no response.
Instead she opened the door and walked inside a circular
room.
That was well lit from large cracks in the ceiling.

In the middle of the area sat a man bound to a chair.
From the looks of him he had been there for quite some
time.
I did not recognize him
Due to his sagging head concealing his face.

My confusion halted me from saying anything.
My host strolled around the back of the chair
With a demeanor similar to a snake and
Graciously felt the man's hair as she circled him.

She asked me about my anger again,
I responded that I had none at the moment.
She smiled at me so seductively

That I momentarily lost myself in her.
She grabbed the man's hair and lifted up his head
To reveal the face of the wealthy man
Who accused me of being a thief.

My heart immediately began to siphon large amounts of blood.
    I felt my chest tighten.
    I involuntarily clinched my fist and
    Constricted both of my arms in revulsion.

My eyes were fixated on the man
    With such intent that they began to water.
    She asked me what I was feeling.
    I told her that I was experiencing rage combined with
anxiety.

She told me not to deny my feelings;
    Not to bury them inside anymore.
    My anger did not fluster long, as
    I began to descend down from my plateau of hatred.
    I asked her what she had done.
    She shrieked in a loud angry tone that pierced my ear
drums.
    The sound woke the man who began rambling
    As to where he was and why he was entrapped.

I ignored him and asked her who she was.
    She gracefully approached me and
    Said that her name was Amon.
    She added that she was here to set me free.

For some reason I had no choice
    But to believe every word that she said.
    She walked around me, dragging her hands across my
shoulders.
    When she neared my front, she caressed both of my hands,
    And placed two daggers in them.

The touch of the metal was soothing to my rough skin.
    The handles fit perfectly within my clutches.
    She was here to offer me vengeance and judgment.
    She leaned forward and whispered to fulfill my inner
thoughts.
    She wanted me to kill the man,
    I told her that I could not do such a thing.
    My comments pushed her away from me.
    She walked back towards the prisoner
    Who was still murmuring about who he was and who he
knew.
    She revealed another dagger and cut the ropes that bound
him.
    He jumped up from the chair in a fury and
    Stated that he would have us both killed for what we had
done.

He caught vision of me and called me a thief once more.
    My anger remained at bay until
    Amon stated that he was the counselor
    Who decided which lands to capture around the city.

I stood there with such animosity conjuring within my body
    That I became hot in temperature.
    The anger rushed through me and gave me no time to
decipher
    Whether Amon was telling the truth or not.

My impulses fell to the persuasion of frustration
    As I gripped the daggers tightly.
    The man did himself no favors by offering insults.

My thoughts and emotions were not enough
    To force me to strike the man
    As my mind was still defending itself.
    Amon knew of my dilemma.
    Her next act would seal the fate of the man.

She offered the counselor her dagger.
    He gladly accepted it.
    She told him that I sold his belongings on the street.
    He became enraged and held his weapon up to me.

He said that he would finish the beating.
    He approached me with such arrogance
    As if his wealth would save him down here beneath the city.

His once great stature in the ranks of society did not matter
anymore.
    My peasant characteristics were washed away.
    We were equals for the first time in our different lives, but
    He did not see that and held tightly to his upper class rank.
    He believed that was enough for him to overpower me.
    His confidence was so great that he saw me as no threat at
all.
    In his mind, no peasant would dare strike a man of his class.
    In my mind, I had already killed him twice.
    He continued to get closer to me
    With no caution or predetermined defense.
    I threw both of my daggers and
    Buried them deep within his upper thighs.
    The pain dropped him to his knees.
    The shock of my attack widened his eyes.
    I could see that he was still holding
    Onto his personal power and rank over me.

I wanted to steal that from him.
    I wanted him to know that I would in fact be the thief
    That he thought I was, but instead
    Of his riches, I would be robbing him of his life.

As I neared him, he swung his dagger in a weak attempt.
    I grabbed his wrist and twisted it until it broke.
    He released his weapon into my hand.
    I felt his pain, however, it did not meet the torment
    That I had received from the guards so I sliced his face.

Blood poured over his rich cloth robe.
 Amon just stood aside me and watched.
 The man's posture was changing now.
 His power was draining as the pain was overshadowing his
ego.
 He began to cling to me and beg for mercy.
 I required that feeling of helplessness from him.
 It empowered me to know that we had switched ranks.
 We may not have been equals in the eyes of society, but
 There underneath the city in that cold room, we were the
same.

I leaned down to look into the eyes of my enemy.
 I needed to know that what he felt was real.
 Did he truly believe that I was his equal?
 I said nothing as I looked to him.
 I saw his eyes twitch as he began to exit his frightened state.
 His begging and pleading was replaced with words of
damnation and resentment.
 He mumbled about how the guards would destroy my kind,
 That they would not rest until every peasant in the city
 Was killed and placed on display for all to see.
 As I slid my dagger across his throat, I never looked away.
 I wanted to follow him into the aftermath; torture him there
as well.
 For now, I settled on being the last vision that he would see.
 He reached up to grasp his throat to hold the wound.
 Blood poured through his fingers like a broken vat.

As he slipped into the trench of death,
 His bloody hands grabbed my cloak.
 I pushed him aside.
 I did not want to provide him any such comfort.

The gurgling sound from his injury came to a halt.
 There were no words to describe
 My immediate sensation at that moment,

But Amon pushed me for a response.

She was always infatuated with my thoughts and emotions.
　　I told her that for the first time in my life I felt powerful
　　And what I imagined God experienced.
　　She immediately smiled at my last comment and
　　Walked over to corpse to retrieve the two daggers.
　　She cleansed the weapons on the man's robe
　　And handed them to me one at a time claiming
　　That one represented vengeance; the other embodied
judgment.

She added that along with these two relics
　　I would bring wrath to those who had oppressed us.
　　The adrenaline from my recent kill was intense.
　　I instantly accepted her task without much thought.

The next day seemed quite difficult and long in duration
　　As I awaited nightfall.
　　However, I was able to acquire my next victims
　　By merely walking down the street
　　And observing how others viewed me.

Any such gesture of disgust or condemnation
　　About my level in society provided me with what I required.
　　The inability to act on my impulses during the daylight
hours
　　Only fed into my anxiousness for the sun to set.

As people passed and shoved me out of the way,
　　I gripped my daggers tightly underneath my cloak.
　　I was becoming a monster
　　And murdered everyone who touched me within my mind.
　　The visions comforted me as the day continued.
　　They allowed me to kill in much more creative ways.
　　Of course, the ability to tear one's head off
　　With my bare hands was unlikely to happen,
　　But the idea was still satisfying.

While other peasants returned
    To their daily rituals of begging from the wealthy,
    I was busy studying their routines and personalities.
    One such man noticed me observing him and walked over to
me.
    I visually deciphered him and gained
    That he was agitated and slightly aggressive in his posture.
    I remained still in my stance as he approached.

He was almost across the street
    When I slipped into a nearby corridor to conceal myself.
    He stopped on the threshold of the light.

If he proceeded into the darkness, he would die.
    Instead he stayed within the light trying to peer down the
corridor.
    I saw his hesitation and weakness
    Even though on the outside he presented a toughened
persona.

If he was truly a strong willed individual,
    He would have easily crossed over into the dark.
    Instead he stayed within his safe haven of the light,
    Even shoved other peasants as they walked by him.
    I allowed him to live as daylight was not my time.
    If I came across him during the night,
    The outcome would be different.
    I grew weary of wandering the streets and
    Walked back to the underground asylum.
    Amon welcomed me and claimed she had something for me.

I followed her again into the hidden circular room.
    I was greeted by the sight of a man who was chained to the
wall.
    He was beaten severely as evident from his bruises.

Apparently Amon had been busy while I was gone.

I did not question her nor the reasoning.
Upon further examination,
The man was the aggressive person I had just encountered.

How she captured and tortured him in the small amount of time
    I could not understand.
    I had no time to question her
    As the rage that I experienced within the corridor
    Fumed within me once again.
    My eyes felt as if they were dripping with boiling water.
    I moved toward him as he dangled from the chains.
    Amon stated that he was a gift for me,
    That she had prepared him to my liking, which was near
death.

She knew my hunger; she knew my anger.
    I slid my dagger of judgment across his bare chest
    Prompting him to awake.

The fresh blood flowed freely
    Down his skin and beautifully combined
    With the previous open wounds.
    His eyes swelled up with tears as he looked upon me.
    He was no longer the strong person
    That he portrayed just moments ago.
    He was no longer the untouchable citizen of society
    That the peasants perceived him as.
    Within such a short time, he had been reduced to nothing.
    He pleaded with me as his true personality showed itself.

We all beg, for different reasons.
    The poor beg to avoid starvation.
    The wealthy beg to avoid death.
    His rambling for mercy annoyed me, so
    I grabbed his tongue and released it from his mouth.
    Amon smirked as even she did not expect that.
    I was maturing with every encounter of death.
    I stabbed my dagger of vengeance deep into his chest

So much that I felt the blade connect with the stone wall.
I pulled his body close as he exhaled for the last time.
I took a deep breath in hopes
That I would swallow his soul as it leaked from his body.
I was not content with the act of death;
I wanted to control him for eternity.

Amon gestured in approval with a sway of her head
And reminded me that the sun was about to set.
The appetizer she had provided me
Was what I needed to control my hunger
As I awaited the main course.

While the sun descended, I emerged from the underground
With pure vengeance flowing through my veins.
My hatred had full control over my actions;
It overshadowed any morals that I had remaining.

Remorse was not my strong suit now.
It had all but withered away.
The uncontrollable beast that lived within me
For so long was set free by Amon who had broken the cage.

I not only killed to fulfill my desires,
I also killed to receive the seductive approval of Amon.
She had taught me well.
She had taught me how to control my anger,
To focus my intentions on my prey.
She taught me to never become unfocused
When tempted by the words of men who were near death.
She taught me that many yearn to be closer to God,
That they would never be as close as I was.
I alone controlled the fates of those in my path.
I alone crushed the destinies of anyone that met my criteria.

I walked the streets with confidence and no fear
As I passed by my fellow peasants.

I could not recall feeling so helpless or deprived of my
freedom.
    It seemed so long ago that I was in their position
    Desperately searching for remorse from.
    I stared into the eyes of everyone that passed me.
    I waited for any excuse to drain their lives.
    My hood provided shadows over my face,
    And only enhanced my vision
    As I was able to see all of their personalities.
    I waited patiently.
    I knew that the corrupted society would offer me my prey.

    And there it was in the sign of a man
    Brutally beating a peasant to the ground.

I moved toward the man as he prepared to strike again.
    With my full momentum, I shoved him into an adjacent
inlet.
    My cloak shielded us from the streets
    As people walked by at a close distance.
    I spared no time in unleashing my daggers
    Allowing them to penetrate the outer shell of his body.

I quickly removed my blades
    As I believed he was not worth the amount of time
    That they dwelled within him.
    I walked out of the inlet as quickly as I had gone in.
    I felt nothing; I had no thought within my head.
    I was a mindless killer, something the city had never seen
before.

I did not remain around long
    To see death reap him of his life.
    Witnessing the reactions of people
    As they stumbled across the dead was not something I cared
for.

The shock emotions and fake sadness was pathetic in my mind.

I knew behind the entire act most people were just relieved
That it was someone else instead of them.
As I walked further away on my journey of death,
I heard his screams for help.
No one ever stopped to help the living,
Why do they stop to help the dead?
There was nothing they could do for him,
They would rush by those in hunger
To come to the aide of someone who was beyond help.
Society was damaged in that aspect.
There was one thing constant with my offering.
Regardless of how powerful they were,
They would all die alone and take no power or money with
them.
It was a simple fact that I alone did not create.
If so, then why would people waste their lives
Trying to acquire more when they take nothing in the end?
The answer, they would feel empowered over others,
Increased their standing in societal ranks.
To me, their rank meant nothing.
The ability to reduce their status by a mere infliction of
death
Was the lifeblood of my way.

I did not seek instant death for my prey,
Which would not be justified as a learning experience for
them.
As much as possible, I wanted to provide them time to
reflect
On their actions; how they handled themselves within
society.

I heard the cries of another nearby servant.
I crept in the room with death closely behind me.
I peered around the corner
To witness a man striking his servant with his bare hand.
The reasoning for the violence did not matter to me.

No one should be punished in that manner.
Before he could strike again,
I reached for him from behind and
Forcefully pushed him towards the wall.
My momentum slammed his face into a self-portrait
painting.
His face smeared against his own as I pinned him
motionless.

The man became terrified at my sudden entrance,
But soon demanded to know who I was.
His strong personality overwhelmed his fear
As he stated that I had made a mistake that would cost me
dearly.
The servant remained on his knees,
Trying desperately to understand the situation.
He could not see my face, but I could see his
From underneath my hood.

I observed both fear and relief on his face from
Seeing his master helpless and subdued.
The man spewed useless words
Regarding his popularity and status;
He was saying those to the wrong person.

Not once did he enter into a plea of sorrow or remorse.
With rarity, I offered my victim a question.
I asked him why he beat his servant.
He responded that his servant was his property,
That he owned him; that he could do as he saw fit.

He was telling the truth;
He did not view his servant as a human, rather a commodity.
Even when faced with violence, he held onto the idea that
He was entitled to discipline his property without regard.
I looked to the servant as his eyes swelled.
I could tell he had nothing left,

The years of punishment had broken his spirit and self-
worth.
    I wanted the master to see his servant in true reality form,
    Not as a slave, but as a human being.

I turned my prey around to allow him to
    Observe his servant mentally destroyed on the ground.
    I stared into his eyes for any sign of pity, but found none.
    He was truly a beast who victimized the weak.

I extracted my dagger of judgment and held it close to his face.
    Reality finally showed itself to him
    While I touched the cold unforgiving blade against his
cheek.

The action allowed for his power to be reduced
    And replaced with fear about his salvation.
    He only showed remorse when faced with his own death.

A true person should fear death for others as well as for
themselves.
    His chin extended upwards to avoid the contact,
    But he could only rise up so high.
    I applied enough pressure to slightly open a small wound,
    Forced tears rolled down his face.
    I looked to the servant who had sobered up from his sadness
    As he witnessed the tears of his master.

That was a personality trait that hardly anyone saw from their
owner,
    I wanted to offer it to him in hopes that he would regain
    His internal power and ego.

I unveiled my second dagger of vengeance
    And inserted it up into his chin so deep
    That I believe I saw the blade within his eyes.
    His screams were loud and deafening, but soon silenced
    By my other blade slicing through his throat.

When no longer supported by the metal,
The master along with his painting
Fell to the ground in a symbolic fashion as if I killed him
twice.
    I did not expect any signs of appreciation from the servant.
    The vision of seeing someone murdered
    Was not a beneficial starting point for a conversation.
    The mere eye contact that I had received
    As I walked by him was enough.
    I did not want to achieve too much on that night.
    I eagerly desired to view the reaction of society.
    I did not want to lessen my skill level
    By becoming greedy with my intentions.
    I wanted to leave with the idea
    That I would live to kill another day.

The next day I awoke to a grey wolf licking my face.
    At first, I was startled,
    But the mannerisms of the wolf were kind and gentle.

Any normal person would have run
    From such an carnivorous beast, but
    I saw something very likeable in the eyes of the animal.
    It reminded me of myself;
    Misunderstood, angry and capable of violent acts.
    The wolf's teeth were coated with blood.
    Her surrounding fur was also drenched in the substance.
    My first thought was that she was hurt.
    After running my hands across her body
    It was determined that she was not wounded.

She led me down into the hidden room
    Where the stench of death was very intense.
    A lone man was shackled to the wall and missing his legs.
    He was still alive, but his lower limbs had been chewed.
    It was apparent that my friend had been feasting.
    Amon must have captured him late.

I wondered if she knew that he was being devoured by the
stray.

I could not have been further from the truth
    As the wolf slowly morphed into Amon.
    I had my suspicions ever since the beast spared me,
    But the idea of shape shifting was even beyond my reality.
    I grasped the concept quickly though as it occurred before
my eyes.
    She offered no reasoning; I offered no questions.
    Wiping blood from her lips,
    She stated that she was no longer hungry and
    I could gift him death if I so desired.
    The decision was easy for me
    As the first morning kill
    Had always been very satisfying.

The man was trembling from the loss of blood.
    He could barely keep his eyes open.
    I presented him death
    With one dagger deep in the temple.

The blade prompted his eyes to widen, but
    They would retain no vision.
    If they did, it would have been of my face.
    I withdrew my weapon with no care.

Amon informed me that the city was alive
    With tales of a hooded assassin
    Sent to taunt the wealthy.
    The news appeased me,
    However, I wanted to see and hear for myself.
    Knowing that my hood would only cause suspicion,
    I walked around the streets with it folded down.
    Amon was correct;
    There was a sense of desperation felt within the city.
    There were an increased number of guards patrolling and
    A decreased amount of wealthy about.

I smiled knowing that I forced
Not only my victims,
But the entire society of wealthy into a realm of fear.

Of course, not all of them were hidden
As there was still a great amount roaming about.
These were the untouchable ones,
Those who believed they had nothing to fear.
Their egos were still intact as well as their mannerisms
Towards those who were not like them.
The peasants viewed the hooded assassin as their savior.
Many of them wore their hoods
To tease those who walked by them.

The guards did not take kindly to that
And provided beatings to anyone
Who was caught wearing one.
The scene of peasant kids running
With hoods and wooden daggers
Brought me down from my murderous plateau.

My emotions became mutated in my mind,
I did not know what to think.
Had I done more wrong than right?
Had I somehow made society worse than it actually was?
I needed time to think.
I had been blinded by my own personal hatred.
I could not see the effects of my actions.
I slid into a corridor where I was greeted by Amon in wolf
form.
She was not her pleasant self.
Her calm demeanor was replaced with snarls and growls.
I told her that I could not kill anymore
And left my daggers on the ground before her.
I walked back out into the street
Leaving her behind in the shadows.

I walked amongst the crowds

And heard the numerous stories of the phantom hooded
assassin.
  I overheard that he would kill the wealthy while they slept,
  Giving their riches to the poor.

I heard tales they he was not a man,
    But a demon built from the darkness
    And that he only appeared at night.
    They also told that he was part dragon
    That would attack from above,
    Take his prey back to a cave
    Where he would feast upon them.

It was obvious that the wealthy and guards
    Were arming themselves for protection.
    I bypassed one such man
    Adding gold tipped feathers to manmade arrows.
    I saw another sharpening his sword.
    All of these tales sounded so much better than the truth.
    Somehow the story of an angry peasant
    Seeking revenge on the wealthy
    Did not have a powerful underbelly.

They would have to keep their stories
    As I was done killing.
    I fulfilled my need and sought out my revenge.
    There was nothing else to kill for.

I grew tired of hearing the tales carried by the wind
    And ventured underground for one last time.
    The place was unusually quiet.
    There was neither screams from the near dead
    Nor the stench of the decayed.

My reign of terror had come to an end.
    I was anxious to start a new life, again.
    That was until I heard the faint sound of whimpering
    Coming from the hidden room.

My curiosity guided me down the tunnel.
I paused for a brief moment to prepare myself
As my mind had weakened a great deal
Since the last I had been there.
I pushed open the door to find Amon still in her wolf form
Lying upon the ground.
I kneeled down beside her to provide comfort
While I searched her body for wounds.
My instincts were correct,
An arrow with gold tipped feathers
Was protruding from her mid-section
Her wound was devastating
With the tip puncturing her lung.
She tried desperately to breathe,
But it was not sustainable enough for her.
My subsided anger that I had suppressed rose once again.
My emotions were so intense that they became
uncontrollable.
They escalated even higher
As I saw my daggers near her lifeless body.
Vengeance and judgment was what I had to offer now.
I could no longer offer the city peace and calm.
There was no room for those emotions
In a society plagued with greed and selfishness.
I provided the balance between the weak and the strong;
Between the poor and the wealthy.

The daggers felt so good back within my hands.
They desired more blood to spill across their blades.
My blinded fury forced me out from the underground
While the sun was still in the sky.

I knew I should have sought out patience,
But my anguish was at its peak.
No words or thoughts would have postponed my desires.
I utilized the small amounts of shadows to my benefit.

It was not as concealing as the dark of night,

But it was manageable.
My anger was relentless
And benefited no one within my path.

Anyone who was standing
Within the shadows to avoid the sun was my prey.
I left most of my victims hidden in the darkness
And posed them as if they were a sleeping peasant.

It was easier than I had imagined
As the crowd never noticed the dead piling up around them.
Some would even step over the corpses as they exited
corridors.
I made it a habit to unfold my hood while in the light
To avoid any confrontations with the guards,
However, in the shadows my hood became an evil veil.

I was moving at such a rapid pace that I had forgotten it was
up.
Two guards grabbed me,
Pulled me inside a room to question me.
They were relaxed in their mannerisms
As the tediousness of questioning
Many people before me weighed heavy on them.

They quoted their standard comments
Regarding the evil prowler and
Asked me if I had seen anything.
My response of yes struck them with much confusion.
I went on to say that I saw a man
Kill another by using two daggers much like the ones I
carry.
To say that they were disturbed
Would be an understatement
As I held my beloved weapons in my hands
Drenched in blood, that clung to the blades
Like rain drops on a leaf.

They were startled by me and
    Fumbled to reach their swords, but
    Their hands would never touch the handles.
    I leaped between them,
    Shoved my dagger of vengeance within the mouth of one
and
    Slid my blade of judgment across the throat of the other.
    I stepped forward in order to avoid
    Being crushed by their falling armored bodies.
    Death was quick and painless for them with no defense.
    I wiped my blades on a nearby cloth chair,
    As they were in desperate need of cleansing.
    They each held the blood of at least five kills
    Dulling their sharpness and beauty.
    After, I exited from the room.
    I kept close to the shadows
    As I moved along the streets
    On my quest for the arrow maker.
    I was a living reaper and the street was my burial ground.

I passed a man sharpening several of his blades
    With his back to the shadows.
    I witnessed him swat at a local boy
    Who was fascinated by the shiny metal.
    The vulgar language of the man
    Scared the child away and provided me with a reason.
    He was very skilled at sharpening the blades
    As his head came cleanly off
    With a lone strike from one of his swords.
    I was impressed and could have benefited from his skill.

My pace increased as I searched for the arrow maker.
    I desired his blood dripping down my palms;
    I needed to taste the essence of his soul.
    I would not have to wait long as I soon approached his
abode.

His table was vacant outside

With various pieces of arrows residing atop of it.
I stepped out from the momentum of the crowd
And slid into the inlet of the door.

I peered inside and noticed nothing unusual
    Except the eerie sound of silence.
    I cautiously crept further inside
    Into the main living quarter where
    I saw the man sitting with his back to me.
    I approached him slowly and drew one of my daggers.
    As I neared him, I was grabbed from behind by two guards
    With a third stepping between me and my prize.
    The old man stood and announced that she was right.
    The guards held me tight and
    Pulled my judgment dagger from my grip.
    The man demanded the weapon and the guards obliged.
    He also demanded that I be weakened,
    The guards obliged to that as well.
    They assaulted me heavily and continuously
    Until I could no longer stand.

The old man halted the attack and walked towards me.
    He plunged my own dagger within my chest.
    He judged me for my crimes against society.
    The pain was unlike anything I had ever experienced,
    But I was not ready to die.

The infliction gave me one last empowerment.
    It allowed me to unveil my dagger of vengeance
    And find every blind joint within the armor of the three
guards.
    I cut them deep and hard,
    Forcing them to assume the position of death.
    As they awaited the reaper, I stood above them,
    Not as a God, not as a savior,
    But rather as someone who was dying slower than them.

I stood in front of the old man

With one dagger in my hand and the other in my chest.
I was dying,
But knowing that I would take him with me
Provided the idea with comfort.

With just enough power,
    I stabbed my free weapon into his chest
    And applied downward pressure on the handle
    To tear through the flesh of the man.
    I wanted to cause him great pain before he died
    And I had succeeded.
    I cleansed the blade on his robe
    To rid the metal of his pungent blood.
    My legs were no longer strong enough to support me.
    I opted for a solution that would
    Continue my wrath long after I was gone.
    I removed my hooded cloak and threw it in the fireplace.

I rotated my dagger to point at my heart.
    The scene in the room would look like
    My numerous other kills and
    Prompt the notion that the assassin was still alive.
    I wanted the wealthy to continue to fear me
    After I was gone.
    I wanted them to constantly look around them
    As they walked the streets.

I wanted them to focus more on me than their money.
    I also desired that my fellow peasants
    Hold onto the empowerment that I had gifted them.
    They needed them to believe that
    Money and wealth did not separate us.
    Fear was a characteristic
    That equalized everyone and made us all the same.
    It was the one trait that we all had in common.
    As blood poured from me,
    I peered out of the window one last time and saw her.
    She stared back at me and

Offered me that infamous seductive smile.
Amon stood in the street
With two grey wolves on either side of her.
My eyes grew heavy,
As I saw her blend into the crowded street.
I believed I had taught the wealthy a lesson,
That they would not soon forget.
I prayed that the fear of me would haunt their dreams.
I worried about the peasants and
Hoped that I had done enough to free their minds.

I was unsure how the future
    Would turn out with my inability to prowl the streets.
    My answer came in the vision of a small peasant boy
    Staring in through window at me.
    I do not know if the vision was real or not,
    I did not care as it brought me peace.
    The boy looked upon me as if he knew who I was.
    He studied the room, the blood,
    The various dead bodies then back to me.

    He was neither afraid of me
    Nor the gruesome scene that laid out before him.
    He gave me peace with his eyes;
    Freedom from his demeanor.

His next action provided me with the answer
    That I had been seeking for.
    He folded up his hood and concealed his face.
    I saw myself within him,
    Stabbed the dagger into my heart
    And waited patiently for death.

I was able to die that day
    Knowing that my legacy
    Would continue within the streets.
    Life drained from me within that wealthy room
    With judgment in my chest and

Vengeance in my heart.

~

I stopped writing for a brief moment
    Due to a small glimmer of confusion
    That brought about a few questions.
    It appears that the past events are being removed from my
mind.
    I know this may sound absurd to those who read this,
    But I can no longer recall what I just transcribed.

The collection of my recent work
    Is written in a language that I am unfamiliar with.
    How could I have possibly written those words?
    The idea is quite the conundrum.

I was away from my quill for quite some time,
    As it seems the mischievous shadows have returned.
    They seem very gentle in appearance overall, however
    I have noticed that only seven reside in the cave now, unless
    I am mistaken.

I am still trying to decipher the language of my past pages.
    My current writings are in my native language,
    But as I end a page,
    The language alters during the movement
    To the completed pile.

I do not believe that my friends approve of the time
    I am spending contemplating languages,
    As the shrieking sounds are echoing through the cave once
again.
    I am too tired to offer any fear to them
    And much too exhausted to continue to write.
    My eyes are very heavy and
    The flickering candle against the dark
    Does not aide me in my quest to stay awake.

III

Mountains were beautiful during that season.
    Trees had begun shedding their leaves.
    Our village was nestled between two mountains
    In a wonderful valley full of nature.

Majority of the residents were farmers,
    I worked as a carpenter and
    My time consisted of preparing the recently cut trees
    To become lumber used in new cottages.

The village was nice and peaceful
    With the sun rising and falling against the mountain
horizons.
    I was the main source for all carpentry needs
    And enjoyed being the center of construction.

Over the past few years,
    Repairing structures became my sole chore.
    Seldom did new construction show itself, but
    It was appreciated when it did.
    Most of my time was spent
    In my carpentry shop or
    In the nearby woodlands collecting lumber.

The village was not nearly as big as other neighboring ones,
    But it was unique in its location.
    The proximity of the land between two mountain ranges
    Provided a picturesque horizon.
    The mountains were well respected and

We even had festivities in honor of them.

Common travel from the west soon led
    Nomads and gypsies towards the village.
    The path funneled travelers of all sorts
    Through the mountains and directly into our entrance.
    Residents did not mind the travelers
    As they brought goods and tales from their homeland.
    The increase in demand for lumber was also welcomed.
    Most of the visitors continued on their journey
    After a brief period of rest, but
    Some stayed behind and even became residents.

I had not seen that type of excitement in the village.
    Some were fearful of sudden change, while others embraced
it.
    However, the merchants all seemed very thankful.
    Elders viewed the change as a threat to their way of life
causing
    Arguments to erupt on occasion, but nothing serious.

The landscape of our village changed dramatically as
    New cottages were erected and new farmlands were plowed.
    We were slowly running out of space and
    Even spread pastures up the base of the mountains
    To maximize the acres within the valley.

Change was gradual over the years,
    Thus allowing for people to adapt.
    Some residents left as they were disgusted
    By the new condensed lifestyle.

I did not mind, as the carpentry needs kept me busy.
    My business grew to meet the demands of my customers.
    I began making wagon repairs, plow equipment and
    Even constructed a water vat to match the consumption.

Travelers brought many concepts and items

To the village from their native homelands.
They gifted us with unique spices, recipes, tools
And more importantly stories of far off places.
Living in the valley for so long, it was quite refreshing
To hear tales from other parts of the world.
They were fascinating and
Included different species of animals, remote civilizations
And heroic tales of warfare.
We had become so isolated within our mountain pass valley
That the stories easily captivated us.
Each night we invited new travelers to come to the
courtyard
And tell us about their homelands.
Residents looked forward to these events each night
And it gave our visitors a chance to feel welcomed.

Of all the stories and tales that the travelers told,
Only one ever raised concern among the residents.
A group of gypsies recited a tale of a great plague
That ravished their homeland
Forcing people to flee in seek of a safe haven.

They told of a flesh eating virus
That consumed everything a man was created of except
bone.
Until then, the stories were light and often humorous, so
The shock of an approaching plague was devastating.

I was not seriously involved in their tale,
But found myself unable to turn away as
They were very descriptive with their words.
They continued by saying that they had witnessed villages
Once full of life being reduced to huge mounds of lifeless
flesh.

The tale spoke that the infected ones would be alive
As their flesh rotted away and was consumed.
I cannot say whether I believed the tale,

But their story telling technique was quite convincing.
I looked around the courtyard and
Could easily decipher who was a believer or not.
There were those who elected to not believe
As that proved to be the easiest option.

No one wanted to consider that a plague was killing people,
Let alone approaching our village.
I took the story for what it was, a story.
I was not going to scream profanities at the gypsies
Like some had chosen to do.
We had invited them to share a story from their homeland
And that was what they did.
Regardless of whether or not someone believed them,
The tale was quite interesting.

Days went by and the gypsies
Were well on their way to their next destination,
While the tale of the plague lingered around longer.
Open invites for new stories were reduced as
Residents were afraid of what they would hear next.

I found it somewhat unique that
We welcomed the peaceful stories
And shielded ourselves from the horrific ones.

We soon felt deprived by not hearing the nightly stories
And began the ritual again.
To avoid any future offerings of death,
We implemented an approval process.

A group of elder residents would learn of the tales
Prior to them speaking and
Would either approve or decline them.
I was sure that the method was not the best option at hand,
But it worked and allowed for the practice to resume.

One traveler had been approved and

She began telling her story to a large crowd in the courtyard.
She spoke of ripened fruit trees as far as the eye could see
And large waterfalls for bathing.
She described her prosperous village and loving family.
Her next words struck fear throughout the listeners
And gained my attention as I carved a piece of wood.
She said her village and family were all destroyed by the
plague.
Silence fell in the courtyard.
Evidence promoting the plague had just doubled.
Two separate visitors within a short time span
Telling of a similar virus rehashed the panic of the crowd.
The elder censors were as equally shocked and
Were instantly blamed for the words of the woman.
People went into a chaotic state over the next season.
They took all precautions to fend off the plague;
Offering a dead animal carcass outside their cottages or
Keeping a smoldering hot fire that would burn the plague
vapors.

Rumors were abundant during that time
With some being more obscure than others.
My favorite was that one could avoid the virus
By simply not allowing your skin to be exposed.
People walked around the village completely covered in
cloth.
I did not pay any mind to the tale
As I was busy selling wood
To feed the fires people were creating to fend off the putrid
smog.
The rumors brought about many coins in my pocket.
We ended the story telling event and never resurrected it.
It was the village's way to avoid the situation.
Our best option was to keep the tale as the fearful
imagination
Of the gypsies and the lone woman.
That mindset would change the following day,
As our village received the first physical sign

That such a plague did exist outside of a stubborn tale.

I remember the events clearly.
    I was busy stripping the bark from freshly cut logs
    In the nearby woods just outside of the village.
    I had a specific area where I retrieved the lumber from
    And did the task at least every other day.

The amount of wood I gathered at any given time
    Would stock my shop for two days.
    I did not gather more wood than I needed
    As I believed that if the wood was allowed to sit for a long period
    That it would dry out and become weak.
    I was almost done for the day and
    Acquired a good amount of lumber.
    As I was loading up my cart, I saw him.
    He was just standing there staring at me from afar.

At first glance the image startled me as
    I am usually alone within the woods
    Except for the occasional wandering deer.
    He was dressed in a hooded cloak that hid his identity.
    None of his characteristics could be viewed
    Especially from that distance.
    I placed the log that I was holding into the cart and
    Wiped off my hands that were covered with dirt.
    I never turned away from him as I cleaned up my surroundings.
    With everything in place and orderly, I called to him.

The sound of my voice resulted in no response.
    He remained in his position slightly swaying from side to side.
    I shouted to him and asked if he needed help,
    But again received no answer.

With the sun slowly sinking behind the mountains,

I knew it was not a good idea for him to be out in the woods
After sunset as coyotes roamed the area.
I took a few steps towards him.
My movement must have scared him as he scurried away.

I laid down my tools and gave chase all the while asking him to stop.
Winding through the rows of trees, I kept after him.
The sun continued to sink further and
I was worried that the coyotes would view him as prey.

I pleaded with him to stop.
Even shouted that it was dangerous to run in the woods at night.
Fortunately, my final words were heard as he came to a stop.
Sensing the race had ended;
I slowed my pace to a walk
And neared him from behind.
His hooded cloak concealed his physical attributes.
As I got closer, I could hear him mumbling,
But could not interpret his words.
He was shaking uncontrollably and continued to sway.
I extended my arm to allow my hand to touch his shoulder
In hopes that my contact would offer him comfort.
I did not succeed in my effort as before I touched him,
He shifted around, grabbing my arm while dropping to his knees.
The words were less mumbled now as he begged for mercy.
His grip was tight on my forearm,
So much so that his nails provided outside pressure on my skin.
From the looks of his hands
I could tell he was pale in complexion and weak in strength.
His bony fingers and dirty nails dug deep into my skin.
My concern was stronger than him and
Allowed me to forego any discomfort he was causing me.
I offered to provide him food and shelter.

My first inclination was that he was a traveler
Who had lost his way; perhaps ventured from the path.
Since the new trade route,
We had seen our share of lost people
Especially in the winter season
As the snow would occasionally shield the road.
However, it was rare to find people straying
During that particular time of year.

The past few days brought about no new groups of travelers, so
    My curiosity increased regarding him.
    It was unwise to travel by oneself.
    The terrain leading to our village through the mountain
ranges
    Could cripple even the strongest of warriors.
    To see a frail person wandering alone was something
    I had never encountered before.
    I held onto the notion that he was accidentally
    Left behind by his group probably while he slept.
    Still, the last group we received was three days ago.
    To survive in that environment on your own for that long
was quite a feat.
    From the look of his hands,
    He had not consumed anything for quite some time.
    I thought it was best to lead him to my cart and
    Bring him to the village so that I could replenish him;
    Treat him back to health.
    Part of me was curious to his story and
    Hoped that he would enlighten me as to how he survived the
mountain trek.

Supporting his shoulders, I guided him upwards.
    As he rose, I reassured him that there was no reason to hide
beneath the cloth.
    With him still gripping my arm,
    I raised both of my hands and folded back his hood.

What I witnessed next would haunt my dreams.

All that I assumed regarding the lone traveler
Would be erased from my memory.
My description of what I saw
Could not translate the level of horror appropriately.

His face was all but caved in
    With sagging skin loosely gripping to his skull.
    The flowing pattern of his skin
    Combined with an abundance of wrinkles
    Was evident enough that he had no excess fat or flesh within
his face.
    I had never seen a human skull before,
    That was the closest I had ever come.
    The top portions of skin clung so tightly
    To his skull and had become transparent
    That I could see the outline and formation of it.

His eyes were loosely held by their sockets,
    But the lack of flesh allowed them to protrude further than
normal.
    The pupils consisted of a black circle
    Randomly shifting within a sea of blood.

I could not tell the direction of his sight as
    His eyes were moving rapidly in different directions
    With no apparent pattern.
    His mouth was filled with rotted yellow teeth
    Outlined with dried caked lips.
    When he opened his mouth,
    I could see that it was filled with a thickened blood
substance
    Which shifted about by the movement of his tongue.

The sight was devastating to me;
    To see a human being in such a state of despair and agony.
    I continued the notion that I needed to get him back to the
village
    To reverse the starvation that was altering his appearance.

As I watched the uncontrollable twitching and
The shaking he exerted while I held his shoulders,
I was reminded about the gypsies
And the stories they told about an approaching plague.

I immediately released my grip on the man by
Prying his fingers from my arm.
I was surprised that my strength did not break his bones.
My release sent him stumbling back downward where
He began to beg for mercy once again.

I distanced myself while rubbing my arms from his touch.
What did I do?
Was the plague true?
Were the gypsies right?

I required a moment to recollect my thoughts.
My demeanor quickly changed
From a concerned citizen
To a selfish protector.
As he whimpered on the ground,
The aftermath of his touch on my arm was very much
apparent.
I looked closely at my forearm
Where his nails left indentations in my skin.
I noticed my blood vessels were darkening in color.
His sharpened disfigured fingernails
Punctured my skin ever so slightly and left four small
wounds.

Much to my displeasure, the skin alterations
Were slowly spreading across my skin.
I quickly scanned my surroundings
For any witnesses.

I desperately concealed my wound by lowering my shirt sleeve
And gripped my arm in hopes to suffocate the disease.
I knew I could not provide any satisfaction physically,

But still I tried.

Fear quickly bombarded my mind
    And was too much to handle.
    I opted to forego the notion of the plague
    And believe that it was just a skin irritation caused by his
nails.

I knew that was not true
    As I could not avoid the utter devastation he was
experiencing.
    I stood motionless as my mind
    Raced through random thoughts
    Trying to decipher the information presented.

Once my mind accepted the terms,
    It came to one conclusion.
    I had received the plague.
    My throat became tight
    As if fear itself was strangling me.

My skin became cold and drenched with sweat
    As the verdict was read to me from within.
    My sentence surely was death.
    My mortality had no defense.
    My life was altered by that touch.
    That mere selfless act of kindness had doomed me.
    With my emotions in a battered state,
    I shifted from worrying to anger.

I snarled down at the sniffling traveler
    Who had so inadvertently donated his curse onto me.
    Still clutching my arm
    In hopes of somehow spiritually extracting the disease,
    I demanded answers from him.
    He offered no verbal response,
    Only uncontrollable body movements.
    His lack of courtesy was an insult.

I kicked him down further to the ground.
I wanted to go back to my cart,
Retrieve one of my tools
And unleash my anger on him
As gratification for what he had done to me.
I pictured myself stomping on his weak skull,
Burying him in an unmarked grave in the woods
So that no one would know my secret.
My conscious would not allow that of course,
As I was never a violent man,
But the latest events would be justification enough.
Alas, I could not as I still had remorse for him.

I did not know what to do.
    My mind was not helping me at all.
    My human instinct filled the void and
    Prompted me to reach for the man.

I heard the faint sound of laughter coming from his mouth,
    Which was half buried in grass.
    He revealed his face slowly and looked up to me.
    He was no longer shaking
    And appeared to have regained energy and health.

He even pushed himself up on his own free will
    From the ground into a standing position.
    The sight confused me slightly and
    I immediately entered into a state that it was only a dream.

The idea of a dream was somewhat comforting.
    It was an option that my mind failed to present me with.
    His statue was still not that of a normal human being
    And his height was much shorter than mine.

Overall his appearance remained small,
    But his skin and face transformed back to normal.
    From the time he rose from the ground

To his current position, he had gained back the flesh and fat within his face.
His low laughter continued.
I witnessed his once blood stained eyes
Turn a dull shade of white.
He momentarily looked around the surrounding area
As if to survey the land.

The silence broke with my first question
Asking him who he was.
Still observing the natural land,
He responded in a clear tone by saying his name was Mammon.
I proceeded to ask him about his disease.
How was it that he was able to seemingly remove it?
He replied in a stubborn tone that he was capable of many things.
I asked if he was alive.
He replied that he was very much alive.
He had come on a very important task
Not only to spread the word of an approaching plague,
But to spread the disease itself.
My depression set in.
I hoped that my retrieval of the disease was a part of the charade.
I folded back my sleeve and noticed
That the grouping of enlarged blood vessels had
Spread further up my arm towards my elbow.

Sensing my sadness with the turn of events,
Mammon offered me some serenity
By stating that he was also carrying a cure.
He informed me that he only had one dosage of the vaccine;
That it would take several seasons for it to be duplicated.
From his own words, I could consume it
And spare my own life
Or I could give the vial to the village elders
So that they may work towards duplicating it.

On one hand I could save myself,
    On the other I could save the village.
    I pondered in my mind a way to have both outcomes.
    Mammon stopped me and said that only one would prevail.
    I could sense him studying my mind,
    Waiting for my response.
    When I offered none,
    He shunned me and grabbed my wrist.
    He pried open my clutched fingers and
    Placed the vial into my palm and closed my hand.

He offered a smirk and told me to think about it,
    But to not take too much time as the plague
    Had the power to reach a verdict for me.
    His words sent me barreling down a spiral of thoughts,
    Many of which I would have never imagined that I would
have.

From anger to stubbornness,
    From sadness to despair,
    From eagerness to resentment,
    My mind journeyed further away from rational thought.

Knowing that he had me completely in a state of emotional
chaos,
    Mammon granted me one more smile.
    He folded up his hood and stated that he would see me soon.
    In a much better physical form,
    He fled through the rows of trees and vanished from sight.
    He left me behind with so many unanswered questions,
    A vial of vaccine and a burning flesh eating plague
    That was slowly consuming my arm.
    Leaving my tools, cart and gathered logs within the woods,
    I ran back to the village.
    The sun had all but vanished
    As the fog from the mountains rolled in
    And blanketed the trees for the night.

Coyotes howled as I ran desperately through the barked
maze.
    I paid no attention to the predators
    As my mind was focused on a more drastic situation.
    I entered into the radius of the village and
    Made sure that my arm was concealed
    As if anyone discovered my sickness,
    I would surely be banished from my homestead.

I imagined some of my neighbors would opt
    For a more deadly punishment
    Like buried alive or engulfed in flames.
    I briefly thought about purposely giving those people
    My present and allowing them to suffer with me,
    But my conscious once again stepped in.

I was not feeling up to my usually happy self
    And gave no friendly gestures
    Towards anyone that I may have passed.
    Straight into my shop I went and
    Shut the door tightly behind me.
    The inside of my abode was relaxing,
    But was quickly overshadowed by the vial I held in my
hand.
    My arm was easily hidden from my sight, but
    The vial was a constant reminder
    That the recent events were not a dream.
    I needed to rid myself of the souvenir so
    I placed the vial upon the table and
    Covered it with a nearby goblet.
    Not holding it eased my mind for quite some time
    Until the burning within my arm brought me back to reality.
    I unveiled my arm and saw that the disease had drastically
grown.
    In a desperate attempt to cleanse my limb,
    I scrubbed my skin in a bowl of fresh water.
    I knew of the result, but I had to try.

A knock on the front door
    Echoed through the inside and
    Startled me as I vigorously rubbed the hairs from my
forearm.

Without venturing towards the door, I asked who it was.
    My neighbor responded that he saw me running and
    Wanted to know if everything was alright.
    I nervously answered that I was just tired from the tasks of
the day.
    He luckily accepted my answer and left me alone for the
night.
    I needed a restful night sleep
    As I believed it would erase the awful dream I was having.

I awoke the next morning
    To the playful demeanor of my pet dog
    And a large amount of tongue lashing.
    The gesture soothed me as a new day had begun.

At that moment everything was in place and orderly in my life.
    I was even confused as to what day it was and
    Whether or not I needed to gather a new wood supply.
    The confusion was a blessing compared to the nightmare I
had just experienced.
    I arose from my bed, but realized that I could not lift my
arm.
    My eyes were astounded from the sight of my dark bluish
skin.
    Numbness extended from my fingertips to my shoulder
blade.
    I had complete immobility with the arm and
    Only had slight feeling which allowed me
    To experience the painful pressure being created from
within.
    During that moment of realizing that it was not a dream,
    I violently pushed my dog away and
    Wrapped my dead arm in a cloth blanket.

To go from a high level of happiness
To the lowest level of concern was devastating on my mind.
The rapid change in emotion made me sick to my stomach.
My vision blurred to where I had to sit back down
Until the chaotic moment subsided.

To not draw attention to myself,
    I dressed myself in my carpentry clothes,
    But did not risk going outside.
    The idea of not being around people
    During that time was partially satisfying and safe.

I am not sure whether the gratification
    Came from me hiding my disease or
    That I would not willingly infect others.
    Either way, I was very happy to be away from the
commotion.

I needed to turn my attention away from my arm
    So I decided to focus on my work.
    Half a day wasted in the woods with my new friend
    Proved disastrous on my work schedule and
    My daily tasks were compounding.
    As I proceeded with my chores,
    I thought that ignoring the situation would benefit me.
    I struggled with only having one working arm,
    But managed surprisingly well considering.

Throughout the day, my accomplishments were adding up,
    How was I going to interact with my customers?
    In preparation, I burrowed a large hole within the front door
    As a means to communicate with my patrons.

Verbal portions of a conversation
    Were more important than the physical.
    My customers did not need to see me.
    Although skeptical at first, they accepted
    My new procedure and rarely questioned it.

Occasionally a few of them would succumb
To their curiosity and try to stare through the hole, but
Seeing my face on the other side normally appeased them.

Considering my new ailment,
   I was actually able to manage my work,
   Finishing quite a few orders.

As I was cleaning, a knock rang out at the front door.
   I announced that I was closed and continued sweeping the
floor.
   Another knock sounded and prompted me to the door.
   Peering through customer hole, I saw him.
   Fear instantly consumed me.
   Those pale white eyes staring back at me were
unforgettable.
   Mammon had returned.
   The squinting fashion of his eyes leaked displeasure.
   He demanded entry, but I ignored his request.
   I pretended that no one was inside.
   He knocked even louder causing
   My tools hanging from the inner wall to shake.
   I hid behind my work bench and peered around the corner.
   I saw those miserable eyes scanning inside.

His fingers entered through the hole and
   Grasped the inner portion of the wooden door.
   When he had enough leverage,
   He violently shook the frame to gain entry.

The rusty hinges held up under the pressure,
   But did loosen slightly.
   After lowering my head during the commotion,
   I rose again to get another glimpse of my visitor,
   But none could be seen.
   I slowly walked towards the door to survey the situation
   And realized that he had indeed left.

Regaining my sense of dignity, I turned to continue my
cleaning,
But I would not succeed.
Instead of facing my chores
I came to face to face with Mammon.
The close vicinity of him was horrifically sudden.
It startled me so much that I stumbled backwards.
He just stood there observing me.
He had an unpleasant aura to him
As if he was disgusted by me and my previous actions.
With his arms crossed, he asked me about my decision.

I knew he was growing impatient with me.
He laughed at my lack of response and
Reminded me that I was running out of time to decide.
He stated that the plague will not stop;
That it will devour my soul.

He also reminded me again of my choices.
That I could save myself or sacrifice my well-being for the
benefit of others.
My fear tried to avoid the conversation
And did not allow me to form words,
But that only enticed my visitor.

In order to help in my decision making,
He said that he would speed up the process of the disease.
No sooner had the words exited his lips
Did my arm become increasingly heavy with dead weight.
I could feel the tension spreading to my upper shoulder.

He smiled at the sight of my increased discomfort.
He teased me by squatting down in front of me
As he glanced closely at my arm.
His eyes moved up my skin
As if he was guiding the disease closer to my shoulder.
He went on to sarcastically describe
How the virus first would clench the blood vessels;

Suffocate them to the point where they become clogged.
Forcing the arm to become numb.

He continued by saying that the blood
    Would have nowhere to flow.
    It will become enraged at its captor.
    The trapped substance would act
    As a thirst quencher for the virus and
    Provide it with the necessary energy
    It requires in order for it to progress to the next area.

Fingertips will be the first area to feel the pressure.
    Followed closely by the frigid bone decay of the wrist.
    He leaned back from me and
    Announced how proud he was of his creation and that
    He looked forward to my answer.
    As he exited my shop, he left behind the fact
    That he would see me again soon.

With no time to contemplate his words
    My arm was becoming progressively more painful.
    It was rendered useless and had fallen to the disease.
    In a state of panic, I came to the conclusion
    I needed to stop the virus from spreading to my chest.

The decision was not difficult to make
    Especially when I looked to my arm
    And saw the blackened pulsating skin.
    The disease had mutated from killing the blood
    To consuming the decayed flesh.

Open sores and blisters appeared
    To tear across my skin
    In order to join one another and forge larger openings.
    At this point I could no longer move my fingers, wrist or
arm.
    The only movement left was in my shoulder

As I could barely rotate it forcing the dead arm to sway
slightly.

I had no time to spare.
    The arm needed to come off.
    I lifted the lifeless limb and
    Slammed it on my work bench in between two braces
    Used on a daily basis to cut wooden planks.
    With my good hand, I twisted the metal brackets
    In order to confine my arm.
    The pressure was not as much as I would have liked,
    But substantial considering the situation.

With a log blade in hand,
    I measured out just enough space
    Between the decayed flesh
    And the healthy area
    To make sure to completely remove the disease from my
body.

All that was left was to commit to the task at hand,
    But it was easier said than done.
    The chore I was about to complete was irreversible.
    My mind halted me because of that.
    I sat there with my arm
    Held to a work bench
    And a saw in the other.
    The situation alone would drain the sanity of any man,
    But alas there I was.
    As my neighbors slept soundly in their beds
    With no concern in the world,
    I was about to dissect myself.

I closed my eyes and
    Placed a wooden peg in my mouth.
    With a downward motion, I
    Allowed the teeth of the blade
    To tear deep into my flesh.

The pain was unbearable at first,
    But soon reduced at the thought of possibly
    Becoming a lifeless mass of diseased flesh.
    The skin and muscle proved easy to cut.
    They gave no resistance to the sharpened blade.

I took a brief moment to allow
    The blood to flow from my arm.
    I saw the lower portion decrease in size
    As the life fluid eagerly escaped from its diseased prison.
    I used a rag to wipe the blood
    To reveal the alignment of my cut.
    The amount of blood was extraordinary
    And easily concealed my previous work.

I found myself squeezing my arm,
    Manually siphoning the blood to speed along the process.
    I even lowered my body so that my arm
    Would be at the highest level thus forcing it to drain.
    The floor surrounding the work bench was coated with
blood.
    A large amount of saw dust combined with the blood
    Formed a red sticky paste that plastered to the floor like
mud.

Satisfied that the blood flow had decreased,
    I raised myself back up and
    Gripped the saw again.
    My once swelled arm was nothing more than skin and bone.
    The disease made sure that no ounce of flesh remained.
    With my next downward thrust,
    The blade hit the opposition of bone.
    The friction sent vibrations throughout my upper chest.
    Every slice of the blade forced my shoulder back and forth
    Along with the motion,
    Which made it difficult to gain a clean cut.

I tried to be fluid and precise, but my blade work was anything
but.
    I dragged the teeth slowly with a tearing motion
    To avoid the blade getting stuck in the hardened material.
    The conquest of removing my arm overshadowed any pain
    I experienced and altered into a challenge of sorts.
    Not once did I come to the realization
    That I was losing an arm,
    But rather focused on regaining control over my life.
    No doubt that my method of dealing with the disease
    Would anger Mammon and deny him of his answer,
    But at that exact moment I did not care about his reaction.

Another thrust of the blade
    Burrowed the teeth deep within my bone.
    Half way through the brilliant white substance,
    I took a moment to retighten the loosening braces
    As the blood was allowing my arm to loosen.

I grabbed a smaller carving blade
    So that I could expose more of the bone.
    With quick motions,
    I removed chunks of my shoulder flesh and
    Wiped away the excess blood to reveal the pearly hue of
bone.

Satisfied with my carvings,
    I switched back to the larger blade
    And sawed through the remainder portion of bone.
    A sigh entered upon my face
    As the last splinter gave way to the blade.
    The flesh and skin on the other side
    Proved to be just as easy as its counterpart and
    Took only a few slices to separate.
    With my arm completely alienated from my body
    And held to the bench by the braces,
    I dropped the saw and sat down into a chair.
    I had become accustomed to the pain.

The excitement that flowed through me
As I looked to my diseased ridden arm was astonishing.
Knowing that the cursed plague
No longer threatened my livelihood
Was overwhelming as if I had single handily defeated the
beast.

I did not care that I only had one arm.
That blackened limb on the work bench
Stopped being my arm a long time ago.
I was happy to be rid of it.
I was proud that I did it myself.

To stop the bleeding from my shoulder,
I heated the saw blade and singed the open wound.
That demonstrated to be more painful
Than the actual act of sawing off ones arm,
But necessary nonetheless.

A blackened crust formed over my wound.
I placed the dead arm within the fireplace and
Happily watched as the skin became engulfed in flames.
The rotted carcass was no match for the intensity of the
heat.
It soon disappeared leaving behind my skeletal remains as
evidence of my ghastly chore.
The smell of burning flesh filled my shop and was
intoxicating.
Freedom from the disease subdued any lasting pain,
But the thought of Mammon's return drew up some freshly
brewed fear.
I did not allow for the anticipation of our next encounter
To dampen my excitement of my new life.
Instead I cleansed my tools, swabbed the work bench
Shoveled up most of the red paste on the ground and retired
for the night.

I was awoken by my dog much like the previous day

With random acts of tongue kindness.
For a brief moment I had thought
That my gruesome task was once again a dream,
But I quickly came back to reality
As my blanket had bonded with my wound and
The faint aroma of my cooked flesh still lingered.

The cloth fibers absorbed with the oozing wound
    And had dried under the newly formed hardened skin.
    I pulled at the blanket, but the skin was no match for the
tightly wound fibers.
    With each tug, the skin pulled from my shoulder reopening
any healing that occurred.

I took a deep breath and gave a violent pull.
    The blanket freed itself and seized a large portion of my
skin.
    The pain was moderate as I had obviously experienced
worse.

While making a pot of tea, a knock sounded from the front
door.
    My immediate reaction was to hide behind my work bench.
    Was it Mammon or just simply a customer?
    I was not prepared to open the door for anyone
    As my missing arm would conjure up questions and
concerns.
    I decided to wait in hopes that my visitor would go away.
    I felt safe enough to move about my shop,
    However the calmness would not last as
    I got struck from behind with an unforgiving object.
    The force sent me tumbling forward into my work bench.
    I held my head and turned over to see
    Mammon standing near me clutching my skeletal arm.

Without haste, he twisted my old hand and pried it from the
wrist.
    He held up the bone and swung it downward at me again.

I managed to shift up my lone arm to protect myself,
But the force was too much.
The contact between the two bones sent chills up my arm.
He continued to swing two more times,
Each more devastating than the last
Until I could hold up my arm no more.
Seeing that I could no longer defend myself,
He lowered his weapon of bone and began to laugh.

Mammon tossed aside my skeletal arm and crawled upon my chest.
He was so close to my face that I could smell his pungent breath;
I could feel his excess saliva spewing from his mouth.
He was angry with me
As if my avoiding his original gift was wasting his time.

As I laid there bleeding and in pain,
He just stood on my chest like a gargoyle atop a steeple.
I could sense that he wanted to physically destroy me, but
Something held him back.

He needed something from me,
He needed my choice.
I was empowered for a brief moment,
Although my body did not reflect that.
My mind was finally clear
Of all of the fearful thoughts that had clouded my judgment.
I did not need to fear him anymore.
I showed my new found faith by offering my friend a grin.
That appeared to calm his anger and resentment towards me.
He leaped back off of my chest
Allowing me to finally take a much needed deep breath.
I wanted to rub my newly wounded arm
But that was physically impossible now.

My visitor sat down at my work bench and merely stared at me.

I could tell that he was conjuring up a new plan
In order for me to fulfill his demands.
He lifted up the goblet that was concealing the vial and
smiled.

He informed me once again of my task and
Insured me that the removal of my arm would not alter my
fate.
I did not believe him as I knew that I had
Strategically removed the threat of the plague from my
body.

I knew I had allowed enough of a distance
Between the decayed and healthy flesh when deciding on
where to cut.
His words meant nothing to me and
My new outlook revealed itself through my mannerisms.

I became rude and arrogant to him,
Which was uncharacteristic of me.
I wanted him out of my shop and out of my life.
He had already taken so much from me,
I was not going to give him anymore so I asked him to
leave.
My words angered him to the point
That I believe I saw him change the shape of his body.
The metamorphosis occurred so fast
That I could not be sure as to what I saw.

His human stature violently twisted and
Became entangled into a grotesque demon-like formation
That instantly shunned me with fear.
The vision was so demoralizing on my mind that
I immediately broke into a cold sweat.

Any such self-power that I had gathered
Up to that point had vanished.
My mind burrowed back down

Into the realm of self-pity and cowardliness.

During that time, he was mumbling in tongues.
    I could not translate his words.
    His body reshaped back into his previous state,
    But his eyes remained an evil shade of red.
    I knew at that moment that I was a fool to try to conquer
him.

I was about to receive my punishment.
    He leaped back upon my chest
    With a force that broke some of my ribs.
    He wasted no time with unveiling his new plan.
    From underneath his cloak he pulled out a small dagger.
    He held up his arm and cut through his wrist
    To release a bright murky liquid that seeped from his flesh
and coated the blade.

With a smirk, he glanced at the dagger then at me.
    Part of me wanted him to shove the blade
    Deep within my skull so that my life would be ended.
    My body wanted to die, but my mind begged him for mercy.

He plunged the knife within my upper chest,
    Not in an area that would lead to my demise,
    Rather a pinpointed area to infect my body once again.
    He leaned hard on the dagger as if to make a personal point
    That I should meet his demands.
    His point was well received that time.

My body was in shambles;
    My mind was deteriorating at a quick pace.
    He stood from me and placed the vial upon my chest.
    As he walked away, he offered me his signature last words
    That he would see me soon.
    As I laid there broken and bruised,
    I quickly realized that the visits with my friend
    Never end well for me.

Throughout the day, customers would come to the door
    Inquire about orders and such.
    I did not respond to them.
    None of my old life mattered,
    None of my customers mattered.
    All of that was useless to me now.
    My friends, my neighbors, my material items,
    Were all rendered pointless.

My only salvation was that vial of vaccine.
    That was the only relic of potential peace in my life.
    The other villagers did not care about me;
    They were only concerned with their orders or repairs.
    They saw me as a means to their greater good,
    As a stepping stone to benefit them.
    I laid there half dead and for what?
    To salvage their existence; to save their livelihood.
    Within me was the monster, a beast like no other and
    I was the gatekeeper for it.
    That small vial that rested upon my chest was the key to all
of it.

The dagger burned deep within my flesh.
    I could feel the newly added disease spreading,
    Contracting my muscles.
    My lungs weakened and gasped for air.
    Mammon was right;
    The disease would suffocate me into making a decision.
    I could feel it creeping up my neck and squeezing my throat.
    My mind was racing through possible scenarios;
    Outcomes to benefit both parties at hand.

However, the greed was strong in me
    When faced with my own demise.
    At that point, my mind was the only
    Working organism left in my body.
    It was trying desperately to create a solution

In order to save the shell in which it resided in.
It portrayed an idea that seemed reasonable at the time.
When unchallenged it would ultimately win.
I would consume the vial and
With my new found life,
I would erect a large wall around the village
To protect everyone from the approaching plague.
The plan was perfect and gave me such inspiration
That it must have been the answer.
With enough strength,
I managed to move the vial up to my mouth and
Used my teeth to pry open the lid.
The liquid tasted like nectar of a ripened fruit.
It was so pleasant going down my ravaged throat
That I did not want it to end.
With my internal organs in such a weak state,
I could actually feel the struggle taken place
Between the vaccine and the virus.
I could feel my lungs filling with air;
My heart funneling the blood.
The relief of making a choice was overwhelming,
So much so that I blacked out and fell asleep.

Next day brought about bright
Sunshine through the hallowed out hole in the door.
Again my dog served as my wake master.
I subconsciously petted him and realized that I had two
arms.

The sight and feeling was a blessing to behold
And much appreciated.
I believed that I had returned to my former self
As the result of meeting the demands of Mammon.
I was completely healthy again
With no physical signs of broken bones or scars
From my previous encounters.
Even my shop was clean with no trace of blood.

My reaction was that I should have consumed the vial
earlier.
    I would have avoided the large amount of pain.
    Regardless, my attitude was renewed and
    Restructured with wonderful thoughts of encouragement.

I opened the front door of my shop
    For the first time in days and looked around the village.
    I was still holding on to the thought
    That none of the other people mattered to me,
    But at the same time,
    I needed them for my own livelihood.

I required their business to better my life.
    Call it selfishness, but they owed me
    For the pain and suffering I went through.
    Regardless of what I thought about them individually,
    They were worth more to me collectively as a group.

To preserve them, I would keep to my word
    I had given myself regarding the perimeter wall.
    I began to construct the barrier within my mind;
    Envisioned how much wood it would require.

I soon started construction of a project
    That would enclose the village and safeguard the residents
    From outside travelers that may be carrying the plague.
    The village was easily convinced
    As I increased the severity of the tales told by the gypsies.
    Fear did a wonderful thing
    When it came down to acquiring volunteers.
    Days went by with no visit from Mammon,
    Which allowed me to fully focus on my task.
    With the wall completely surrounding the village,
    A main gate was the last piece of the puzzle.
    The structure was even more beautiful than I had imagined.
    I had designed the perimeter with extra height
    To deter travelers from scaling it to gain entrance.

A local blacksmith forged the massive gate
    That proved to be the most pivotal aspect of the
construction.
    From the characteristics of the structure,
    One would think that we were defending ourselves
    Against a vast army of barbarians.

Some said it was too much,
    In my mind it was necessary
    As I had experienced the pain and torture
    That the plague could unleash.
    I offered the naysayers no response to their claims
    As the wall was already built.

The village was indebted to me
    As they should have been.
    My selfish act would be their salvation.
    My selfish encounter would ultimately spare their lives.
    I never mentioned my near death experience to anyone,
    Although I did ponder sharing my story
    If we had not ceased the nightly ritual.
    I wondered what they would think of me
    If I had told them that I had beaten the plague.
    Would they have seen me as a hero?
    Would they hold a feast in my name or even worship me?

It was tempting, but the time was not appropriate.
    Some residents thought I had lost my sanity.
    I understood why they would think that as
    I had built a huge wall that blocked the beautiful horizon
    To fend off a fictitious approaching plague.
    I knew it was coming though,
    I knew that Mammon would be the one escorting it.

Peace fell within the village as
    Travelers were turned away from a safe distance.
    We did not allow visitors or anyone who was not like us

Within the inner vicinity of the wall.
We forced hungry travelers
To continue on their way and bypass our village.
The idea was brutal in its intentions
As most of them would not make it to the next town.

The once healthy resources of our village
   That were offered to starving travelers were no longer
gifted.
   Groups after groups were denied free passage through the
gates,
   Which often times resulted in riots and violence,
   It came to the point that residents were cautious
   To exit the gate as they were afraid
   That they would be denied reentry.

I saw firsthand several attempts
   By plague-ridden peasants to scale the wall.
   They were met with brutal hatred
   And thrown rocks that persuaded them otherwise.
   Due to my history, I was able to spot those who were
infected.
   Most tried to conceal a certain limb
   Or completely cover themselves,
   But they were not fooling me.
   Even in the crowds outside,
   The plague infested ones were not wanted.
   They were beaten severely if anyone found out.
   Some non-infected people were even punished
   Merely because another traveler accused them.

We turned away those begging for food and water,
   Even half-starved children.
   We wanted no one who was not already within the wall.
   The task to keep people out was a daunting one.
   Each of the villagers had a common cause so
   We equally shared the burden through night watches.

We had to deny access to all who would threaten our
lifestyles.
    We gave them no pity or remorse.
    The travelers sought out charity,
    We denied them of their request.
    We became a selfish stronghold in a plague infested world
and
    We thought nothing wrong about it.

With Mammon gone, everything was at peace within my life.
    I had given him his answer and not only saved myself,
    But saved the village as well.
    The pay for erecting such a mighty wall
    Had made me wealthy and content.
    Orders were exceeding my expectations as
    People required reinforced lumber to increase the security of
their cottages
    As if the plague would not penetrate hardened wood.

As with every day, I arose to the loving touch of my dog.
    When prepping the shop for my daily chores,
    I was greeted by my neighbor.
    He appeared distraught and after further questioning,
    It was revealed that my dog had bitten him.

Apparently, he was tending to his garden late at night
    When my dog became estranged.
    He was not worried about it as it was just a scratch and
    He blamed the shadows of night as the reason for the
confusion.

His concern did grow a little as he showed me his wound.
    I looked to his arm and my chest began to tighten.
    It was as if Mammon himself was standing on it again.
    There was a small scratch that was surrounded by the
blackened blood vessels
    I had known so well.
    My immediate reaction was to strike my neighbor dead.

My rational thought prompted me otherwise.
I asked who he was in contact with.
He replied that he did nothing unusual
That he greeted everyone as he did each day.

My throat immediately became dry,
    I tried desperately to swallow.
    I called for my dog and noticed that his eyes were blood red.
    He snarled at me as I reached down to touch him.

My neighbor was concerned and kept asking me questions, but
    My attention was directly upon my dog.
    He had been infected all along.
    Each day that I struggled with the curse of what to do,
    My choice had already been established.

I had made the wrong decision.
    I should have chosen to duplicate the vaccine.
    What had I done?
    I witnessed the darkened blood vessels creep up his neck.
    He grasped his chest as his wandering eyes searched
    For some sort of rational reasons why it was occurring.
    He would never retrieve those answers
    As he soon fell lifeless to the ground.

I walked out the front door and
    Gazed upon the village courtyard
    That was littered with decaying bodies.
    I had single-handily murdered everyone within our village.
    Those still alive tried eagerly to scale the wall,
    But the height was too much for them to handle.
    The village became their grave;
    The wall served as their tombstone.
    Within a matter of moments I was the only one standing
    Within my beautifully constructed wooden perimeter.

I did not feel remorse,
    As I watched my fellow neighbors slump to their death.

It was almost soothing to not have to fear the plague
anymore.
    I offered no pity even as my dog collapsed.
    I was alive and healthy amongst a sea of contamination.
    I had what no others had and I was not about to offer it as
charity.

Loud pounding on the front gate
    Rang out through the barren courtyard.
    Even at that moment, travelers wanted in;
    They sought salvation.
    I walked over to the gate and unlatched it.
    People flowed in like a newly formed river.
    They clung to me with their blackened fingers and hands.
    They begged for help, but I could offer them none
    Nor did I want to.
    I looked upon them as mindless animals
    And treated them like cattle as I herded them inside.
    I had spared myself
    That shameless period before death and
    I was disgusted to be around them.
    I wanted to speed up the process of the plague
    Just to rid myself of their babbling moaning and agony.
    I climbed atop the gate and watched as miles of infested
    Travelers funneled through my wall.
    At that moment I realized the purpose of my construction.
    It was not meant to keep the plague out,
    Rather to serve as a place to house the dead.
    With everyone lifeless or on the verge of dying,
    My carpentry business obviously decreased.
    To fend off the insanity that was brewing within me
    From being the only living person,
    I began to construct coffins for the dead.

I would randomly select a dead corpse from the courtyard and
    Search through their belongings.
    If they had any kind of money or relics on them
    Then they would pay me for a coffin.

I referred to them as the rich dead and
Their bodies were placed within a special pile near my shop.
Those with no money or valuable belongings
Were considered the poor dead and were
Thrown within a wide deep trench that I created.
If I was approached by an infested living person
Who begged me for help,
I had them first empty their pockets.
They would then be led to the appropriate pile
Depending upon what they revealed.

I had no personal connection with anyone;
    I considered myself alone on a dead island.
    However, my burial services proved profitable.
    I had to eventually construct a shed to house all of the
    Belongings that I was receiving.

To avoid utter isolation, I propped up a few corpses
    Around the entrance of the village
    To serve as my welcoming committee.
    I only used the freshest looking bodies as
    I did not want to scare off my visitors.
    Due to the decaying method of the human body,
    I had to change out the committee on a regular basis.

On one particular day while rotating my unpaid staff,
    I noticed Mammon waiting in line to enter.
    The vision of him struck me like a heavy mallet to the head.
    How could one person cause so much fear in me?
    I decided to withhold my emotions and waved to him.

I greeted him and told him that he did not have to wait in line.
    We walked together into the courtyard with a bitter silence.
    Part of me was afraid that he was here with another
question,
    But I tried not to think about that as he surveyed the two
piles.
    While looking into my pit of poor corpses,

He told me that he had forgotten to inform me
About a small part of the question.
My heart began to beat extraordinarily fast.
My vision began to blur once again.

My brow instantly started to collect sweat beads as
	He went on to say that he had forgotten to tell me
	That the vial of vaccine was only temporary.
	He said that the elders who were to receive the vial
	Were also going to add the finishing touches to it,
	Most importantly the longevity.

I tried to swallow, but no saliva had built up within my mouth.
	I saw myself in Mammon for the first time.
	He looked upon me as I did my infected visitors
	With no remorse or pity.
	With the words he offered me,
	He also brought me the gift of death.
	I was not saddened by his visit nor did I dwell in his words.
	He gestured me one last smirk and
	Said that he would see me again.
	He added that he was proud of my choice.

He leaped in my death trench and
	Vanished amongst the tangled corpses.
	As I stood on the threshold of the pit,
	The line of visitors continued flowing through the village
gates.

I decided to build one last coffin
	With the most prized pieces of wood.
	I deemed none of the previous dead
	To be worthy enough of that quality.
	As I felt my chest tightening under the pressure of the
disease,
	I lifted my coffin and carried it well away
	From the pit to the inside of my shop.

I walked passed my pile of riches
    That I had been collecting from the dead,
    I emptied my pockets of any coins and relics
    And paid for my own coffin.

I moved my work bench and placed the coffin in its place.
    My legs began to slump and become weightless.
    I felt my ankles breaking as the disease hollowed out my
bones.
    Leaning over the edge of the coffin, I managed to fall in.
    As I laid there on my back awaiting death,

I pondered what my life would have been like
    If I had made the other choice.

~

Why must you deny me access
    To my previous transcriptions?
    Why am I not allowed to understand what I am writing?
    Am I not doing what you have asked me to do?

I am so alone with my thoughts that
    The ability to read my own words would be a blessing.
    I require more interaction as
    The solitary confinement within this cave
    Is deteriorating my mind.
    I demand more than just this quill and paper.
    I demand more than shadowy figures
    That do nothing more than lurk in the dark.
    I demand...

~

I...I apologize for my previous thoughts and words.
    I will never demand anything again.
    I am grateful for what you have given me.
    I graciously accept the quest you have offered.

I will do whatever you wish.
I beg you to keep the shadows confined to the walls.
I will never ask for anything again.
My intentions are neither to anger you
Nor betray you in anyway.

I have come to the realization
That I will not know what I have previously transcribed.
The knowledge of that is a relief.
From the numbers of my shadowy friends,
I see that two are missing now.
I view this positively,
However I am very concerned
With reaching the point where none are left.
Does that mean I have finished my task
And can go back to my farm?

Surely once I fulfill the needs of God,
He would allow my exit from this cave.
I can only pray that my past memories
Would be restored within my mind.
How wonderful that would be?
To be able to interact with other people
Would also be a pleasant gift.
The inability to hear any words
Not coming from my mind is wearing on me.
I can only talk to myself for so long
Before I find myself annoying.
I dread the fact that I am viewing my inner thoughts as an
enemy.
I know this sounds strange,
But I often hear my thoughts
And wish they were no longer there.

I would imagine that complete silence
Would not be any better, but I sometimes hope
That my rapid thought patterns would decrease.

I find that I am starting to argue with myself
   Which is undoubtedly gratifying to my shadowy friends,
   But only provides me with pressure that is uncontrollable.
   It is probably for the best that I do not know my own name.
   I would only use it to tell myself to be quiet.

IV

Sloth

I woke to the sound of thunder,
　　Which was a blessing as there was much
　　Unfinished work to be done on the farm.
　　Storms were abundant that time of year,
　　The rain was much desired from the
　　Dry spell the previous season brought.

The output of my wheat had reached its peak.
　　Even had me plowing new fields
　　To fulfill the demands of the nearby cities,
　　Which was gradually increasing.

I had always handled all operations of my farm by myself.
　　Labor during the days was long and tiring,
　　But my effort was precise and stringent.

My work ethic alone was the basis
　　For overshadowing my competitors.
　　Several new farms were erected over the years,
　　I countered them by increasing my output and service.

For many years, I had been the sole supplier of wheat.
　　My product was unmatched by any competitor.
　　With the construction of new villages and towns,
　　Demand for wheat grew to the point where my fields
doubled.
　　My passion for work allowed me to fulfill the demands
　　Although the increased production

Provided me with much fatigue.
I soon became accustomed to the change in my sleep pattern
And even found it refreshing.
I believed that if I worked while my rivals slept,
My farm would remain successful.
Less time sleeping translated into more time working.

One aspect that I did not anticipate
  Was the large variety of usage for wheat.
  As the villages grew in size,
  Different influences spread across the region,
  People began to experiment and create new recipes
involving the product.

New ideas mixed with trade specialties
  Forced the consumption of wheat to increase dramatically.
  For the first time since running the farm,
  I was falling behind in my output and
  Demand for my product intensified greatly.

I worried that if I did not meet the orders
  More competitors would arise.
  New competition would not be a welcomed sight for me.
  I viewed my inability to meet demand as a weakness and
  I was determined to do whatever in my power to stay ahead
of my rivals.
  I came to the understanding that I could no longer handle
the farm by myself.
  As much as the notion of acquiring help disgusted me,
  It became apparent in the quality of my product.
  In order to meet the daily requirements,
  I had to concentrate more on the quantity than the quality.
  That was against everything that I stood for.
  I needed to swallow my pride so that my output would not
suffer.

Finding an assistant would prove to be difficult.
    My criteria was impossible to conquer.
    I met many people who had the skills for the task,
    But my personal preferences were never satisfied.

I turned away highly proclaimed farmers
    For the sole reasons of selfishness.
    My ego would not allow me to seek those
    Who I believed were less than me.
    And unfortunately, that was everyone I encountered.
    The task seemed hopeless
    Until I met Belphegor, an irrigation specialist in the region.
    Belphegor was recognized for his moral ethics
    And quality of his product.
    I had never met him before,
    But his customers spoke highly of him.
    Unlike all of the other candidates who came to me,
    I actually had to seek out Belphegor.
    During the winter season when the crops were at the lowest,
    I traveled into town in hopes to meet up with him.
    In a strange coincidence, Belphegor happened to be in town.
    I approached him and introduced myself.
    Apparently my reputation proceeded me
    As he stated that he knew who I was.

He even appeared gracious to meet me,
    That made the conversation easier than I had imagined.
    It also reduced my appearance of being in a needy situation
    Even though I was very desperate for help.

We walked for awhile around the town and
    Discussed architecture and agriculture.
    The conversation was so splendid that I felt at ease with
him.
    We shared the same ideas and beliefs towards nature.
    We had the same understanding regarding
    The concept of benefiting and replenishing the land.
    He had passed my personality test with ease,

But I was more interested in this work ethic than anything
else.

I shifted the conversation
    In hopes to gain a sense of his lifestyle.
    He offered everything that I required
    By informing me that he lives for his work,
    That he rarely gets to step away and venture into town.
    He continued by saying that being away from his work,
    He actually missed it.
    His thoughts matched mine as I too missed my farm.
    I wasted no time in offering him a position on my farm.
    He was very accepting of my proposal and continued
    That he could start as soon as he could gather his
belongings.

We parted ways and I went back to my fields
    With an increase in determination,
    Which was not what I was anticipating.
    My hatred for assistance,
    Viewing it as a weakness had dramatically decreased.
    I even amazed myself by showing signs of relief.

The following morning, I arose at my regular time
    And was met by Belphegor on the farm.
    His punctuality was a blessing
    As I still had a few lingering doubts about the whole
situation.
    His anxiousness to get to work
    Quickly erased those doubts and replaced them with
enthusiasm.
    Any awkwardness that I had predicted
    During the first day of working alongside another person
    Was non-existent as the day moved along smoothly.

Regardless of whom I had chosen to assist me,
    I was going to analyze their work ethic ability the first day.
    I spared no time in testing Belphegor

By bombarding him with tasks and chores,
Some more desirable than others.
He absorbed everything that I required for him to do.
He managed his time swiftly;
Adjusted his pace in order to meet my demands.
He reminded me of myself and my own work ethic.

Over the next few days,
It was evident that Belphegor was a perfect match.
He would work late and rise early the morning after.
His responsibilities were completed with such accuracy and
quality
That he even enhanced certain aspects of the farm.
He was such a blessing that I could not imagine the farm
without him.
Together we formed a productive process
That destroyed any current competitors and
Those that would be forthcoming.

Our first structural addition that we designed together
Was a storage unit to house the oversupply of product.
His knowledge of architecture surpassed mine and
Was apparent within the beautiful facility he had
constructed.
I will say, that it was quite nice to converse with another
While working on the farm.
For so many years, I had been alone with my thoughts.
It was refreshing to hear different ideas
Involving the fields regardless of how beneficial they were.
We had many discussions regarding the land.
How to increase production.
Reap more benefits from nature.
Some of the smaller ideas
Such as enhancing the sturdiness of the tool shed
Or cleansing the paths between the fields
Were quickly implemented without haste.
Most were handled by Belphegor during off hours or

While I was tending to the daily chores.
I do not know how he was able to take on as much as he did,
To wake up the next day and
Have an idea completed was quite gratifying.
Larger notions would gradually consume our conversations.
Often times the ideas would remain just in our thoughts,
Occasionally one would be so beneficial
That it pleaded for more attention.

Such an idea was to increase the irrigation flow
To the wheat by constructing a large canal system.
With the constant threat of dry seasons,
The idea proved to be a potentially noteworthy one.

The conversation was enhanced
To include particular specifications.
One main barricade was the vast amount of wood
Required to build such a large structure.

I was a little hesitant
As an irrigation system that massive had never been
constructed
And I worried about the sturdiness of it.
He always had a response to counteract my anxiety.
And was very persuasive in his choice of words.
For the first time,
I had entrusted my farm in the hands of another.
That was not an easy task for me to unleash.
My land was the treasure of my life,
But I saw something in Belphegor that day
That would convince me to rely on him.
I saw creativeness and excitement within his eyes.
It reminded me of how I felt
When I came across an idea that I thoroughly believed in.

He had gained my approval, but
We still struggled with the issue of lumber.
Belphegor stated that he knew of a large area of oak trees.

He thought they would be the perfect shape for the task.
He was not sure that they were still there
As he had not ventured there in quite some time.
Apparently, he had stumbled upon the area while traveling.
Since then he stated that he had been in several nearby towns
And had not observed oak being used in any of the architecture.

He was convinced that they remained there.
The idea of using oak for the structure was an excellent idea.
I had no previous encounters with such wood, as
I constructed the farm mainly from pine.

I had never even touched oak before so
My excitement grew since
I was expanding my knowledge.
I imagined what my competitors would think
Knowing that my farm was the first in the region to utilize oak.

I predicted their frustration of not knowing
Where to find the oak trees.
It provided me with some pleasure.
That was the enhancement my farm needed
To keep my product ahead of the others.
It would only be a matter of time
Before they found the tree source and copied my methods.

I followed the guidance of Belphegor
Merely that he was a master at constructing irrigation systems.
I could tell the sheer size of the structure
Would be a challenge for him,
I was anxious to see his design implemented.
It was established that we would travel the next day
To the valley of oak and collect the needed supplies.

I slept easy that night
Knowing that the irrigation enrichment was greatly needed.
The ability to spread water across the fields
In equal portions was an improvement
That would counteract the sporadic rainy seasons
We had been experiencing.
Belphegor stayed up all night developing plans.
He finished the details of the project while I slept.
Next day we set out to lay claim to the oak trees.
I had not traveled that far in quite some time, however
Conversations and sharing of ideas lessened the duration.
Belphegor showed me sketches of his design and
I was amazed by the detail that he used.
The vision was wonderful and I had no concerns,
Which was unusual of me especially
When the topic involved altering my fields.

Toting two large wagons,
We journeyed through thick pine forests and gaping ravines.
On occasion our wagons got wedged within the terrain
Particularly when we crossed the drained riverbed of mud.

I could not help but think about the journey back.
How we would be able to handle the same path
With our wagons filled with the heavy oak?
I did not let it discourage me,
I had faith that my partner had exhausted all potential
threats.

We traveled through vast grass fields
That proved not too difficult for our wagons.
The long blades of grass lied down beneath the wooden
wheels
And provided us with a path to return on.

The more difficult passage proved to be
Pulling of the wagons uphill.
We struggled for quite some time

Before we were able to rest on the crest.

I was about to ask Belphegor how much further,
  He interrupted my question by gesturing to the valley
below.
  Our long journey had ended
  As I overlooked a valley filled with oak trees.

The sight was very inspiring with
  Rows of beautifully aligned oak trees packing the valley.
  The trunks were perfectly rounded
  Which exploded at the top with powerful branches
  And clusters of splendid green leaves.

The scene was further enhanced
  With streams of sunlight highlighting the tops of the trees.
  It was an awe inspiring natural sight.
  As if the heavens leaked perfection on to the ground
underneath.

The outlook filled my mind with creativity that
  Soon was replaced with visions of my jealous competitors.
  I imagined their reactions
  When they first would learn of my oak structure.
  Then depicted their facial expressions when they gazed
upon it.
  I looked to Belphegor with high approval.
  He offered a smile in return.
  The structure that was only an idea was turning into a
reality.

We remained on the crest of hill for a brief moment as
  I was in no rush to end the satisfaction that I felt.
  However, the longer I stared, the more hesitant I was
becoming.
  Something was too flawless about the circumstances;
  Something was too flawless about the trees.

It was not until I witnessed a runaway lightning bolt
    Exit from a picturesque white cloud above the valley
    That I realized what the place was.
    The valley and the trees were on holy ground.

I shared my thought with Belphegor.
    He immediately took offense to my words.
    It was unlike him to get upset with me about anything
    As we had always shared ideas without any negative tones.
    He accused me of insulting his judgment;
    He questioned our friendship.
    The quick outburst startled me and
    Caused my thoughts to become entangled with confusion.
    I assured him that it was only a feeling that I had,
    That my words meant no harm.
    He withdrew his anger and apologized for his comments.
    I accepted his apology,
    But his previous mannerisms still troubled me.
    I had never seen that side of him before.
    I could tell that he was still physically upset
    By the way he forcefully pulled his wagon
    As he began his decent down to the valley.
    Setting aside my beliefs,
    I pulled my wagon and followed him.
    The surrounding area was so serene
    That it made the journey pleasurable.

The cool breeze combined with the warmth of the sun was
relaxing.
    I envisioned myself lying upon the grass and sleeping.
    The crisp air felt good as it filled my lungs.
    For now, I kept the thoughts to myself.
    I was not about to mention the topic of sacred ground again.

We neared the outer perimeter of the trees.
    They made us feel small in comparison to their mighty
heights.
    They were spectacular in all aspects of their characteristics.

I could only imagine the massive root support systems
That built such relics.

As I stood at the base of one of them and looked up,
    They were extensions from the ground straight up to
heaven.
    The way the green leaves contrasted
    Against the blue sky was breathtaking.
    These were the visions
    That dreams were comprised of.
    I slid my hand along the bark of the mighty tree and
    Instantly felt its strength and power under my fingertips.
    Belphegor walked towards me carrying two axes.
    He pointed to the tree I was touching,
    Announced that we would start with it.
    My first response was that these axes
    Would never penetrate the armor of bark.

I hesitantly grabbed the axe and
    Watched him circle to the opposite side.
    As I choked up on the wooden handle,
    I noticed a carved symbol of a lion in the bark.

The symbol was so detailed.
    The lion was alive on the brown canvas.
    I looked to the other trees and
    Saw that they each had similar carvings of different animals.
    My assumption of holy ground was becoming clearer,
    I struggled as to how to bring up the topic again.
    I would not have to battle long as
    My physical actions would speak for me.
    While Belphegor raised his axe, I was lowering mine.
    He halted his swing and gave me a disapproving gesture.
    I took a few steps back and
    Announced that we could not proceed
    As we were on holy ground.
    I saw his frustration with me growing within his eyes,
    However, I was certain that we should not be here.

He spoke about the trees,
    Saying these are the only ones capable
    Of withstanding the pressures of the irrigation canals.
    I replied that I could not destroy God's land.

His muscles flinched as he gripped his axe.
    For a brief moment, we stood there with axe in hand
    Staring at one another.
    I was unsure what his next move was going to be.

I could see that he was contemplating
    Through his facial gestures.
    I was neither a fighter nor an angry person,
    However, I held tight to my axe
    In the unfortunate event that I needed to defend myself.

Part of me hoped that it was all a misunderstanding
    That he did not know the trees were marked.
    My anxiety grew with each passing moment without sound.
    He showed signs that he was thinking
    About how to respond to me.
    The scene made me nervous
    As I translated it as he was about to lie to me.

My hands suctioned to the axe handle
    From the sweat pouring from my palms.
    I was praying that he would not strike at me,
    Then I realized that no man would hurt another on holy
ground.
    That would be considered an act of cruelty.

It calmed my nerves slightly,
    It still did not change the fact that he remained silent.
    He broke the tension by speaking and
    Told me that he had made a mistake.
    That maybe we should not harm the trees.

The comments were a relief to hear
    As I did not know how to properly defend myself,
    Especially against an axe.
    I stood there still confused
    As he pulled his cart away from the trees.

Part of me was hesitant to follow him off of the sacred ground.
    I imagined him luring me to an unholy area and attacking
me.
    I did not give that thought much backing as
    I believed that he truly had made a mistake.

Traveling home dwelled on forever.
    Discussions were not nearly as exciting as the journey there.
    I was still uncertain as to the truth regarding my friend.
    I determined that his outburst was due to the notion
    We traveled that great distance and returned with nothing.

When I looked through his eyes, it even made me upset,
    But I was not about to become disloyal to God;
    Desecrate such beautiful trees on sacred ground.

I had made my living from the land that God created.
    I had to respect his wishes.
    I dared not think about what would have happen
    If I followed Belphegor's wishes.
    I had time to contemplate such outcomes
    As the journey back to the farm was long.
    I imagined season after season of draught
    With no relief in sight;
    No water to flow through the new canals.
    I predicted powerful thunderstorms destroying the fields,
    Saturating my newly plowed lands.
    I even thought of a pack of savage wolves
    Tormenting my crops and feasting upon them as I slept.
    Next morning I arose from a peaceful slumber.

I walked outside in amazement and disgust.

Throughout the land was a massive new irrigation system
Funneling water to the wheat fields.
I walked over to the nearest canal and touched the wood.
Although it was beautifully carved to perfection,
I could not help but realize that it was
Constructed from oak.
My hand glided down the smooth wood as I walked
alongside.

My emotions were so entangled
That I did not know what to think.

It was literally amazing in all aspects of design.
I soon became angry as my fingers
Floated above the indentation of a lion's head.
As I savagely scoured the fields for Belphegor,
I could not ignore what type of punishment
God would unleash upon us and the farm.

I had told Belphegor not to touch the trees;
He had disobeyed me.
He had broken the trust that took time to build.
I had determined that I would first allow him to explain
himself.

I followed the canals to each of the fields.
The more I was around the structure,
The more I began to admire it.
It was ideal in all aspects except the wood source.

My chaotic search for my partner slowly decreased.
It was replaced with the admiration and quality of the
system.
The craftsmanship was extraordinary;
The joints of the canals were handled with expert carpentry.

I began to question the notion of scared ground.

Why would God deny us farmers such a high quality of
wood?
Surely, he could plant new trees.
By the looks of the system,
Belphegor probably only used a few of them.
Are we not using the wood to replenish God's land
With the nutrients that he provides us?
The idea that we were taken from the land
In order to give back to the land
Pacified my anger towards my partner.
When all of my irritation had subsided,
Belphegor suddenly appeared next to me.
It was as if he was monitoring my anger level.
I could not be upset with him
After he constructed such a wonderful system
That would greatly benefit the farm.
As for the outcome with God,
The trees were already destroyed,
It would be a shame for the wood to go to waste.

Over the next few days
My fear of a backlash from God diminished.
I even doubted my original idea of the oak valley being
sacred.
With no signs of turbulent storms, sun drenched droughts
And tormenting wolves in the near future,
I was never given proof that the trees were holy, so
I drifted away from the concept.
My worrying was replaced with acceptance
My concern was replaced with influence.

Days on the farm returned back to normal.
They were filled to capacity with tasks and upkeep.
The new irrigation proved invaluable and
Improved the quality of the wheat.

Belphegor and I worked from dawn to dusk and
Even through the night on certain projects.

I had never seen a work ethic that equaled mine
From anyone before.
I had always viewed others as weak and lazy
Compared to myself.
The farm was my life, a successful life
Due to my commitment to work.

Over time, Belphegor's work capacity continued to grow.
I was amazed at the amount of work that he could handle.
Most times I was unsure how
He actually accomplished the tasks with such speed.
Each day he would take on more,
Even crossed over to some of my tasks.
I did not believe in personal angels,
But in this instance I did.
He did so much work
That I was actually acquiring free time,
However I did not know what to do with it,
But it was still pleasant nonetheless.

The amount of free time increased
With the turn of every season.
I was even able to oversleep.
He never woke me as he believed that I needed my rest.
The extra sleep felt good so I did not argue with him.
As long as the tasks were being completed, I was happy to
oblige.

I do not know exactly when I noticed, but
I could tell that my physical attributes were changing.
For instance, my weight had increased substantially
Along with a reduction in my overall stamina.

They were no more apparent
Than when I tried to complete simple farming chores.
I blamed it solely on the amount of free time I now had.
I began to set aside tasks until the next day
Which was rare for me.

One should always finish the work of the present day
    As the next day would bring about its own amount.
    However, I now saw nothing wrong with postponing the
work.
    I enjoyed my free time so much,
    I was not about to decrease it even for my personal beliefs.

One morning after I had overslept,
    I peered out the window and
    Saw Belphegor busily working in the fields.
    My first thought was to go out and help,
    But I knew he could handle it, so I went back to sleep.
    That had occurred on many separate occasions and
    Was growing more abundant as the days went by.
    I failed to believe that I was becoming lazy,
    Instead settling on the excuse that I had worked so hard,
    I was entitled to the much needed rest.
    Next morning I decided to get back out on the farm.
    I awoke earlier than I had in a long time,
    Which was difficult to do.
    I greeted Belphegor at the edge of the first field where
    He was mending to one of the irrigation canals.
    He was shocked to see me up at that time and
    Even presented me with an attitude
    Similar to the one I received in the oak tree valley.
    I thought he would be happy that I was there to help;
    Instead he was more annoyed at the offer.

He said that all of the tasks were in order
    That I could go back in and rest.
    He pushed so much that I became upset.
    Even went so far as to say that the farm was mine and
    No one would tell me what to do.
    He responded with that same eerie silence he had done
before.
    That contemplating silence;
    That stare that made me question him so long ago.

I broke the silence by asking him what he wanted from me.
He replied that he was just here to help and
If I wanted him to leave then he would.
His statement caught me off guard,
Forced me to instantly coward.
I stated that I did not want him to leave
As the farm had never run so smoothly.

We apologized to one another.
    He said that if I wanted to help
    That the tools in the shed needed cleansing.
    I accepted the task and headed off in that direction.

As I walked, I could feel him staring at me.
    Why did I doubt him?
    He had done nothing wrong to me.
    He had only increased the production of my farm,
    Even allowed me some freedom,
    Which I really enjoyed.
    And still I questioned him, but why?

There was something about his personality
    That changed for the worse
    When he was approached about his intentions.
    In the past, he would desire the ability to share tasks with
me,
    He had recently begun to push me away.
    I thought he just likes to work alone.
    I could understand as I once desired the same thing.

I entered the tool shed and looked around.
    As he had said, the dirty tools were abundant.
    At first the task seemed daunting and unexciting.
    I stood in the doorway with a feeling of anxiety as
    I gazed upon the massive chore at hand.

I used to do the job with such love and care for my tools.
    The cleansing of them for the next day

Was considered a relaxing chore for me.
I did not consider it work as I enjoyed handling it.

Now I stood there trying to avoid beginning.
    Part of me thought that if I walked away
    Belphegor would do the task,
    Probably at a quicker speed.

Perhaps I still had a slither of work ethic left.
    With a deep sigh I reached for my first tool.
    It was painful to scrape the dried dirt from it.
    My facial gestures matched my decreasing desire to
continue.
    I am unsure how the next events unfolded,
    But it would alter my life greatly.
    After finishing my first tool,
    I reached for another one on the floor
    When the shed began to tremble.
    The tools hanging from the walls
    Vibrated in a perfect rhythm and
    Soon began to become unhinged.
    I noticed that I could not retract my arm from the ground.
    I pulled at my arm, but something had it tightly secured.
    There was nothing visual there to hold me.
    I stared at my wrist and
    Saw the indentations of gripping fingers.
    I looked up and witnessed what I believe
    To have been a spirit with dark red eyes.
    It was leaning backwards while pulling my arm towards it.
    I immediately grabbed my arm with my other hand and
    Applied force the opposite way.
    During the struggle, the tools hanging from the wall fell
    With knives stabbing into the dirt in a close proximity to
me.
    My held captive arm would shift closer to the falling tools.
    Some carving knives were in line to fall next.
    The sheer amount of them made me nervous.
    One by one the vibrations of the shed

Enabled them to plummet towards me.
With each knife that successfully avoided my arm,
I breathed a sigh of relief.
I was able to wrestle my own arm
From its captor to evade all of the blades thus far.

As I continued to try to break away
From the clutches of the spirit,
I heard a loud rattle above me.
The noise was so distinct that it quickly drew my attention.

A large tree axe supported by two hinges
Vibrating directly above me.
I gave so much thought to the axe that
I was losing the battle for my arm.

I remember that tool in such detail.
It was the only one that was perfectly shiny and clean.
The first hinge holding the handle broke free
Allowing for the axe to shift positions and swing downward.

The spirit pulled even harder on my arm now,
But I gained some spare energy that I fed into my resistance.
My upper arm was becoming sore from the struggle,
I felt my shoulder pull from its socket.
My arm immediately went numb and
I was unable to continue my full onslaught of its retrieval.
The fear I had of the dangling axe
Prompted me to support my held arm with my free one,
But my resistance was dealt a devastating distraction.

I could only fight my captor for so long.
The spirit knew that and waited patiently
While my stamina drained.
I noticed that my captor only pulled my arm when I resisted.

The knowledge wore me down.
I knew I would not win the battle.

I stopped providing any thought
And power to the recapture of my limb.
It revealed itself within my posture as
I prepared myself for the inevitable.
Instead of dwelling in the spirit itself,
I tried to fixate on the axe,
But the dirt and dust from the vibrating shed clouded my
vision.
The last hinge supporting the tool broke loose
Supplying the axe full freedom to descend.
I desperately prayed that the handle would fall first,
The odds were not in my favor as
The blade easily sliced through my arm near the wrist.
Separation from the tension of being pulled
Sent me falling backwards.
The pain was unbearable and so intense that
I did not even ponder the whereabouts of the spirit.
I cried out loud for help and Belphegor came running.

He supported me
As I walked to my room.
He cleansed my wound and
Stayed with me until the pain subsided.
I tried to explain the accident to him,
He offered nothing more than a bewildered look
When I mentioned about the spirit pulling my arm.

I resided in bed for the next few days while
Belphegor tended to all aspects of the farm.
What I realized during my free time
Was that he never required pay for his work.

He never once asked about money
Or his share of the profits.
I was receiving all the money from the farm
Without doing any of the work.
Maybe the accident was a blessing;
Maybe it was a sign that I did not need to work.

I could reap the benefits of the farm
Without exerting any effort.

It was bound to happen,
    The thought of doing chores and tasks
    Left a disgusting taste in my mouth now.
    I had no work ethic anymore;
    No desire to tend to the farm.

The ideas only increased
    While I laid there incapacitated
    From my recent misfortune.
    I had given up on my ideas.

The thoughts only bothered me now;
    Disrupted my sleep.
    I imagined what kings must feel like,
    The ability to rule from their thrones
    Without having to exert energy.

Maybe I could acquire more help on the farm,
    Rule my wheat kingdom from the comfort of my bed.
    I believed that it could happen.
    I would get to work on expanding my help the next day.
    Later that night,
    I awoke to Belphegor standing next to my bed.
    The sight startled me at first until I realized who it was.
    He said he had a question for me;
    He needed my full attention.

I slumped up in my bed and
    Gave him what he asked for.
    I was so tired
    I may have even given him a rude look
    While I adjusted my eyes to the candle he was carrying.

He stated that he was there to present me with a question,
    That he required an answer from me.

I obliged as long as I did not have to get out of bed.
He continued by asking me if I wanted my hand back.
I was not anticipating such a question so
I asked him to repeat himself.
Instead he unveiled my severed hand from a cloth shirt
And held it before me.
My hand was in perfect condition and healthy in
appearance.
The sight baffled me
To the point where I could not speak.
He continued to say that he was the spirit who stole my
hand.
I laughed at the idea of him being the spirit,
But I quickly changed my attitude when
I witnessed his eyes starting to leak a red gassy substance.
I asked him who he was.
He responded that his name was indeed Belphegor,
He was not here for the reasons that I believed.
He said he was not here to help me nor tend to my farm.

He said I had a choice to make.
He held up my hand again and said that if I desired it,
I could have my hand back along with my original work
ethic.
He said that if I chose my hand,
I would not be able to rest nor have free time as long as I
lived.

The alternative was to keep my newfound injury;
My restful, sloth lifestyle.
I would still be able to reap the benefits of the farm
Without having to work.
He went on to say that I had until the next morning
To make my choice.
He placed my hand on a nearby table.
I replied that I did not believe him.

My comments angered him,

He immediately morphed into his spirit-like state
And hovered above my bed.
The incident was too much for me to comprehend.
I sank further down into my bed and
Pulled my blanket up over my head.

I shivered uncontrollably
As I felt his presence getting closer to me.
He must have taken my denial for eye contact as an insult.
He physically ripped the blanket from my clutches.

Being exposed to him struck me with instant fear.
I was not about to open my eyes
To witness what I believed to be in front of me.
I felt my body being lifted from my bed
For a brief moment and twisted within the air.
I kept my eyes tightly sealed
Until the duration of the event had subsided.

I sensed that the evil aura was no longer near.
I peered from beneath my tightly closed eye lids
And noticed that I was alone.
The conversation ended as quickly as it had begun.

With Belphegor out of my room,
I ran through my options,
It was quite difficult with my old hand pulsating on the
table.
My hand was still alive just separated from the rest of my
body.
My mind remained in control of my severed limb.
I witnessed my fingers move and bend from afar.
I was able to think about forming a fist,
The hand would follow through with the orders.
Whenever I believed that I was dreaming,
I needed only to look upon the table.

I was not very diligent with the goal presented to me.

I viewed it as a task and much like the other tasks on the
farm,
 I gave no energy to it.
 My mind had followed my physical attributes
 Down the bothersome path of laziness.

I decided to postpone my answer and
 Retire for the night.
 Belphegor had given me until the morning for my answer,
 So I did not need to decide at that moment.
 Why should I have bothered with the confusion?
 I told myself that I would be in a better mood in the
morning;
 More apt to apply energy to the situation.
 I awoke late in the morning
 With the sun already high in the sky.
 As I gravitated towards the window to look out over the
farm,
 I was reminded about the choice I had to make.
 I still was undecided.

The art of work alone had become tiresome for me.
 Someone asking me to do something
 Was even more dreaded within my eyes.
 I did not want to achieve anything for myself.
 Why would I want to achieve anything for anyone else?

I viewed people as pesky insects;
 I just wanted to swat them away.
 I remember when I was open to the offerings
 Especially when I was in town.
 I wasted no time with helping people,
 Even listening to what they had to say.

Everybody needed something from me
 And now I only wanted to be left alone.
 It reached the point where I desired no contact with them.

If I needed something from the town, I would send
Belphegor.
    If I needed to meet with customers, I would send Belphegor.

My outlook on competition had also changed.
    I no longer gazed upon rivals as a challenge,
    Rather as an insult to my character.
    I never use to have resentment towards others.
    I had grown to hate people, customers and competitors so
much.
    It was easier to remain in bed than to risk having a
conversation with one of them.
    Belphegor was different
    As obviously he was not human.
    That was the reason why I got along with him so well.
    He was not like the others.
    He demanded nothing from me;
    Allowed me to be alone at the same time.

He never once asked me for a favor
    Nor to help him with anything.
    He just let me be.
    It was the perfect relationship.
    I believe that I could not have had with anyone else.
    Everyone else caused me stress to even look upon.

I did not forget that he was a shape shifting demon
    Who cut off my hand, but rather focused on the positive
aspects.
    I was allowed to live off of his labor and profit from it.

I was willing to overlook the events of the other night
    As long as he continued completing his daily tasks.
    The farm no longer needed me as it did in the past.
    My suggestions were pointless and lacked enthusiasm.
    All of the enhancements that benefited the farm came from
Belphegor.
    I was satisfied with that.

Developing a new idea took too much energy.
I still was the controller of the farm and all enhancements.

Most were approved without much thought
    In order to speed up the process.
    I entrusted in the ideas portrayed by my friend.
    I no longer believed that he was there to help me.
    I believed that he was there to ease my life.
    He made everything easy for me.
    He removed burdens from my life
    By handling all aspects of the farm.

I came to the brutal recognition that
    My help was no longer needed on the farm.
    I believed that was fair, as long as I continued
    To receive the profits of Belphegor's labor.

I started to leave my room,
    But had the feeling that I was forgetting something.
    I looked to the table but my hand was no longer there.
    I had apparently slept through my deadline for my choice
    Since I did not attach my hand, I obviously chose the latter.

I was not upset at allowing my physical state to answer for me
    I was going to choose my new livelihood anyways.
    I viewed the whole situation with my hand and
    The question regarding it would affect others in a different
way,
    But it did not bother me.

I had not used that particular hand in awhile.
    If losing it was the worst that would happen
    Then I was satisfied with that.
    The idea of never having to work again
    While profiting from the farm was a hard choice not to
make.

Eventually, I ventured outside and

Saw that the farm was in working order.
I strolled over to the storage unit and
Saw that it was completely filled to capacity with wheat.
My next stop was the tool shed
That was unaltered by the vibrations of the other night.
I peered inside and noticed the shiny clean tools.I then
walked along the irrigation system and
Followed it to each field
The sparkling water flowed within the oak canals.
All of the fields were so beautiful and compacted with
wheat.
The current state of the farm was something to behold.
Everything was in perfect order,
I dared not touch anything.
All I saw from the farm was not the quality of the wheat.

Rather the large amount of profit that was established
By me not lifting a finger.

I walked back up to the house and
Noticed Belphegor loading up a wooden cart.
As I got closer to him,
I found that he was packing up his belongings.

I asked him what he was doing.
He responded that his time on the farm had ended.
I immediately went into a confused state.
He interrupted me and said that I had made my choice.

I tried to decipher as to how my choice involved him, but
I could not reach a verdict.
He read my confusion and
Stated that he was never here to help me with the farm,
But rather to help me choose.
He held up my severed limb and tossed it into my chest.
Instead of the once healthy appearance,
The hand was rotted and decayed in color.

I dropped it to the ground as soon as I came into contact
with it.
 The cold touch of it disgusted me.
 Belphegor smiled at my reaction.
 He thanked me for my decision, but
 I told him I still did not understand.

He tried to comfort me by being very blunt in his words.
 He said that he helps people to realize
 That there was more to life than work;
 That he tests the limits of their work ethic.

He informed me that he was only here for one task;
 Not the irrigation system,
 Not the storage shed
 Not to cleanse tools.
 His only task was to push the boundaries
 Of my strong work ethic and exploit it for weaknesses.

He told me the results of his findings
 Was that my work ethic started off strong.
 He continued to say that the gradual lessening of my daily
work
 Was when he noticed a decrease in energy.
 He increased his own work load in order to suffocate mine.
 He saw his task threatened when I was cleansing the tools
and
 Feared a rebound, so he took my hand.
 That proved to be the event that would derail me
 Further into laziness with no hope of returning.

I pleaded with him to stay.
 I asked him how I could possibly
 Profit from the farm without him here.
 He replied that I would be able to reap the profits
 Without working for a few days
 Before the tasks needed tending to.

I desperately bent down to retrieve my hand
    Eagerly trying to connect it back on my arm.
    I begged him to give me my work ethic back,
    He informed me that he could only take and not give.

He reminded me that I had a choice.
    My newly found attitude chose for me.
    I dropped to my knees while holding my hand
    And continued to beg him, but
    He ignored my plea and focused on packing his belongings.

His once friendly personality looked to me with no remorse.
    There was a time when he would do anything to help me,
    He now turned away when I needed him the most.
    I watched him walk away;
    I was left alone on a highly productive farm
    With no work ethic and one working hand.

I spent the next few days
    As he said reaping the benefits of the completed tasks.
    I not only lived off of the land,
    I had been living off of Belphegor as well.

I could no longer support
    My livelihood with my current personality.
    I had adapted to require the labor of others.
    That was the very trait that disgusted me in the past.
    I dwelled within it and admired it so much
    It would change the outcome of my productivity.

I never thought that Belphegor would leave.
    I assumed he would stay on the farm forever, but
    That would not be the case.
    In the past, I was able to oversee the farm
    And duties all by myself,
    However, the increase in production was too much.
    I should have at least checked on the supply
    During the few days following Belphegor's departure,

I opted to sleep instead.
My once strong work ethic was in such disarray.
My laziness continued well after the wheat crop ran out.
The output of my farm decreased.
It was felt by the towns that I supplied.
I did not realize how many people depended on my product
Until my farm stopped furnishing them.
I could hear people complaining and knocking on my door.
They meant nothing to me.
I only viewed them as beggars and trespassers.
I misread how my work level affected others,
At the same time I did not care.
I fully intended on supplying them with wheat
When I managed to get around to it.

Over time my prosperous fields
    Became overgrown with weeds and shrubs
    That choked the life from the beautiful crops.
    The algae infested canals of the irrigation system
    Clogged the flow of water.

My productive farm had deteriorated and wasted away.
    New rival farms formed all around and
    Fulfilled the demands of the people as
    I could not provide for them anymore.
    I wanted nothing more but to provide a high quality product
    For the citizens of the region
    Through my strong work ethic and excellent crop.
    But at that moment, I only wanted to sleep.

~

I am growing tired of writing now.
    The darkness of the cave and
    The constant flickering of the candle
    Wears heavy on my eyes.

The frustration of not knowing

The details of the events
That I transcribe about is increasing within me.
The ability to read my own pages
Would help me with the boredom that I often feel.

I am finding myself very lonely
    Especially since my shadowy friends
    Are diminishing; another one has vanished.
    I suppose I should view this in a positive manner,
    Instead I feel sorrow for their departure.
    It is difficult to have a positive demeanor
    On my situation as there is not much to look forward to
    Within my darkened cave.
    I am somewhat saddened
    That I am alone with my thoughts.

I never imagined life without any companionship
    Would be this devastating on my mind.
    If only I could converse with a single living organism.
    My friends in the shadow get me by,
    But they do not respond to me.
    I try to befriend them,
    Even greeted them on one occasion, but
    It appears that my acknowledgment
    Frightens them deeper into the darkness.
    Am I not allowed to ask
    For the simple conversation
    So that my mind stays healthy?
    I know no one will answer me and
    It fills my heart with emptiness;
    My mind with severe depression
    To know that I am the only one
    Who will respond to my words.

I am starting to question
    My understanding of my situation.
    My religious beliefs are also changing
    As I believe more due to my present state.

However questions still plague my mind and
Cloud my judgment about the heavens.
If there is a God, then why is there suffering on the planet?
Why do people hunger and thirst?
Some things are beyond my realm of thought, but
That does not stop me from pondering the questions.

If I could just walk outside of this cave;
Breathe air that is not comprised of dirt and dust.
I promise I would not venture far,
I just desire to feel the warmth of the sun
Or even the cool wet of rain.

I am growing so tired of my surroundings.
My mind is beginning to lose control.
I often find myself laughing uncontrollably for no reason.

My mind is budding with more power.
It feeds from the confinement.
I am still in control, but I have to scold my mind
To stop the rapid patterns of thought.
I know it is working against me and
Trying to lure me into a chaotic state.
Sometimes it is tempting to release my control,
To allow it to guide my soul,
But my body resists the notion.
The thought patterns and rapid images
Are so strong that I pound on my head
To relinquish them, but fail.

If I close my eyes,
The images worsen and become more realistic.
They are showing me visions of death
That are so vivid they are producing emotions
Of sadness and despair.

Is it not enough that I am confined
And stricken of my life to be a servant?

Provide me with my sanity;
Provide with an understanding.

I do not ask for much,
    I only ask for some sort of consultation.
    Please slow my mind so that I may relinquish the battle
within.
    Please make them stop, I beg of you.
    I have done all you have asked of me.

Please spare my mind from any wrath
    You may require of me as the pressure is intense.
    I need release;
    I need to get the thoughts out of my head.

If no one will help me,
    Then I will take matters into my own hands.
    I will use the solid wall of the cave
    To persuade the thoughts to exit.

I will control my mind with physical exertion
    No matter how grave the result may be.
    I will punish my mind for controlling and
    Depriving me of my rational judgment
    And the ability to freely think for myself.
    If I do not return to my quill, then I have succeeded in my
quest.

V

gluttony

The approaching blizzard
    Was supposed to be the worst
    The region had seen in quite some time.
    The prophets warned of wide spread panic
    And drastic devastation across the land.

They told of the land changing
    Into a frozen wasteland
    With entire species of animals
    Being eliminated from the planet.

They preached how God was disappointed
    In how the human race treated his world and
    The lack of respect they provided
    To its natural resources.

The gifts from God were tossed aside
    Along with the desire for longevity in one's life.
    God would punish all
    With the blistering frost and relentless ice
    In an attempt to alter the ideas of those who strayed.

The prophets spoke of no salvation.
    An impending death would be the final gift from him.
    Redemption and avoidance
    Would not be an option.

Only death would greet those in the path.

The frost reaper would not be shunned.
The prophets were stern in their voice and
Articulated with their words.

However, these self-imposed prophets
Were also viewed as unstable by the citizens of the city.
They would stand on the street corners to
Spread their insanity to anyone
Who would lend them an ear.

Most of the responses
Were in the form of rotten food
Thrown at them by their judging audience.
As they dodged the objects,
They continued to broaden their word of destruction.
They never condemned those
Who critiqued them and even
Intellectually challenged such individuals,
But the battle of the minds never ended well.

Nothing broke the spirits of the prophets.
They would always return to their stage
Each morning to begin again.
I never faulted them
As I truly felt that they
Fully believed their own words
Regardless if anyone else followed them along their path.

As for me, I did not hear
Their words too closely
As the region in which we lived
Was not known for its frigid winters,
Let alone blizzards.
We experienced the typical
Decrease in temperature
Between the seasons, but
Nothing so drastic as to alter our livelihoods.

What worked against the prophets
    Was that they had been preaching
    Their tale for several winters.
    Prior to last winter, we were to be destroyed.
    The warm winter that we had
    Only added to the insanity
    In the eyes of the citizens.
    In defense of the prophets,
    They never mentioned any time frames
    That the destruction would occur,
    But as each cold season passed,
    Their words lessened in power and belief.

I knew about the prophets
    And their speeches
    As one was located directly outside
    Of my merchant store.
    I was a popular vendor
    In one of the busier sections of the city.
    My location allowed me to survey
    Many varieties of people and on slow days,
    I would sit outside and watch as the crowds walked pass.

Business was always good for me,
    Considering what I sold, in comparison to other merchants.
    My store was the main supplier of food
    Consisting of bread, fruits and vegetables.

I was known for always having a full supply.
    I worked closely with the local farmers
    To have the freshest crop
    Delivered to me and they never disappointed.

I had always gone out of my way
    To insure the happiness of my customers.
    I believed that a happy customer
    Was more likely to return than an angry one.
    I took pride in my relationships

With the farmers and always reevaluated
My pay for their products.
I knew the key to my prosperity
Was the farmers and their crops.

I knew most of my regular customers by name
And made it a point to welcome new visitors.
I believed I was not only selling fruits and vegetables,
But also selling my personality.

I felt it was important
That the people entrusted me
To provide them wonderful staples
Accompanied with a splendid attitude.

The ability to not bargain successfully
Was death to most vendors.
Bargaining was a part of our society,
It was important that it be done in a respectable manner.

Otherwise, one side of the party
Would always become angered.
The transaction and any potential business
Would be destroyed.

I learned that lesson very early in my venture
And adapted it quickly.
I was a master of persuasion and
It was transparent to my customers.
I allowed them to think
They were achieving their bargain
When in fact they were not.
My tone of voice was never raised and
My words were chosen carefully.
The combination allowed the customer
To feel that they had humbled me.

My large amount of customers

Allowed me with an increase in opportunity.
I had survived through the toughest of times
The city could inflict upon me.
My thought process and belief
Was that people always needed to eat,
Regardless of what type of situation was occurring.

Business was the most successful during war times.
    The army would stock up on food items prior to leaving the
port.
    The amount of food they purchased
    Was enough to keep me in business
    For several seasons at a time.
    Unfortunately, no such battles
    Were occurring as the world was at an unfortunate peace.
    My section of the city
    Had all the vendors
    The citizens needed to survive
    Except for a butcher for meat products.

I was always in awe
    That no meat vendor existed.
    Everyone traveled across town
    To purchase their meat products,
    Which proved to be a tiresome act.

I had thought about establishing
    A second store,
    However, the amount of work
    Would be too much for me to withstand.
    I was barely able to meet the demands from one.
    I am glad that I did not venture into the area
    As a new butcher soon entered into the city
    And opened across the street from me.
    I was excited for the arrival of my new neighbor, as
    I believed a butcher was the last piece
    Our section needed to be a powerful portion of the city.
    Less traveling of our citizens

Meant more opportunities for them to buy locally.
I did not want to bother my neighbor
On the first few days of his arrival.
I wanted to give him a chance to settle in and
Establish his store before I welcomed him.
I was anxious to meet him;
To offer him my support.
I knew opening a new store was a challenge.
Days went by and
When I saw that his store was for opened for business,
I walked over to introduce myself.
I doubted that he would be busy on his first day.

The store was well organized
   With a large collection of meats
   From all types of animals.
   The butcher across town
   Never had a supply of meat like that.

The aroma delivered a sense of freshness and quality.
   I would often times have to hold my breath
   When purchasing meat from any vendor.
   Occasionally I even had to battle
   Swarms of flies for the staple,
   But his store was different.
   A wide variety of knives hung from the wall
   Arranged by size and shape.
   When I first entered
   I was alone, but soon greeted by a short thin man
   Who came from the back.

He was wearing a typical white butcher apron
   That was smeared with blood
   And random chunks of excess meat clinging to the cloth.
   He was carrying two butcher knives,
   Each equally coated with blood.

My initial reaction

Was that he had just murdered a person,
But his warm smile and demeanor was inviting.
He mistook me for a customer
And was very appreciative of my presence.

He reminded me of how I always
Cherished my own customers.
He quickly set down his knives and
Headed over to where he kept his freshly cut slabs of meat.

He proceeded to ask how he could assist me.
I informed him that I was his neighboring vendor.
His face lit up with excitement
As he walked from behind his meat counter.

He said his name was Beelzebub and
That he had been a butcher in another region
For quite some time.
He had decided to travel here
As he heard that the quality of meat
Was better due to the warmer climate.

From the look of the current stock in his shop,
I would say that he was correct.
I had never seen such beautiful cuts of meat.
The marble of meat and fat was artwork to my eyes.
I was used to slabs of meat that were cut with dull knives
And no care for the level of fat within each piece.

I told him that I was glad that a butcher
With high quality standards was here.
I had brought him over a complimentary basket of fruits,
Which he was very grateful to receive.
Although he was covered in blood,
His store was spotless and cleansed.
He took excellent care of his tools.
When not in use,
They were shiny artworks displayed on the wall.

My reaction of the new butcher
    Was that of excitement and acceptance.
    Not only did he fill a void in that part of the city,
    But he complimented my own business very well.
    To be able to purchase all of one's food products
    In such close vicinity
    Would surely attract new customers to our area.
    We said our farewells as I could tell
    He needed to handle more chores.

The mornings are very busy within our area
    As all of the vendors open up their shops.
    Most place tables outside along the streets
    To entice customers with visuals of their products.

I usually displayed a few baskets of varying staples
    Mainly as a reminder of the types of
    Fruits and vegetables that were currently in season.
    I had been open for business in the city for so long
    That I did not need to lure customers in.

It had been known for some time
    That if one needed fruits and vegetables
    That I was the man to see.
    All of my products came from nearby farms.
    I had established a friendship with the farmers
    Where I would pay them a good price for their crops.
    In turn I would raise the cost slightly
    So that I would gain a profit from the sell.

I treated the farmers well and
    Stayed competitive with my purchases.
    Every few days I would receive a delivery
    With new stock and paid them by quantity.
    It was beneficial for the farmers to sell to me
    Instead of the citizens
    As the amount of time they would have to spend

On the streets would take them away from their farm.
I believed they made more money
Selling large amounts to me
Than they would selling individually to random people.
I was not alone in that style of business
As several others vendors used the same method.

While I placed some ripened apples
    Within a basket outside my store
    I saw Beelzebub doing the same.
    We waved to one another
    As the street began to fill up with people.

I noticed him making his way across and
    I waited for him to approach.
    His height concealed him within the sea of people and
    I actually lost sight of him for a brief period.

He soon emerged from the crowd,
    Before he did, I had thought he got swept down the street
    From the momentum of the rush.
    He patted me on the shoulder and
    I could tell that he needed to ask me something
    So I gave him my full attention.

He said that he had concerns
    About a particular matter.
    I asked him what it was he was concerned with and
    He replied that he had been hearing tales
    Of an approaching blizzard.

I immediately smiled
    And reassured him that no such blizzard existed.
    He told me that he had heard the story
    From a lone man standing on the corner
    Preaching to those who walked by.

I informed him of the local prophets,

That they had been preaching
About the blizzard for many years.
I calmed his nerves by revealing that the city
Had not even received a drop of snow in quite some time.

My words appeared to ease him, but
I could tell that he was still hesitant.
I could relate to him
As the prophets were very harsh in their tones;
Very luring with their words.
He soon became relaxed and
Said that the details of the frozen event were very
convining.

I agreed with him as
I sometimes questioned the notion of the tale,
But my belief that no one could foresee events
Always won the conflict.
I noticed that he had customers and gestured.
He quickly dove back into the river of people
And surfaced on the other side.

Business was prosperous
As usual during that time of season.
With the approaching winter,
I purchased more fruits and vegetables
Than I usually did in order to
Keep my profits steady until the spring.

The back portion of my store was used to house excess.
During that period, I instructed the farmers
That they should deliver me the unripe fruits and vegetables
As they would last longer than the fully ripened ones.
They always obliged my wishes.
I had faith in the fact that I was able to supply customers
With perfect staples
Even during the cold days of winter.

The next morning I talked with Beelzebub,
    I told him about my winter method of storage.
    He agreed that it was a good idea and
    Said that he would also begin storing meat
    In preparation of the possible lower quantity.

Normally I would not share my
    Strategies and methods to other vendors,
    But I felt Beelzebub had become my friend
    And that his product was not in direct competition with
mine.

The conversations that I had with Beelzebub
    Were gratifying to me.
    I thought that he respected me not only as a fellow vendor
    But as a friend.
    I got the sense that he confided in me more than anyone
else.
    That only increased my willingness to assist him;
    To make sure that his business would survive the season.
    I had never done anything like that before
    For any other vendor, but
    I was drawn to the butcher.
    His success was my success.

Over the next few days leading up
    To the beginning of the winter season,
    I felt that Beelzebub and I were well prepared.
    Our storage units were stocked completely full.
    So much so that we could barely close the door.

The winter trust that I always provided
    To the customers began a long time ago.
    They knew that they could purchase food
    From me no matter how cold the weather reached.

I gifted Beelzebub that trust that I had worked
    So hard to achieve.

I believed in him and his shop.
I was more than content to watch other vendors fail and
crumble,
However, my feelings for my new friend were different.
I enjoyed his presence.
I wanted him to remain my neighbor.
If there was anything I could do to make that happen
Then I would not hesitate to do so.

The prophets were out in full force
As winter rapidly approached us.
The sense of annoyance amongst the crowded streets
Grew to match the increased intensity of the prophets'
words.
They spoke of the mighty blizzard.
The burial of the city underneath snow.
I did not give them my full attention as
I was mainly focused on setting up my visual table,
However, I was hearing random words.

I found myself only capturing the strong words
Such as destruction or disastrous.
One portion stood out in the statements of chaos and
Lured me in like a hook to a hungry fish.

I had never heard them use
The word madness before.
The crispness in the tone which he used struck me as odd.
I had heard so many negative words spill from their mouths,
but
They were always the same each day.

Using the new word was unpredictable
And prompted me to halt my work and look to the prophet.
He spoke of the damage that the lands would receive
The punishment that would reside deep within the soil.

As he continued, I found myself dwelling in his words.

130

I even took a few steps towards him.
He proceeded by saying that the animals and vegetation
Would be depleted and would not
Return as long as the frost covered the land.

He spoke of freezing rain and large ice storms
    That would slaughter the livestock as they grazed upon the
fields.
    As I stood there with a piece of fruit in my hand,
    I pondered the idea of a land without that type of food.

It was as if the prophet was speaking directly to me that day.
    That time I actually heard him.
    In the past, their words never meant anything to me.
    They were focused mainly on the global aspect of the storm
and
    Not at a level that I could properly understand.
    I could not control the atmosphere or
    The destruction of mountains and valleys.
    But the notion that the vegetation would be in danger
    Was something real that I could associate with.

My life was based on vegetation.
    Without vegetation I was nothing,
    The idea of losing everything I owned caught my attention.
    What if he was telling the truth?
    What if all of the crops were to be destroyed?
    My livelihood could not survive such a devastating attack.

If I were to avoid the onslaught of the approaching storm,
    I needed to prepare to the best of my abilities.
    I needed to store as much fruits and vegetables that I could.
    I imagined the amount of food that would be required
    To feed all of the citizens of the city.
    I needed to acquire a level of food that would meet that
demand.

As I surveyed my current stock of product,

I was reminded that the prophets
Had also mentioned the suffering of animals.
I had to inform Beelzebub as his store
Would endure the pain as much as mine.

The day proved to be too busy
    To spread my concern.
    I planned to visit with him the next day.
    The morning came quicker than I had liked,
    But the store of a vendor never waits
    And the customers did not either.
    I crossed the street before the crowds got too heavy and
    Was welcomed by Beelzebub inside his store.

I did not want to startle him with my new found claim
    So I began the conversation by asking about his storage
facility.
    He said he was nearly full to capacity,
    That he would need to begin turning away product
    For the time being.

I gradually brought the prophets into our conversation
    And asked him his thoughts regarding the blizzard.
    He said that he had no concern about it
    Since our last conversation about the subject.

I wanted to choose my next words carefully
    As I did not want to portray the idea
    That I believed the full tale.
    I told him that maybe we should expand our storage
    To acquire more stock in case we experience
    An abnormal winter season.

I specifically did not mention the word blizzard
    As to not cause panic.
    He agreed with me as more storage of stock
    Resulted in more money.
    Regardless of whether we received poor weather or not,

The extra space was a good idea.
Over the next few days,
We worked busily on expanding our storage areas.
We were able to double my space
Due to the amount of store floor space I was able to remove.

Beelzebub did not fare as well as I,
However we were able to increase his space substantially.
The extra area filled up quickly
As the farmers enlarged their delivery amounts.

Each day I heard new threats from the prophets
That seemed to be pointed directly at me.
The main reoccurring statements included
The deprivation of crops and vegetation.

Their words involving the topic
Were painful to my ears.
I could not avoid or ignore them.
I tried to not hear them,
But their tones echoed through the streets.

It was as if they were the only sounds I could hear.
Normally the rustling noise of the outside streets
Filtered their words, but lately the prophets
Had been subduing all other sounds.
I felt my anxiety of the situation rise
With each sermon I heard.
It was slowly affecting my work and my concentration.
A new concept from the prophets did catch me off guard
Involving the mass starvation
That would occur due to the lack of crops.
I had never ventured too much further
Pass the notion of destroyed vegetation.
I did not realize the severity of such an event.

I imagined people fighting for food,
Possibly dying from starvation.

I needed to store enough food to feed everyone
To help them to survive the catastrophe.

I needed more food than I originally thought.
    My store was not capable of handling such a quantity.
    To meet the new demand, I tore down an adjacent wall
    To the next door shop, which was vacant at the time.

No one ever used the space,
    So I did not think that anyone would ever notice.
    From the outside, the two shops remained separate,
    But served as one large room from the inside.
    I did not want to give the idea
    To the outside world that I was expanding
    So I only removed a small portion of the wall
    To provide me with access to the other side.
    To hide the pathway from my patrons,
    I stacked up boxes in front to conceal the hole.
    I now had plenty of space to store the food,
    Much more than I actually required.
    When speaking with Beelzebub,
    He did not have enough area to expand.
    The vicinity of his walls to his neighbors forbade him
    From gaining more.

He informed me that in his current state
    That he would not be able to take in any more supply.
    In a gesture of good faith and
    Without giving too much thought to it,
    I offered him the opportunity
    To share the space of the vacant store next to me.

The area was twice as big as his store
    And the storage was sufficient for both of us.
    The openness shared between the two stores
    Would allow for more conversation even during the busy
times.
    We got along so well

That I did not have any concerns
And never resented my idea.
He thought the gesture was a wonderful one
And asked when he should begin moving his supplies.
I needed to still clear some debris from the space
So I offered to assist him the next day.

A new morning sun rose and
    The warmth of it did little
    To heat the environment as winter had begun.
    The season always had a way to defeat the sun
    And shun it from the sky.

Beelzebub and I met early at his store.
    We loaded up his stock, tools and supplies
    And quickly unloaded them within the new area.
    Once everything was transferred,
    It was apparent that we each had plenty of room.
    The large storage space in the back
    Was more than adequate to hold our overstock.

The customers loved the idea
    That they could buy their vegetables and meat
    Within the same shop.
    Word spread throughout the city and
    We soon became known as the largest vendor in the region.

Although the business merger was a success,
    I could never really enjoy the outcome
    As the words of the prophets continued
    To bombard my mind and pierce my thoughts.

No matter how much I focused on my customers,
    There was always a portion of me
    That I gave to the prophets each day.
    I became so accustomed to hearing their stories
    That it was part of my daily routine.
    I tried desperately to avoid them,

But the cold wind delivered their ideas directly to my ears.

The continuation of time
    Led us further into the winter season each time the sun set.
    The chill in the air grew more intense every night.
    Each day that followed became colder and
    Was well announced by the prophets
    Who started their rants early.

They claimed it had begun,
    That soon the frost would reap the ones who did not believe.
    The scene of the prophets saying their words
    While their breath froze in contact with the air
    Added to the intensity of their speeches.

The crowded streets paid no attention to them, but
    I could not rid myself of the forecast.
    The only vision that provided me with comfort
    Was the amount of food we were collecting.

My worrying decreased every time
    I gazed upon my storage space and
    Saw the mass amount of food.
    I slept well each night knowing
    That I would easily be able to feed my customers
    Throughout the duration of the storm and amid the
aftermath.
    The salvation of the citizens was my main concern.
    My preparedness would be felt by them
    In their time of need.

With every turn of a new day
    The weather turned for the worse.
    It was not so much the temperature,
    Rather the wind that made the outside unbearable.

The wind would barrel through the city streets
    Striking everyone within its path.

It was relentless and unlike anything
The city had experienced before.
It spared no one from its chilly persona
And weaved its way through every street
Like a snake through a grassy field.
The cold only added to my concern
That the prophets were correct.
I found myself paying more attention
To them as others passed me by.

I desired more details and a scheduled time frame,
But they could offer me none.
Each sermon brought about new clues
Regarding the blizzard and I was there to collect them.

I became fascinated with the topic and
Even showed up on the streets
Before the prophets would appear.
I noticed that I was even defending them
When the crowd would insult them.

They spoke of a never ending snow
That would fall from the heavens, blanketing the city.
They said we must fear the blanket as
It would suffocate us and conceal us from the region.

Others balked at the idea, but I did not.
I knew they were telling the truth;
I knew they were only trying to help us prepare.
I was going to make sure that I heard their words;
That Beelzebub and I were going to be ready.
We owed it to ourselves, our livelihoods and
Our customers to be well prepared.
With that day's knowledge
Embedded within my mind,
I told Beelzebub the latest news.
I spoke of how we needed to
Deliver the food to citizens of the city

Prior to the blizzard.

He was hesitant in his approval of my plan.
    I asked what he was concerned about and
    He said that he worried about his own safety,
    Which was something that I never thought about.

His small pause escorted me down a path
    I never knew existed.
    A path of self-conservation and salvation.
    If we gave away all of the food,
    Then how would we possibly survive the duration
    And aftermath of the storm?

His point made me reorganize my whole outlook;
    Take more of a selfish glance at myself.
    I looked to the stockpile of food and
    Realized that we could survive for several seasons
    After the winter had vanished.

If the prophets were indeed correct in their words,
    Vegetation and animals would cease to exist.
    The outcome would prove to be more deadly
    Than the storm itself.

We would require as much food as possible
    In order to survive.
    I could not sacrifice my hunger,
    Face possible starvation
    For a crowd of people
    Who chose not to believe the prophets.

Beelzebub and I worked hard to collect the extra food,
    We should be able to do with it as we see fit.
    My tumbling of emotions were
    Obviously was written on my face
    As Beelzebub smiled at my confusion.

He added that seeking personal salvation
    Would not make us bad people;
    The others chose to not listen to the warnings of the
prophets.
    He said that we could not change the fates of others;
    That we were only in control of our own actions.

He was correct in his words.
    I could not alter the fates of those who did not believe.
    It was not my task to work for the welfare of others and
    Spend my thoughts in order to prepare them.
    I could tell that my partner was no longer concerned
    About not having food for others.
    His brief moment was all I needed to change the course
    Of my ship and all the cargo that was on board.

We could not simply stop the selling of our products,
    But we could reduce the quantity
    That our customers were purchasing.
    We could ration the amounts that we brought
    Out of storage and placed within our storefront.
    It was determined that we would
    Tell our customers that the food levels
    Had decreased due to the winter season.

Over the next few days, we implemented our plan and
    Sold low quantities of food to our customers.
    Some became irate when informed
    That they could not stock up for the season,
    I told them that anything was better than nothing.
    We made sure to keep our main storage area
    Hidden from anyone entering into our store.
    My tolerance of people walking out
    With food was decreasing
    As I viewed a bundle of food equal
    To a day of survival after the storm.

I felt like I was selling

One day of my life away with every customer.
Beelzebub had the same thought.
He came up with the idea to lessen
The quantities within the bundles.

We did not think anyone would notice
    The reduction and we were right.
    They were just happy to receive the food.
    Each day the weather got colder,
    We matched the decrease in temperature
    With a decrease in the amount of food.

Later in the days, we would not replenish
    The storefront with food.
    We told people that we had none left.
    After the store closed,
    Beelzebub and I would eat to keep up our energy.
    The once clear skies turned to a dark grey.
    The snow started out light and was
    Quickly absorbed by the ground.
    By the end of the day,
    There was a light coating of white coloring the streets.

Beelzebub again showed signs of hesitation,
    I was not about to close my store off to a line of hungry
people.
    We needed to provide them with some level of service
    Regardless of how small it was.

I viewed the line of people as several days of my survival.
    My partner agreed with me.
    We lowered the level of food offering
    Even further to the point where the amount
    Was barely enough to feed one person for a half a day.

I had no remorse knowing that just behind my back wall
    Was an abundant supply of food
    That would feed me through the storm.

The food was mine.
The crowd was lucky
That I was not selfish and supplied them with some.
The next day, Beelzebub noticed
That a portion of the food had become rotten.
We both decided to trim the decayed food
And place them in the bundles to give out.

I reassured myself that rotten food was better than no food at all.
The people did not seem to notice.
I received a surprise visit the following day
From a few of my suppliers.
The farmers did not wait in line
Like the others and barged into the store.

Due to the frost that was destroying their land;
They were demanding back the crops that they sold me.
With the storage area well hidden,
I told them that all the food we had
Was going to the people of the city.
If they required food,
They would have to wait in line.

My words enraged them
As they began threatening to cut off my stock
For future seasons
If I did not return their product.

I replied that I could not
As it was dispersed amongst the people.
In a sudden turn of events,
The people began to fight along side me
As they did not want the food that they were to receive
To be given back to the farmers.

With the farmers outnumbered and
Being forced from the store,

It was apparent that I had won the battle.
As they were pushed,
They proclaimed that I was hording the food, but
The people were only concerned
With their current status in the line
To believe such nonsense.

We continued to give out the contaminated food as
We did not want it to alter the fresh supply.
The amount of rotten food was more
Than we had originally thought as
We uncovered more that was buried deep in storage.
We increased the amount of food in the bundles
In order to cleanse the store.

Outside, the snow enlarged in density.
A bitter wind howled through the streets.
The city was completely covered with a white cover
That was thickening with each coming day.

With their robes glistening with white crystals,
The prophets continued their tales and
I was there to hear every word.
They spoke of snow as the tears of a demon;
The frost as its coffin.
They enlightened me by saying the freezing rain
Will slay many and alter few.
Were they talking about people or animals?
They never answered my questions,
Which was quite frustrating.
The line in front of the shop became larger
With every day that went by.
I still saw every person as a day of my survival.
To see several hundred people lining up was a bit
depressing.

I told Beelzebub my worries,
He suggested that we could close the store and

Claim the food was depleted.
He said it was my choice
And that he would abide by my decision.

The choice was difficult
As I was giving food away, albeit some of it was
contaminated.
Was it not my right to preserve my own salvation?
I had acquired the food in good faith,
So I should be able to do with it as I see.

I should not have to suffer for believing in the prophets.
Everyone had the same opportunity to prepare for the storm;
Instead they chose to ignore the words.
I should not have to suffer for the ignorance of others.
I looked to Beelzebub with a smile and made my choice.
He was very satisfied to say the least
As that meant more food for him as well.

I stood upon a table and acquired attention.
I announced that we would no longer be able to offer food
As the supply had run dry.
My words instantly sent everyone into a panic.
They desperately laid claim to any food that was present.
Arguments and fights sporadically
Showed their ugly faces as the thought of no food
Entered into the minds of the customers.
The word spread quickly outside
Where the line wrapped through the streets.

People began to shove one another
In hopes to gain access inside.
Beelzebub and I started to funnel the people outside
In hopes that we could rid the store of chaos.
He grabbed two of his butcher knives.
The threat of violence led the customers out through the
door
And onto the cold, bitter streets.

We barricaded the door and breathed a sigh of relief.

I was not concerned about their safety
    Or how they would weather the storm.
    I was only concerned about my survival through the blizzard
and
    My partner shared my fears.

With no one inside, we opened up our storage
    Simply to look upon it with satisfaction.
    I felt relieved not to give away any more food.
    I saw the pile as my complete salvation.
    The morning after, we did not open.
    It was the first time that I did not
    Welcome customers since starting the store.
    It was quite relaxing
    To not have to set up the visual table.

I only wanted to hear the words of the prophets.
    The new speech brought about more concerns
    Of the freezing rain that would soon arrive.
    They said the rain would seal doors, crack streets
    And would serve as the first sign of devastation.

They advised everyone to stay
    Within the safety of their abodes.
    No one except me would listen.
    As I walked away from the prophet,
    I was approached by two men who demanded food.

I told them that I had no more to give.
    They were in a state of starvation
    With their thin appearance and sunken cheeks.
    I myself was very healthy and
    Was nourished quite nicely each day, but
    My appearance did not seem to help the cause.
    They became violent and began to shove me around
    And accused me of hording food.

I denied their accusations as they pushed me to the ground.
Beelzebub came out of the store armed with his knives
And stood by my side.
The inclusion of blades halted my attackers' progress.
They backed away slowly, then ran the opposite way.
To calm myself from the recent incident,
I sat down with a ripe apple and stared at the pile of food.
My power came from knowing that the men
Who attacked me would weaken in the days to come;
That I would continue to be healthy.

The next hazy sun brought about the freezing rain.
It pounded the city and all who dared to be outside.
From the haven of the shop,
I could hear the screams of people outside.
There was no physical warning.
The sharpened rain droplets appeared at a blistering speed.
Several people banged on our door in hopes to seek shelter,
But Beelzebub and I were performing inventory of our food.
We ignored their request as we were quite busy.
The screams got louder and distracted
Me from counting the bananas.
It was very annoying.

I opened the front door ever so slightly
To hear the shouted words of the prophets.
They were no longer standing at their usual places.
Instead they sought shelter underneath an overhang.
Their robes had become tattered from the frozen falling
daggers,
But still they preached in hopes to save lives.

They spoke of a massive hail storm
That would destroy buildings and scar the city.
I began to worry as everything they had foreseen
Had come true.

Before I could close the door an arm

Penetrated from the outside and kept the door ajar.
Someone was trying to overpower me to gain access.
I pushed at the door but the inclusion of the arm
Made it nearly impossible to close it fully.
I called to Beelzebub who came to my aid.
He held the door and told me to get a knife.
Without much thought I grabbed one from a nearby table
And tried to give it to him.
He told me that there was no time,
That I must handle the situation myself
As our stockpile of food was in jeopardy.
The pressure was too much for me,
I stalled in my actions.

Beelzebub hurried my thoughts
While the man was pushing open the door.
I gripped the knife and slashed the blade across the arm.
The man cried out in pain.
Beelzebub told me to do it again.

I slashed one more time as the man withdrew his arm
Allowing us to close the door.
I looked at the blood dripping from the knife.
I knew that it was necessary in order to preserve our
salvation,
But the pain that I caused another human
Made my heart sink into my stomach and drown itself.
Beelzebub took the knife and smiled at me in acceptance.
From that day on, I knew I had to protect the food
By any means necessary.
I knew the starvation was making people desperate.
I vowed that I would strive to never feel that pain.
I did not want to die by hunger.
The steps that I accomplished would help me avoid it.

I awoke to the loud knocking
On the walls and ceiling.
The hail had begun to fall.

It sounded like the city was being
Bludgeoned to death with heavy stones.
God pummeled the buildings with great authority.
The weak human constructions and materials
Were no match for the sheer power of the almighty.

The impact of the heavier hail
Splintered and cracked the wooden structure of the store.
The grey haze of the outside leaked through the cracks
And holes that mother nature was creating.
The dull rays of light spilled into the shop
With full force and extended across the entire floor.
We overturned tables and leaned them up against
The storage walls to provide reinforced protection
In case the hail storm intensified.

The newly created holes in the front wall
Provided me with the opportunity to peer outside.
I saw many people running to seek shelter
Through the snow ridden streets.

The ice on the ground made it almost impossible
To gain traction as several people lost their balance.
The large ice chunks exploded upon impact
With the land and buildings.
The shattering of the ice bombs glistened
Against the grey glow of the city.
The noise of the blasts shook the very foundation
Of my spine and forced uncontrollable twitches in my
muscles.

I surveyed further down the street and
Witnessed bundles of cloth submerged in the snow.
At first I thought that someone lost their cloaks,
But as the wind shifted the material,
I was able to view the lifeless body of a woman.

Her skin was blue in appearance

With an expression of fear frozen upon her face.
The vision did not startle me as
I knew that death would reveal itself within the storm
eventually.
    I looked down the other end of the street and saw more
bodies
    Being buried in the snow.

A man forcefully started beating on the front door
    While I looked to him through a hole in the wall.
    When he received no response,
    He ran across the street to another store
    When a large piece of hail struck him in his back.

The power of the hail forced him face down into the snow.
    He was slowly moving and
    Managed to raise himself with his arms.
    As he struggled to get to his knees,
    Another piece of ice smashed into the back of his head
    And silenced his movements.

The boulder of ice exploded on impact with his skull
    Robbing him of his life.
    The bright red blood flowed into the street
    Crystallizing in the freezing environment.
    The cold wind that crept through the hole gave me chills, so
    I walked into the food storage and sliced up some bread.

During our meals, as Beelzebub and I sat with food,
    It was not uncommon for us to be serenaded
    With the chilling sounds of screams from the outside world.
    We tried to have at least one big meal each day
    In order to keep our strength up.
    To my surprise, I was even gaining weight
    Which was welcomed as the excess fat provided me with
warmth.
    On one particular day when the weather was so horrid,
    I could not even see the street from my hole,

I heard a knock on the door.
Through the random shifts in the wind,
I was able to catch a glimpse of a dull red robe of a prophet.

He was standing outside the store
And was simply knocking on the door.
I called to Beelzebub and showed him the visitor.
I struggled with the dilemma of whether to allow him entry.

Beelzebub said it was my choice and that
He would once again agree with my decision.
I thought about how the prophets were the ones
Who warned me of the blizzard;
How their words prepared me for my survival.

On the other hand,
It was one more mouth to feed;
One more stomach to satisfy.
I wanted Beelzebub to assist me in my decision,
He offered me nothing as usual.

I opted to remain silent,
Denying entrance to the prophet.
From past experience, I knew that my denial of entry
To anyone would ultimately lead to their death.
The survival rate on the street had decreased dramatically.
I looked through the hole and did not see the red robe
anymore,
I knew that my dilemma had subsided.
Beelzebub, for some reason,
Forced me to make all of the tough decisions.
He only offered me a smile after the choice was made.
The latest choice proved to be the hardest so far,
I believed that I made the right decision
Since our food pile was slowly diminishing.

Moments after, I imagined the prophet
Pummeled by the hail as he froze to death.

I desperately looked out the hole to see if my vision was
correct.
    Beelzebub must have seen my desperation.
    He wanted to ease my worry so
    He summoned me for a meal.
    My hunger took precedence over my concern for the
prophet.
    It prompted me to sit down at the table with a plate of food.

After I was full from my meal
    I discarded the excess that I could not eat
    Within a wooden crate that we used for waste.
    The crate began to smell so horribly
    With the mixture of food
    That we decided to empty it outside.

The front door was sealed shut from the ice,
    But I managed to jar it loose.
    The air was so cold outside
    That my fingers immediately turned numb upon contact.

I tilted the crate
    Allowing the waste to spill out onto the ground.
    The warmth of the food released steam
    Upon blending with the snowy terrain.

I could not cleanse the crate completely
    As the weather was too unbearable
    For me to stay out long enough.
    I slammed the door closed
    Trying desperately to remove my chill,
    But was drawn to the hole in wall
    As I heard a loud commotion outside.
    I peered through the hole and saw several people
    Rummaging through the food waste.
    Their skin was a pale blue and hardened from the frost.
    Icicles hung from their mouths and noses
    In an eerie fashion that presented a monstrous persona.

As if the cold had consumed their bodies
Making them slaves to the blizzard.
They were uncontrollable in their mannerisms
While devouring the food rinds.

The cold starvation that plagued their bodies
    Had made them monsters in my mind.
    The frighten images of their crystallized eyes
    Haunted me for the next few days
    As the weather turned even worse.

The intolerable wind pounded the structures and
    Ripped roofs from buildings.
    An uneasy whistling echoed through the store
    Caused by wind that found its way through the crevices.
    The safety of the store shielded
    Us from the hail, snow and wind, but
    The cold could not be avoided.
    No matter how we blockaded the walls,
    The cold was relentless in its destiny to find a way inside.
    We ate to keep warm,
    Even when we were not hungry.
    We gorged ourselves to add more fat to our bodies.
    We needed the gluttony in order to survive as
    The cold was growing more intense with each day.
    I always kept the hole open
    To get an insight of the storm
    From an outside perspective.
    I saw more frozen dead corpses
    Lining the street every time I looked out.
    I did not stay near the hole for too long
    As I feared the sight of the savage human monsters.

That night as the streets darkened and the wind blew harder,
    I could feel the front wall of the store begin to tremble.
    Small splinters of the wood shifted loose
    Caused by the storm beating from the outside.
    Beelzebub and I feared the worst so

We sought shelter inside the storage area.
We secured the door and sat amongst the pile of food.
I was so cold that I was shaking uncontrollably.
My lungs were contracting from the intake of the air.
My wet nose solidified closed.
I had to loosen the ice
By rubbing it with my sleeve in order to gain air.

Beelzebub seemed to be in better shape and
Was able to handle the cold much more than I could as
He was barely shivering.
He used his energy to offer me more food
So that I would stay warm.
I was so cold that I began to see things
That I could not explain.
I saw Beelzebub grab an apple
That instantly froze upon contact.
I blamed my icy mind for presenting me
With such ridiculous images,
But what happened next was not so easily avoided.

While he handed me a cut of meat,
I mistakenly grabbed his wrist instead.
His skin and flesh was ice to the touch,
Yet he showed no signs of being cold.

I looked up to his eyes as he began to smile.
I noticed that when he exhaled,
His breath could not be seen.
Mine instantly battled with the frigid air,
But his blended equally.
How could that be?
I looked deeper into his eyes and
Saw the pain and suffering of the blizzard.
I saw the snow, the hail and
The frost circling around his pupils.
He was not the same person I had met so long ago.

Had he become a victim to the storm like those savage
people?
    He could not have as he never left the shop.

The wind pounded against the store with more force.
    We heard what seemed to be
    The front wall buckle under the pressure.
    The howling of the storm was extremely loud now
    Without the extra barricade.

The wind swirled around the storage area
    As if it was an ice dragon trying to find a way inside.
    The cold combined with the increased pressure of the wind
    Wreaked havoc on my mind
    Forcing my eyesight to fade in and out.

I felt like a prisoner of the storm
    With my arms and legs shackled to the frost.
    The wood construction of the storage area
    Began to warp and misshape
    From the freezing onslaught of the weather.

The grey atmosphere spilled in
    Through any crack that would allow it.
    Beelzebub showed no signs of concern
    For the approaching weather.
    His eyes were fixated on me.
    His mannerisms were calm as the cold
    Continued to assault all of my internal organs.
    He had always worried about my wellbeing,
    But no more.

He approached the door and unlatched it.
    My eyes squinted at the action
    Which was the only motion that did not cause me pain.
    He leaned down to me and placed an apple upon my chest.
    He said that I had done well.
    I had no idea what he was talking about.

He informed me that he was the cold and the frost.
He said that he was the prophets and the hail.
He said that he was the blizzard.
I tried to understand his words, but my mind was so cold.
He stood from me and push opened the storage door wider
Allowing the snow and wind to filter freely inside.

Through the grey haze of the storm,
    I saw them enter into the store
    Where the front door used to be.
    Those savage humans
    Finally had the opportunity to creep in with the cold.
    As they blended with the snow that swirled within the air,
    I could tell they were seeking food.
    Some had no clothes on,
    But they were completely adapted to the weather.
    Their skin had altered in a hardened shade of blue.

The starvation had negative results
    As their rib cages protruded from their concaved chests.
    They used their primal instincts to sniff out my location.
    Their eyes widened at the sight of me lying upon a pile of
food.

They climbed upon me and rummaged
    Through the food trying to find something
    That was not frozen and somewhat edible.
    They soon turned to my warm fatty meat
    That I had built up on my body to keep me warm.

As they tore through my shivering body,
    I felt no pain.
    The coldness had numbed me.
    I saw Beelzebub fade into the atmosphere
    While my limbs were being fought over.

As I laid upon my frozen food supply
    Being eaten alive by those that I forced into starvation,

I could hear the words of the prophets
Being carried through the bitter wind.
They spoke of an end to the blizzard
And the prosperous return of vegetation.

~

The air within the cave is quite dense now.
    For some unknown reason.
    I am unable to satisfy my lungs
    And provide the proper amount of air they desire.

I find myself with brief moments
    Of shortness of breath.
    With no opening to the outside world,
    Is it possible that the air is fading?
    God would not allow me to suffocate.

Another one of my shadowy friends has left,
    But I do not imagine that they consume any of the air.

I must have completed some transcriptions
    As my hand is sore from gripping the quill.
    I do not try to read my recent work
    As I know I will not be able to understand it.

I will abide by God's wishes
    In hopes to accelerate the process
    And reach the end of my stay.
    I have received no punishment;
    No harsh treatment as a result of my writing.
    This leads me to believe that I am fulfilling his desires.

The notion that God is possibly
    Reading my words is met
    With a mixture of emotions.
    The fact that I do not know
    What exactly I am writing

Is somewhat disturbing.

I only pray that my words
    Do not insult or anger God.
    I realize that I will never know this,
    But I continue to worry about the outcome regardless.

I am beginning to think that the shadows
    Within the cave are somehow
    Associated with my work.
    It appears that when I complete
    A large amount that one will exit.

I am not sure how the two are related,
    If they indeed are at all.
    Maybe it is my boredom providing me
    With puzzles to keep me preoccupied
    Or maybe I am trying to bridge
    Two separate items together that do not belong.
    Regardless, the amount of my shadow friends is decreasing
    And I am unsure as to why.

VI

I loved her.
 I loved her more than she would ever know.
 She was the source of my desires;
 The source of my dreams.

My thoughts were overwhelmed
 With visions of her and
 My heart was filled with the passion
 That I saved for only her.

She was everything to me, the backbone of my existence.
 However, she did not know me.
 She had never laid her eyes upon me
 Nor heard my voice in her ears.

I did not exist in her world
 As she was royalty and
 I was a mere tailor
 Dwelling in the unforgiving streets.

If she only knew how much I loved her,
 She would see into my soul.
 No woman could resist
 That amount of love and
 The possibility of everlasting desires.
 My days were spent weaving,
 Sewing, creating and repairing
 Cloth items outside of my store on the street.

My stool was in a perfect position
    Directly across from the palace gates
    Where I could witness
    All the activities and commotion
    That took place each day.

My life was consumed with her.
    I had even memorized her daily patterns.
    She exited the gates along with her guards
    Every morning to shop at the market.

She was beyond beautiful,
    Which makes her difficult to describe in words.
    Her long, straight brown hair
    Was the color of bark from the finest trees.
    I imagined that if given the chance
    To get close to her
    I would lose myself in her eyes and
    Feel complete prosperity from the vision.

I always battled with myself
    To halt my feelings as
    I know that I would never
    Get the opportunity,
    But my desires were so strong that
    They often clouded my judgment and rationale.

My occupation gave me the ability
    To frequently observe the palace gates,
    Which only aided in my deception of love.
    I worried about her when
    She did not appear on time
    Or if she returned later than usual.

I became depressed if I missed an encounter
    Due to customers or the weather.
    I needed her in my life

For balance and became unstable
If the usual moments were not consistent.
She provided order in my life
When I needed it the most.
She offered me dreams
Full of passion and unconditional love.
She gifted me all of that
Without realizing my existence.

I was a master of my trade and
    Well-known throughout the city, but
    I kept my secret passion
    To myself as to not show weakness.

My obsession was strong on the inside and
    Transparent on the outside.
    It never got in the way of my tasks,
    Except if customers demanded attention
    During my ritual visions of the palace.
    I was never rude to them,
    But I never missed an opportunity to view my beloved.

During the slow peaks of business,
    I often tailored special outfits for her and
    Kept them in the back
    In case she ever ventured my way.

My future thoughts always allowed me
    To be well prepared for that first encounter
    As I had run through the scenario many times in my head.
    The conversation was well scripted
    Although I had altered it quite a bit from the original
version.

I shared my secret with no one.
    I believed that they would have
    Looked upon me with judging eyes.
    I never dwelled in how people saw me

In any other instance, but my secret was different.

I had grown accustomed to people staring at me and
    Deciphering my clothes on any particular day,
    I was immune to their torments and rude gestures.
    I guess I prompted the looks and comments
    As I did sit outside the middle of the city turmoil.

I did not consider myself strange,
    Only different than the others.
    Everyone tried to collect items and dress
    In order to draw attention their way.
    The fascination with wealth and relics
    Was a belief I did not share with them.
    I believed that a keen personality
    Was the key to a flourishing life.

Some called it inner beauty,
    I liked to refer to it as inner reality.
    A person could be dressed in the finest of fabric and
    Give the persona of a high quality soul,
    But the inner reality of their being
    Would show a different vision.

I grew to despise the citizens of the city.
    Mainly due to them always wanting more than they had.
    They were never satisfied with their present belongings
    And always judged others who had more
    Or less than them.
    I could not understand the concept as
    I never wanted something that someone else had.
    I was given items for a reason and
    I also did not receive items for a reason.
    It was not my right to distinguish between the two.
    There was no element of surprise
    If someone constantly wanted additional things.
    When will the want stop?

I imagined that once people acquire the item they seek,
That they would soon discard it
In order to make room for their next desire.

The endless loop disgusted me and kept me humble.
For me, I had no desire for items
Or treasures to increase my approachability.
No, I only had one desire and
It was my beautiful goddess
Who resided behind the palace gates.
For the most part, my secret desire
Had remained invisible to all,
Except for one of my frequent customers.

On a particular day,
She caught me staring at my beloved.
She was an aged widowed woman
Who was once married to a palace guard
Before he died in battle.

Her name was Asmodeus and
She was always kind to me,
But on one day she startled me.
While I was off on one of my daydreams,
She whispered into my ear
That the palace woman was beautiful.

The small comment immediately
Sacrificed any such dream I was having
And replaced it with the heavy hammer of the present.
I felt panic and stress
As if my desire had been uncovered.

I also experienced slight disappointment
For allowing myself to dwell so deep
In my dream that it was apparent
To someone walking by.

She placed a hand on my shoulder
    To calm my nerves and told me
    That she would not reveal my secret.
    That she once looked to her husband
    With the same emotional eyes.

Her words soothed me slightly as
    I felt that we had something in common.
    I pulled a vacant stool and offered her a seat and
    She graciously accepted.
    She appeared tired and weak
    For a reason I did not know.

I had never talked about my inner emotions
    To anyone before.
    I always thought that the sharing of emotions
    Was pointless due to my belief that others
    Cared nothing about who I was internally.
    When I was younger and more apt to share feelings,
    I could tell that the person
    I was talking to was not listening to my words.
    Instead, they were contemplating their own feelings.
    Once I established that,
    I was no longer the same and
    My conversation techniques changed dramatically.

I found that most people
    Do not truly listen
    So why waste my words.
    My observation for distinguishing
    Between those who listened and
    Those who did not was quite simple.

I often times would come up with fake topics
    Involving my feelings and approach people.
    As I shared my thoughts,
    I could tell by observing their eyes and mannerisms
    That they were not listening,

But the main sign was the length
Of the pause after I finished my words.

There would always be a brief pause
    From those who truly listened,
    Which allowed for the words
    To be consumed by their minds.

Non-listeners always had their own thoughts
    Prompted and ready to unleash
    Even before I had finished.
    With no pause and no real consumption of my words,
    They told their story,
    Which was always more drastic and lengthy
    Than the original.
    It was as if they never heard any of my thoughts.
    How could they have
    When they were conjuring their own stories while I spoke?
    A true listener would hear a story from another and
    Offer questions or comments related to what they had just
heard.
    An immediate change of story
    To involve one's self was not a sign of respect.
    I found it easy to set aside my beliefs
    And thoughts in order to listen to another.

I did not discard their words
    That they so eagerly wanted to share
    In order to tell my own version of the story.
    For that purpose,
    I chose to keep my emotions to myself and
    My comments directed towards anyone who would truly
listen.

Something was unique about Asmodeus.
    She offered me something
    That I had not received
    In a long time and

That was the art of listening.

Her eyes did not wander when I spoke.
    Her mannerisms were not agitated with my words and
    She never followed up my thoughts with her own story.
    She allowed for the conversation to flow naturally
    Without embedding twists and turns.

It was a beautiful art of conversation
    To experience as she always prompted me
    To continue by using questions and comments
    That related to my story.
    I still had hesitation with sharing
    My complete desires with her
    So I only offered her basic dialogue.
    At first, I only replied to her original comment
    By saying that my fair maiden was indeed beautiful.

She prompted me for more
    By asking me why I thought she was beautiful.
    In a glazed over state as I watched
    My queen walk from the palace gates,
    I answered Asmodeus that I believed that she was
    The essence of beauty and everything
    That I imagined the heavens would be.

My new friend offered me only a smile
    As acknowledgment of her listening.
    I was a bit overwhelmed
    With relinquishing a small portion of my secret
    To someone that I barely knew,
    But Asmodeus made it very easy to confide in her.
    She knew my every belief and frustration with the common
man.
    It was somewhat nice to have
    A productive conversation with someone
    Other than my own mind.
    She thanked me for the delightful discussion,

However, it was me who should have thanked her.

I continued to work throughout the day and
    Only stopped briefly to watch
    My maiden return to the palace
    After a day of chores in the city.

    I often thought about following her
    On one of her day trips to discover
    What it was that she did in the city,
    But my work did not allow it.
    I did not want to possibly ruin my safe ritual
    By venturing too close.

The guards that escorted her
    Would make sure that neither I
    Nor anyone else would get near her.
    She was a dream, a fantasy.
    One that I knew would never come true, however
    My desire was still strong and I held tightly to it.

I chose not to realize that my outcome
    Would not match reality.
    That would be very depressing and
    Would gift me no contentment
    Within the present.
    Instead, I protected the idea of
    What could be instead of what would be.
    It was less complicated that way and less stressful.
    It allowed me to function in my daily life and
    Actually presented me with an unreasonable goal.

There was not a moment that passed
    That I did not think about her and
    Envision a life shared with her.
    I admit that occasionally reality would creep upon me and
    Torment my emotions, but it was rare.
    The onslaught usually occurred after

A harsh day of work
Or an unsatisfactory meeting with another person.
My dreams when I slept
Would always allow me to drift back
Into my peaceful haven of solitude and
Provide me with a pleasant encounter with my maiden.

The next morning I was greeted by Asmodeus
While I sorted through various fabrics.
It had been a long time since
I actually welcomed the sight of another
The way I did her.

She was different in my eyes
Compared to the others.
I received a sense of acknowledgment that others lacked.
She was not afraid to listen to me
Without any selfish acts.
She did not push me away
With her demeanor or lessen my words with her own.
She simply offered me understanding,
It was a rare relic to find within a city
Where so many were eager to please themselves.

As she sat down, I could tell that her age
Was bothersome to her,
She sighed upon leaning back.
Her smile was pleasant and warm
Without any misconceiving notions or plans.

She prompted me to speak
By asking me how my lady was.
The ability to be open about my desires made me smile.
I eagerly wanted to tell her about my dreams
During the previous night,
But I sheltered my excitement for the time being
And replied that I believed that she was doing well.

Asmodeus was able to decipher my demeanor.
    She was the same as me
    With the ability to acknowledge one's hesitation and
    Translate it into stubbornness.
    There was an uncomfortable pause of silence
    As each of our powerful minds resisted the other.

She wanted me to release my emotions.
    I believed that she was truly requesting it, but
    I was not ready for full disclosure regarding my inner self.

She probably was just offering conversation
    Since we had nothing else in common,
    She predictably asked about my desire as
    It was the only trait she knew about me.

Regardless of her intentions,
    I was put into a situation where I felt uncomfortable.
    Being open was not my strong suit.
    Being around someone who wished to talk
    About it was not something I was accustomed to.

She knew I was uneasy
    About her prying into my chest.
    It felt as though she was pulling apart
    My rib cage in order to attack my heart.
    Searching around for any lingering emotion.
    My thick exterior armor shielded my thoughts
    From portraying any rude gestures,
    Plus I believed that she meant well in her questioning.

Instead of digging more on the subject
    She opted to change the topic to the weather.
    We talked about the mediocre theme
    For a small amount of time.

I felt bad by sheltering myself
    From her original question and

Possibly signaling to her a threatening tone,
So I voluntarily established the topic again.
Her smile let me know that her fake
Weather conversation was as much
Enjoyable to her as it was to me.
As I spoke about my secret,
I felt unburdened by it
As opposed to keeping it trapped within me.

Asmodeus and I met frequently
  Over the next few days.
  With each conversation I revealed more
  Of my darkest desires.
  She never interrupted me;
  Never changed the conversation.
  She was as infatuated with my desire
  As I was with my beloved.
  I even found myself anticipating
  Our discussions when she was not around.
  On one day while Asmodeus and I were conversing,
  I unintentionally missed an encounter
  With my lady as she left the palace
  For the day in the early morning.

I leaped up from sitting down and rushed outside,
  But she was already gone.
  I was angry with myself for being preoccupied
  And felt betrayed by Asmodeus
  Since she was the one that had stolen my consistency.

My friend tried to calm me
  But my anger blocked any such
  Invasion of comfort that tried to
  Penetrate my skin of rage.

It was the first time I had
  Ever not been there for my lady.
  What if something were to happen due to my absence?

What if the cycle of safety was harmed?
Visions of her death haunted my thoughts
Due to my mere selfishness.

I needed desperately to see her return,
    I knew it would be quite some time before that were to
occur.
    I needed to know that she was safe;
    I needed to know at that moment.

I became flustered in my actions and speech
    So much so that I could not function properly.
    Asmodeus tried again to relax me, but I blamed her for the
chaos.
    She went running down the street
    After her attempts to calm me were denied.
    Normally, I would have felt sorrow
    For the rudeness towards my friend,
    But my desires were upset like a river underneath a violent
storm.
    The weak minded emotion of pity would not see the light of
day.
    The rest of the day was spent angrily working
    While staring at the palace gates.
    Time appeared to slow as her return took forever to arrive.
    Down the street I saw the cluster of palace guards and
    I knew my lady had returned safely.
    My angered immediately subsided and
    Bowed down in submission to the emotion of relief.
    Her return meant that I did not cause her any harm
    By my selfish act.

I truly thought my life
    Would have ended that day
    If I did not see her enter back
    Through the palace gates.

I dwelled in my own demise and

Fed upon the anguish
That I could have caused.
It was the deepest trench
I had ever resided in and
She graciously pulled me
From the depths upon her return.
For that I was thankful, as she was
Always kind to me in that manner.
I slept easy that night
With a conscious of what nightmares
Would have awaited me
If the outcome had been different.

I envisioned the dark pit
That I would have plummeted into
If her safety was in jeopardy.
I imagined God blinding my eyes
So that I could no longer see her or
Cleansing my memory
So that I could no longer imagine her.
The mere thought chilled my spine and
Made me appreciate her return even more.
I vowed and prayed that I would no longer
Miss an encounter as long as I lived.

In the morning I found myself
Back on my regular schedule and
It was welcomed with honor and respect
As if I had discovered a long lost treasure.
I did not want to experience that amount of stress again.

One element that was left untouched
Was my friendship with Asmodeus.
I had not talked or seen her since the argument.
With me and my lady back on track,
I began to feel remorse for my actions towards my friend.

I realized it was not her fault or intention

To cause me to miss an encounter,
But my rational judgment was enraptured
By the situation and she was the only one
Who I could release my anger upon
Without relieving my secret.

As I sat there awaiting my maiden
To exit the palace gates,
I could not help but miss my conversations with Asmodeus.
Part of me wanted her to return
While another portion wanted to be left alone
So that I did not have any more distractions.
If she did give me another chance,
I would let her know of my timely tradition
So that she would understand
If I had to leave in mid-conversation.

As the days went by
With no sign of return of my new friend,
I felt remorse from my anger.
The sadness I encountered grew to a level
That I was unaccustomed to.

It affected my sleeping patterns and
A few of my small daily rituals.
I was not used to having a close friend
That I enjoyed the company of.
I did not have any practice
When dealing with the emotions of them either.

I had since moved beyond my anger
As time was the essence of my forgiveness,
I soon realized that others may not follow my procedure.
The complicated nature of handling
Disruptive scenarios between parties
With various outlooks and personalities
Was enough to turn me away from acquiring new
acquaintances.

Having others close to me became a hassle;
    Unproductive to my overall life.
    The situation with Asmodeus was evident enough, but
    I continued to feel for her as
    She was the only one in a long time
    Who actually listened to me.

I am not sure as to whether
    I needed her friendship
    Or her listening ability, but
    Something was missing in my life and
    She was involved somehow.

Maybe I was not prepared to return
    To the idea of talking to myself,
    Especially after conversing with her.
    However, I was not a changed man
    When it came to the general population.

My beliefs that no one listens was still intact,
    But I allowed only Asmodeus
    Inside my emotional wall and
    It felt comforting while she was there.

I did not need her friendship
    Or her personal memories.
    What I needed was her ability
    To sit in front of me
    While I shared my thoughts.

I needed that smile of acknowledgment;
    That gesture of acceptance that had been missing
    In my life for far too long.
    No one else in the city could provide me with that.
    Even worse, no one would even think of trying.
    Asmodeus had a gift of listening and
    I chased it away with my sudden outburst of rage.

The heavens must have heard my cries
    As they delivered me a gift in the form of Asmodeus.
    I saw her walking towards me from down the street.
    The way the sun glistened off of her small physique
    Made my sorrow vanish like fog in strong sunlight.

She approached me and gave only a smile.
    I immediately offered her my apologies and
    Reassured her that she had done nothing wrong.
    That my anger and misconception
    Of my scheduled encounters
    Was the essence of my horrible words.
    I took full responsibility for my actions and
    Realized that I had not shared
    My strict time schedule to her prior.
    Truth was that I was afraid as to how she would see me
    If I told her about my rituals with the palace gates.

At times I even felt that I
    Was over stepping my boundaries and
    Even viewed myself as a wolf stalking a sheep.
    I believed that it was not a crime to give into one's desires.
    Why else would God entitle them to us
    If we were meant to bury them?

I had always kept my desires secret;
    Contained within my mind and heart.
    I never acted upon them
    As I do not believe that I was strong enough
    To act out scenes from my internal play.

I was content with my desires and
    The level at which they resided.
    The visions of my beloved were enough to satisfy me.
    When the butterflies stopped fluttering
    Within my stomach garden prior to an encounter,
    I imagined that my level of desires would alter.

Until that day, I was quite content with my life.

With Asmodeus sitting
    In front me after a long separation,
    I talked constantly
    As there was plenty to catch up on.

I truly felt that her
    Walking into my life was a blessing,
    She held up her hand to halt the conversation
    In order to remind of an approaching encounter.

I had never felt such a friendship like hers before.
    She was truly a friend to me and
    I would work hard to not break that bond again.
    Instead of running out to the street by myself,
    I asked her if she wanted to join me.
    She agreed and we faced towards the palace gates.

While we waited, she asked me what I admired
    About my visions the most.
    It was a difficult question
    For me to answer
    As there was plenty to list.

After a brief pause,
    I responded that it was just simply the woman
    That I admired the most.
    It was the imagination
    That she represented perfection;
    The equality between love and respect
    That formed her beauty.

As the gates opened,
    I realized that it was the first time
    I was sharing my cherished ritual with another.
    I was at peace with that
    As she did not speak during the vision.

She simply allowed me to be myself
  Without sheltering my feelings or desires.
  It was as if she understood what I was experiencing.
  From there on, my encounters
  Would be shared with Asmodeus as
  I believed that she increased my enjoyment.

It was unique to express my feelings
  While in the moment and have someone
  Accept them with courtesy and respect.
  I never worried how she viewed me
  As I did not need to.
  She knew my inner most needs and
  Welcomed the discussions regarding them.

Our friendship grew with each day.
  My trust in others conjured itself up
  From the deepest valley of my untrustworthy soul.
  Trust was not something that I gave away easily.
  I kept it as my last line of defense.

I had seen regular people destroyed
  By their free spirit way of releasing certain emotions
  To anyone who would have them.
  Whether it was love, trust or happiness,
  People often spread their wings
  And leap from the ledge of emotions
  Before testing the depth of the canyon.
  Most would fall quickly
  While a few would soar and
  Fight their way back to the ledge
  In order to salvage the remainders of their lives.

I held on to the idea that God provided us
  With these emotions
  Not to give away aimlessly,
  But rather to seek out those amongst society

Who we deemed fit to receive them.

Releasing emotions like a mindless farmer
    Randomly tossing seeds in a field
    Only destroys the holder.
    Instead, a farmer who strategically
    Placed the seeds in predetermined positions
    Would allow for a more controlled outcome.

The random hurling would only provide chaos
    As the crops would battle with one another.
    Then there was my idealism,
    Which most would consider extreme.

I tested my potential friendships
    For flaws prior to releasing emotions.
    I always had a fear of leaping off of the ledge and
    Not being able to grab the edge.
    I preferred to think of myself
    As having one foot on the ledge at all time
    So that I could easily control the situation if a problem
arose.
    That concept made me not as social within society,
    But it also allowed me to avoid plummeting off of the cliff.

Due to the proximity of my store
    Within the city streets,
    I had been able to observe many
    Different types of personalities as they walked by.

I actually made a game out of differentiating
    Between the weak and strong minded people.
    I could tell who was on the verge of a mind collapse and
    Who was sheltering themselves from others.

Full disclosure of one's feelings
    Was an action that I felt to be a flawed joint in the mind's
armor.

There are those who prey upon it.
Some falsify their expressions
To gain the emotional release from others.
They take advantage of the trust
They are given and use it to destroy its giver.

It was a common practice within the streets
Even in nature to lure prey
In order to reap their rewards
Whether mental or physical.

I take pride that I had never been lured
Into situations that were out of my control.
I believed that I was able to distinguish
Between false and real emotions
When looking into the eyes of a person.

Asmodeus was unlike anyone
I had ever met before.
She was the complete package
Of what I looked for in a friend.
She was kind, patient and most of all forgiving.
I also believed in her consumption of my words.
My only hesitation was that her personality
Seemed too good to be real.

My response was that she relinquished
All of her emotions at a younger age.
Now that she was older,
She desired to hear the feelings of the young.
Regardless of her reasoning,
She was very skilled at the art of listening and
I was very willing to help her in increasing her level.

We experienced many encounters together
After her return and
Had several quality discussions
Regarding my maiden, but

Our friendship reached a new level on one beautiful day.

During that day, as we both anxiously stared
    At the palace gates for my lady to arrive home,
    Asmodeus said something that would alter my dreams.
    She ever so softly whispered that she could
    Get me closer to my maiden if I so desired.

I did not know what to think by the comment.
    At first I thought that she was fooling me,
    But she held strong by her words
    Even when I pressed her for more detail.

She continued to say that her late husband
    Had been a palace guard before he headed off to war.
    She said he had many friends in the palace
    Including several of the guards
    Who currently protected the gates.
    The hesitation that I previously felt
    Towards my friend suddenly crept back into my life.
    Maybe she was being truthful with me
    Or maybe my hesitation came from the mere idea
    That my desires would turn into actions.

It was new unexplored territory that I often avoided.
    I had always been cautious, but Asmodeus
    Spoke so easily about the situation
    That it made me question my beliefs.

She said that if I so desired that
    She could arrange a close encounter with the maiden.
    The mere thought of being in the same vicinity
    As her sent chills up my neck.

I imagined smelling her aroma and
    Maybe touching her skin.
    My hesitation was bombarded
    With what could possibly be.

I no longer was satisfied with visions
    As the potential physical portion of my desires
    Now reigned over all my other emotions.
    I had no chance to judge her idea
    Nor deny it as my mind focused solely
    On the opportunity to be near my maiden.
    All of my dreams of what could have been
    Flashed rapidly on the backs of my eyes lids.
    At that moment,
    My dreams were meeting reality and
    The partnership they were forming
    Would be permanent in my mind.

With so much running through my head,
    I actually cared not about the visionary encounters.
    I even at one point turned to look at Asmodeus
    While my maiden was in sight.

My friend opened up a whole new area of my fascination;
    One that I believed could not exist.
    The potential of her idea was endless;
    The journey would be exciting and new.

I always thought that I would never
    Get the opportunity to meet
    My beloved and there I was
    With a gift of chance in the palm of my sweaty hands.

Once my nerves and emotions subsided
    They allowed me to think logically,
    I began to ask Asmodeus questions regarding her plan.
    She stated that she could easily get us
    By the palace guards
    As they all still respected her late husband.

Once in the palace, I would take up the persona
    Of a servant and make my way to the maiden's quarters.

After that, she would not be able to help me
As my words would be my own.

It was not a well thought out plan,
    But at that moment I did not care.
    Asmodeus thought that it was a good idea
    For her to try to gain entry into the palace
    So that she could see whether the plan would work.
    I agreed and asked her why
    She was doing all of that for me.
    Her response was that she wanted
    To give me the opportunity to meet my desires.

She said that she could only provide me
    With the means to reach my dream
    That once I was there,
    All of the choices would be my own.

She said she was interested in knowing
    How far my emotions would take me;
    If my conscience would allow me to swallow my wants.
    I told her that I wanted nothing more
    Than to be in the same vicinity as my maiden,
    That my rational thought had no place within the palace.

We left each other that day
    With the understanding that Asmodeus
    Would enter the palace through the guards and
    Survey the situation from inside.
    The first part of the plan would occur
    Early the next morning
    When much of the palace servants were asleep.
    I awoke much earlier than I usually did
    As my nerves were tumbling within my sleep and
    Presenting me with visions of blood scarred battlefields.

I sat outside and waited to catch sight of Asmodeus.
    She did not fail me as I saw her from a distance

Approach the palace guards.
The demeanor of the guards were at first abrupt,
But as she spoke, their mannerisms became much more
relaxed.

They even extended out their hands to welcome her,
    Which put a smile on my face.
    After a brief period of conversing,
    The guards opened the gate and allowed her inside.

The sight of her disappearing through the gate
    Was a blessing to me as I now believed
    That I was also capable of entering the palace as well.
    I waited for Asmodeus to exit the gates.
    It took quite some time for her to reappear.

To my surprise she emerged at the exact moment
    That the maiden was returning to the palace.
    I saw my friend speak with her and
    Even witnessed my beloved touch Asmodeus' arm.
    I was amazed by her ability and the calmness
    That she showed throughout the first part of our plan.
    She gave me such confidence in my own ability
    That I never doubted her judgment from that moment on.
    She was a true friend.

She scurried as fast as her little old legs
    Could carry her and greeted me with a smile.
    I did not speak
    As I did not want to miss anything that she had to say.

She began by stating that the guards
    Did remember her and her husband.
    Once inside, she said that the palace was beautiful
    And went on to describe every detail that she saw.
    I did not care about the look of the palace, but
    I was not about to be rude to her
    After what she had done for me.

She finally reached a topic that interested me,
Which were the maiden's quarters.
I had her describe the scene exactly as she saw it.
It was everything that I imagined it to be
With the finest cloth, beautiful artwork and ripest fruits.

She stated that the best time
Would be to enter the palace when the maiden was away;
To be within her quarters when she returned.
It was to be the most perfect encounter that I would ever
have.
I envisioned it every time I closed my eyes and
It was all that I had dreamed.

The day came faster than usual
As if time increased its speed for my reasoning.
Asmodeus met me in front of my store and
We went over the plan that I was an old servant to her
family.
She was offering me to the palace as a sign of respect.

She even acquired a servant tunic
That I wore for the occasion.
We waited patiently for the maiden to leave.
As we neared the gates, I was quite taken back
By the sheer size of the guards.
I had always viewed them from afar and
Did not realize how strong and powerful they were in
person.
To say they were intimidating
Would be an understatement
As they were massive barbarians with heavy armor.
Their strict posture broke tradition when they noticed
Asmodeus.
I could tell they admired her by the way
They lowered their defense and in a most loving way,
As much as a barbarian could, touched her arm.

She acknowledged them and
    Introduced me as her private family servant
    That she would like to gift to the palace.
    I dared not get eye contact with the guards
    As I imagined they were skilled in the art of noticing liars.
    Their pupils would offer me nothing except
    A blistering, painful death.
    I merely bowed my head and stared
    At their armored plated boots that could
    Easily be used to shatter my skull if I ever found
    Myself underneath of one.
    A pause allowed me to envision
    Them ripping the flesh from my body and
    Constructing a chair out of my bones.
    I felt my forehead give in to the heat and begin to bead.
    The tunic did a decent job
    Concealing my nervous shaking, but
    It was the involuntary expressions on my face
    That worried me the most.

My throat became dry and I began to grind my teeth,
    All while I was being surveyed by guards.
    Apparently they believed our story
    Which was something that I was struggling with myself.
    They allowed us passage through the gates.
    As I saw the gates slowly open, I could not help
    To think that metal doors represented the opening of my
coffin.

I kept my eyes fixated straight ahead and
    Followed closely behind Asmodeus
    I could feel their blood scarred eyes piercing my mind.
    It took all of my effort to not look at them.
    I feared the worst if they were able
    To mind control me by looking into my eyes.
    Their breaths were that of large horses and
    Weighed more than me alone.

The shifting of their arms prompted their armored metal plates
    To grind against one another.
    The sound pierced my right mid-section, forcing me to twitch.

I felt as if I was walking through a valley of giants
    With a mind full of fear as my companion.
    Uncomfortable and uneasy are decent words, but
    They do not fully detail the amount of suffering I was enduring.

As we walked through the main courtyard,
    I managed to conjure up enough courage to peer around.
    The courtyard was filled with perfectly structured horses,
    Wonderful statues and flowing fountains.
    There were a few more guards walking about,
    But they paid no attention to us
    Since we has already crossed the threshold.

My tunic provided me perfect concealment
    And allowed me to blend in with the other servants.
    My confidence began to unhide itself
    From behind the wall of fear and stress.
    I could feel my curiosity peeking over my shoulders
    Like a creature seeking knowledge.

I realized that no one within the palace
    Was looking at us;
    We were of no concern to them.
    Everyone had tasks to tend to and
    They did so quickly with no spare time to give to strangers.
    I lifted my head up and walked
    With a complete understanding and confidence
    In the plan that Asmodeus had constructed.
    I did notice that none of the servants spoke,
    So I held back my tongue while in the courtyard.

We came to the main doors
    Leading into the palace
    Where two smaller guards resided.
    My courage once again fled the scene
    And buried itself deep in my stomach.
    Fear and stress gladly stepped in to fill the void left behind.

The guards asked our purpose in the palace.
    I kept silent and let Asmodeus handle the situation.
    She stated that she was here to deliver a private servant.
    She also said that I had served under her late husband.
    The guards nodded in acceptance and
    Allowed us entry into the palace.
    The inside of the palace overflowed
    With wealth and riches
    That I had never seen before.
    The amount of relics and statues
    That aligned the main hallway
    Was breathtaking to say the least.

The glistening marble that constructed
    The floor and columns was enough to make an artist weep.
    The surroundings were so magnificent
    That I had a hard time understanding
    How people could live like that.
    The palace had so much
    When regular citizens of the city had so less.
    I had never been wealthy.
    Even with my own business.
    To witness that amount of wealth
    Proved difficult for me to relate to.

It was as if I had entered into a completely
    Different world or realm of society
    Where the poor were no longer
    Sleeping on the streets, but rather transformed into servants.

Everyone was clean in appearance

Regardless of their status in rank.
Just crossing the threshold
Onto the marble environment
Gave me a sense of purpose and prosperity.

I was so accustomed to the outer streets
That the inside of the palace felt odd to me.
I imagined that the maiden felt the same way
When venturing into the city each day.
Everywhere I looked there were priceless
Historical relics that dated before my time.
Although I wanted to touch them
In order to feel their power, I dared not
As they were worth more than my simple life.
Instead I merely followed Asmodeus
As we walked through an endless labyrinth of hallways.
My mind was so thoughtless
Due to my surroundings
That I paid no attention to where
We were going and how we managed to get there.

I began to have second thoughts
Regarding the plan
Once I witnessed how the maiden lived.
She had so much more compared to me.

I voiced my hesitation to Asmodeus
That prompted her forward progress to stop.
She turned to me with her kind face and told me not to
worry.
She briefly eased my anxiety;
However my calmness would not last.

We rounded a corner and into a large banquet room.
Endless tables crossed over the marble floor
Holding a large buffet.
The amount of varying food was astonishing and
Would feed all of the poor in the city.

The seats around the table were occupied by large burly men
    Who were engulfing the food at a high rate with no care.
    As we passed one table,
    I could not help but compare my statue to the men.
    Their arms were perfectly etched with muscles
    As if they were sculpted by God himself.
    I saw muscles that I did not even know existed in a human
arm
    While they devoured full legs of lamb.

I felt so weak in their presence and not much of a man.
    Even the legs of meat were bigger than my arms.
    What little dignity I had left escorted me out of the banquet
room
    And into another larger hallway lined with various artworks.

My hesitation with the plan
    Showed its ugly face again and
    Was backed with the onslaught
    On my manhood from the banquet room.
    I must have sighed louder than I imagined
    As Asmodeus turned to look at me without a smile.
    She repeated that I had nothing to worry about, that
    The plan was working exactly as we had discussed.

She was right in her words.
    It was going very smoothly,
    However my mind was plaguing me with delays and
    Uncontrollable thoughts of indecision.

I do not believe she accepted my reasoning.
    She ignored my words and continued walking.
    She disregarded my feelings like a piece of fruit
    At a barbarian's table.

She had always been so accepting
    Of how I felt until that moment.

I continued to follow her,
However my mind was flourishing with disappointment.
How could she ignore me?
Her plan was to benefit me not her.
What was she to receive from the plan?

I must have pondered the notion
    For quite some time as Asmodeus
    Announced that the maiden's quarters
    Were just up ahead.

Reality struck me
    With such an intense power
    That all of my confusion and
    Hesitation were slaughtered.

Asmodeus always knew exactly
    What to say to me in order to
    Completely alter my outlook
    On any given situation.

We neared the main door of the maiden's quarters.
    I instantly fell back in love with her.
    The aroma of the freshly cut flowers
    That stood on either side of the door
    Heightened my desires.
    They awakened the sleeping butterflies
    Living within my stomach.

My chaotic nerves prompted
    My hands to tremble
    As I reached to touch the solid door.
    Asmodeus plucked a single rose and handed it to me.
    She also gifted me a small silk cloth tied with a golden
thread.

I opened the cloth and revealed a petite golden dagger
    That was so beautiful in design.

I was immediately grateful to my friend,
But disappointed in myself for not preparing a gift in
advance.

She told me that she could no longer continue with me.
She said that she was able to execute the plan
To allow me access to the maiden's quarters,
But her portion had come to an end.

She continued to say that I was to wait
In the room for the return of the maiden.
She also informed me that the choices
That I make within the room would be my own.

At that moment, I had no idea as to what
She was talking about as my mind was fixated
On my first physical encounter with my beloved.
Whatever it was that she said must not have been
Important as she did not stay long enough to get a response.

Instead she hurried down the hallway and
Left me alone standing in front of the door.
I reached for and felt the cool handle in the palm of my
hand.
With an effortless push,
The door squeaked open and allowed my entrance.
The room was everything I had imagined it would be.
The relics and treasures that were displayed
Added to the rich environment.
The chairs were draped with the finest fabrics.

Statues of what I assumed were her ancestors
Stood guard along the walls and
Watched me as I stared wide eyed at my surroundings.

Questions bombarded me as I waited.
Where should I be when she arrived?
Should I offer her the gift before or after we converse?

Not knowing the answers to the questions
Added to my confusion as my nerves took hold.
Being alone in the room did not benefit me at all.
The extra time to dwell in the plan and reality
Of where I resided only served to attack my senses.

The varying shifts of my emotions
Were enough to make any sane person go mad.
The only true satisfaction that I received
Was from the red rose that I held in my hand.
It served as a symbol of my passion and
Desire for my beloved.
The red pedals were perfectly shaped.
The green stem provided me with strength
During that crucial time.
In the land of free roaming thought and mental confusion,
The rose was my physical anchor
That kept me from being swept away.

By looking to the flower,
I was able to calm myself and imagined my maiden.
Her beauty soothed me
As it had always done in my time of need.
She was perfection in my eyes even if only a vision.
I was so excited to meet her that my breath become short
And my heartbeat became uneven.

My nerves sent me into a downward spiral.
My emotions ran wild like released farm animals.
I went into a labyrinth of panic and could not find my way
out.
I dropped the gifts and raced towards the window.
The height would not allow me to exit that way.
I stood in the middle of the room praying for an answer,
But received none.
I was alone and felt trapped.

My desires had led me there and my conscious wanted me
out.
    I sat down in my self-made prison
    And grasped the gifts as if they would provide me with
answers.
    The red rose once again calmed me.
    It comforted me for the remainder of my isolation.

With my mind quiet,
    I was able to hear the faint sound of footsteps
    Approaching from the hallway outside.
    The rhythmic patterns on the marble floor were my fate.
    My heart fed off the rhythm and matched the pace precisely.
    With the gifts clinging to my palms by a thin glaze of sweat,
    I waited.
    With my eyes wide open and my throat dry,
    I waited.

The moment that I had envisioned
    For such a long time was about to happen.
    The only thing between me and my lady
    Was a wooden door.

I wanted to leap up and swing open the door
    To reveal myself, but my shaky,
    Unstable legs would not allow that.

The door slowly opened and prompted me to stand.
    The quick movement blurred my vision,
    But graciously allowed me to remain vertical.
    That moment of not knowing
    What was to come was a time period
    I wished I had back
    As the choices I would make from there on
    Would alter my fate.

The door opened to reveal a large man
    Dressed in a white robe.

The image immediately shocked me
As I was expecting my beautiful maiden.

The vision of me also confused the man
As we stood there facing each other with
Our eyes full of astonishment.
His eyes broke the weird pause
By gazing down at the rose and dagger.
I could see the anger in his eyes building,
But I had no idea who he was and why he was there.
We both spurted out a question at the same time.
He asked who I was and
I asked why he was there.
In the heat of the confusion
We each actually answered our own questions.
I stated I was here to see the maiden.
He answered with something that
Would devour my inner demon and
Alter it into something much more devastating.

He stated that he was her husband.
The words pierced my skull and
Allowed me to die inside over and over again.
I felt complete emptiness and hollowed.
My desires were all drained with his words.
Everything I had done for her,
All of the time I gave her had been stolen from me.
I did not know who I was without those desires.
The darkness consumed any light
That my heart leaked and forced my soul
Into a pit of despair from which it would not return.
I plummeted from the ledge
Without any hope of grasping the edge for support.
I allowed my emotions to rule my life
And for that I would suffer.

The husband went into a blind rage and lunged for me.
I was too distraught in my mind to avoid any such attack.

I felt every swing of his fist connect with my face,
    But the pain did not compare to what my heart had
experienced.

My vision went in and out with every strike,
    But my mind portrayed visions of disloyalty and
resentment.
    I felt my body collide with the ground,
    But it was of no concern to me.
    My body became weak, but
    My mind remained strong.
    They were two separated entities and
    Cared not for one another.

My body was only concerned
    With the brutal assault it was receiving
    While my mind only cared about
    The emotional scars that it had received.
    My body was bleeding, but my heart was bleeding more.

I felt the cool air combine with my open wounds on my face,
    As the husband continued to beat me.
    My mind shifted from thoughts of pity to thoughts of
revenge.
    My body was energized by my mind and
    Allowed me the option of one swift motion.

With dagger still in hand,
    I stood and stabbed the man deep in his heart.
    The force of my attack allowed me to overpower
    The weakened man and push him back towards the door.

His back slammed into the wooden door
    With me and my dagger holding him up.
    I twisted my weapon
    As if to drain his heart of any love he had for his wife.
    I felt the blood spill over my hand and
    Drain the admiration into my pores.

His eyes glazed over,
But I was not done with him.
I dragged my dagger around his chest
And pulled his heart from its case.
His body crumbled to the floor
With no love or heart remaining for my beloved.

I had no time to contemplate what I had done
As more footsteps could be heard in the hallway.
I dragged the husband's body away from the door and
Tossed his heart back on his chest.

It was not the idea first encounter
I had envisioned for her
As my face was bloody and bruised,
Plus her husband was heartless on the floor, but
She was tainted in my eyes now.
She had lied to me the entire time.
Every shared encounter,
Every dream and fantasy was all for nothing.

She tempted me with her beauty and false hope.
She had none of the traits
That she had portrayed for as long as I knew her.
She hid secrets from me; a marriage from me.

She would realize what she had done to me.
She destroyed me and forced me to do evil things.
She was everything to me and
Everything was what she took from me.

As the door opened, I hid to the side to allow her to enter.
She closed the door behind her and felt the blood-stained
wood.
Her eyes widened as she looked to her red coated fingertips
And saw her lifeless husband on the ground.

She was so terrified

That she could not gather the breath
Needed to form a scream.
She had not seen me yet, but I was very close
And was able to smell her hair.

The scent was beautiful and relaxed me.
It was an aroma that would be with me
Long after my stay on earth.
Her lure was strong and overpowering to my senses.

I lost myself in her for a brief moment
Until she turned around and yelled.
She quickly stepped away from me in defense.
Her eyes were a brilliant shade of green,
But were overshadowed by the tears and strain from the
stress.

Her lips were moist and quivering from the fear,
But were beautiful nonetheless.
She did not remember me,
Even after everything we had been through.

Every day we saw each other and shared so much,
And yet she had no memory.
She looked to me as if I was a stranger, a murderer.
If she could only look deep in her heart,
I believed that she would remember me and
The love that I offered her with every encounter.

How could she not understand me?
I had given her so much.
Her husband did not love her like I loved her,
No one could.
He lied to her about his love and
I exposed his heart to prove it.
She was as beautiful as I had envisioned from so far away.
I ignored her fear and uncontrollable crying.
I looked into her eyes to find what I was looking for.

She truly had no idea who I was.

Her lack of memory angered me
  More than her secret marriage.
  Her denial to accept me and my love
  Enraged me to where everything in the room
  Received a coating of red.

I had two gifts in my hand.
  She was to choose only one.
  I held out the rose as a last sign of faith.
  She could have a life with me.
  We could be happy if she would only accept it.

My blood boiled at her lack of support
  For our relationship by not taking the first gift.
  I dropped the rose on the ground and
  Prepared to offer her the second gift.

She needed to know that it was always about her.
  Everything I did was for her.
  Every dream, every fantasy was for her.
  Every need, want and desire was for her.
  She was the reason I was alive and
  The reason why she had to die.

She corrupted our relationship through marriage
  And the avoidance of memory.
  She would feel the pain and suffering that she had caused
me.
  She would feel every heart ache and
  Every anxiety that she gifted me.
  Her mouth dropped open as she realized
  That it was time for our love to end.
  She tried to run, but the strength of my hand holding her
hair
  From behind was too much for her.

I ran my blade across her throat and
    Heard her betrayal leak from her wound.
    Her gasps for air were only more denial for our love.

I lowered her body to the ground
    With respect as she had once loved me.
    I took a moment to kiss her warm lips
    One last time before I proceeded to carve her heart out.
    I would always cherish her heart
    As long as I lived no matter how much
    She ventured away from me.
    I had always believed that her heart was mine for the taken.

The mood in the room was somber
    Until Asmodeus opened the door and joined me.
    I predicted nothing but shock on her face,
    Instead she greeted the situation with a smile.
    She told me I had done well.
    I was not sure how the removal
    Of the hearts out of two people was perceived as doing well,
    But I accepted her comment.

I asked her if she knew about the secret marriage.
    She said that the marriage was no secret.
    She said I was the only one who did not know about it.
    She said my lust for my beloved
    Would not have allowed me to believe it.

She could tell that my anger was increasing
    Towards her and she denied my feelings by informing me
    That I could not kill what was already dead.
    I wanted to try so badly,
    But her smile penetrated my mind so deep with an evil
arrow
    That I actually became fearful of the unknown.

I asked her what she was.
    She only stated that she was a demon.

After what I had been through,
I had no choice but to believe her.

My anger subsided and
    I asked her in a calm voice
    About what was to occur next.
    She grabbed the handle of the door and
    Said that the encounter had to end.

She pulled the door open as she vanished.
    In the doorway stood four palace guards
    Each with a shocked expression on their faces.
    There I was covered in blood
    Standing over two corpses
    With a dagger in one hand and a heart in the other.

~

I am growing accustomed to the darkness in the cave.
    Being in here for so long with the only light
    Coming from the small candle
    Has allowed me to adapt my vision.
    I predict a negative effect
    When I am allowed to exit into the sunlight.
    Even the thought of the sun
    Makes me squint against the brightness.

I think I am becoming friends
    With the darkness and often times
    Speak to it as if it were alive.
    The black can secure and hide any evils
    That lurk or allow them to show themselves.

It is the true ruler of the cave.
    It allows me just enough light
    So that I may continue my task.
    It is gracious and kind to me.

I dare not think about angering the darkness
As I do not wish to feel its sheer power.
I could see how the darkness
Could be quite relentless in its actions
If it were not a friend.

I wish to stay on the good side of the darkness
And do nothing to provoke it.
I will follow its orders and meet its demands.
I owe it at least that for listening to my worries and
Not judging me for my actions.

I will offer it the same in return.
I will hear its cries and
See it with non-judging eyes.
For now, I will sleep
Knowing that the darkness is my friend.

VII

Ore was my source of life;
    My source of business.
    I had never desired anything else except for it.
    It was my passion.
    My thirst for it was never quenched.

Even though I would
    Receive a large quantity of it,
    I still wanted more.
    The sound of the wagon wheels
    Rotating and squeaking
    Along the path appeased me.

Once I heard the sound,
    I would stop working and
    Watch as the wagon neared.
    I could often judge the amount of ore
    The wagon was toting
    By the different depths of tones
    That the wooden wheels would emit.

A low grinding noise reflected
    That the wagon was empty
    While a high pitched sound
    Meant the load was full.

Obviously, a high sound
    Of an approaching wagon delighted me.

More ore meant more opportunities
And larger products.

Most blacksmiths opted for certain
    Types of ore and sought it out.
    While others craved other ores
    Such as copper or bronze,
    I focused mainly on iron.

I always felt at ease with the ore and
    Harnessing its strength.
    I was a master of iron.
    The weapons and armor
    I produced was evident of that.

I never ventured away from weaponry
    Even when the popularity of
    Precious metals was introduced.
    An abundance of trinkets
    Infiltrated society at a rapid pace.

To keep up with the demand,
    Most turned to creating relics.
    I tried my hand at the new market,
    But constantly found myself back at weaponry.

I found no power and strength
    In goblets and plates.
    The output was unsatisfactory for me,
    Especially since most of the precious metal
    Creations were for monetary gain.

Holding a well-made goblet
    Was not the same as holding
    A well-made sword.

No one personalized with trinkets
    Except when they would increase

Their personal standing within society.
When someone held a sword for the first time,
You could see the empowerment
Within their eyes as their face
Reflected off of the blade.

A well-built sword tested a man's will and strength.
　The weight of the metal,
　Length of the blade
　Had to be right and built
　To match the persona of the owner.

That was not the case with trinkets.
　Anyone could randomly use them,
　But not weaponry.
　I believed a single sword
　Was constructed for a single person.
　A single shield was constructed
　To protect only one person.

To watch someone bond
　With such a weapon was satisfying to me.
　I had seen it so many times in the past.
　That moment of transfer released ownership
　Of the weapon from creator to owner.
　It was my gift; my talent to the world.

The iron ore that I worked with
　Came from a nearby mountain range.
　Each blacksmith employed strikers
　For many reasons including holding the metal
　While the blacksmith strikes it,
　But the main reason was to retrieve
　The ore from the mountain.

Some of the more wealthy blacksmiths
　Like those who created trinkets
　Were able to employ more strikers.

I did not have internal strikers
To help me forge the metal.
I was able to handle the process on my own.

I had only one striker
Who retrieved the ore from the mountain
And delivered it to me.
His workmanship was not the best,
But it was difficult to fill the role
Since the task was an undesirable one.
The mountain was separated into zones
Equally owned by all the blacksmiths within the region.
Each zone had an entrance point into the mountain
Where the striker would venture into the mine
To retrieve the ore.
It was common knowledge
That the strikers would stay only within their designated mine
And not creep into others as ore thievery
Was not looked well upon.

The process worked and
I was fortunate enough to lay claim
To a portion of the mountain
With an abundance amount of ore.

Others were not so lucky
As once you lay claim to a section,
You own that area regardless of whether
You can generate ore from it or not.

To avoid confusion, the mines were clearly marked
On the outside and throughout the inside
With flags and banners representing the blacksmith.
There was no reason why a striker
Would mistakenly venture into another blacksmith's mine
Other than to steal ore.

The mountain range supplied
    Plenty of the resource for everyone who needed it,
    So the concept of theft
    Proved to not be an issue.

However, the quality of the ore was another factor.
    The highest quality of ore was the key to success.
    The higher quality of the ore in its rawest form
    Carried over to the higher quality of the end product
    Thus making the output more desirable.

The strikers were not trained
    In the art of deciphering
    Between low and high quality ore.
    That task was only for the most skillful blacksmith,
    Plus the fact that the ore was caked with dirt and mud
    When the striker was in possession of it.
    It was not until the cleansing process
    That the ore could be rated by quality.
    For this purpose, the strikers mined all ore
    Regardless of what they believed the quality to be.

It was possible that a delivery wagon
    Would only consist of low quality ore
    While others were overfilled with high quality.
    One never knew until the ore was released from its dirt
prison.
    Part of the excitement was uncovering the high quality and
    Pondering the levels that I would receive each delivery.

Along with iron, I also instructed
    My striker to collect and mine any findings of coal.
    The mountain range was also famous for its coal output.
    That was a common practice with most blacksmiths
    As the infusion of coal into the products
    Benefited them greatly.
    I personally would forge the coal with iron to produce steel,
    Which I would use in my weaponry designs.

The amount of coal was sufficient in the region and
Allowed me to create a wide variety of products with steel.

The process of forging and
Smelting the ore was a tedious one.
Only a blacksmith with high tolerance
For heat and strength could handle the daily process.

I for one welcomed the heat and
Enjoyed the strength and endurance
That my occupation provided me.
The challenge to bend and shape
Some of the most hardened natural materials
Into usable weapons was a desire of mine.

The role of a striker was an unusual one.
It was not an occupation for the light hearted.
They did a maximum amount of work for minimal pay.
It was hard labor and undesirable long working days.

Rarely did strikers have families
As they would venture into the mines
And not resurface for several days at a time.
Armed with only a pick axe and shovel,
They would spend most of their lives
Surrounded by darkness with the only task of acquiring ore.
Several days of work would reveal
A wagon full of ore that would be unloaded at a workshop.
The striker's role allowed for the blacksmith
To focus on the construction of the products
As it would be impossible to both mine and create.
The task of mining required too much time.

Most strikers were treated well,
But the egos of a few blacksmiths were known
To apply hardships on anyone that worked for them.
As for me, I tried to give honorable pay for honorable work.

When business was good and I was able to pay more, I
would.
    When high quality was received; high pay would be given.

I was fortunate due to my tenure in the region,
    To have laid claim to several
    Prime zones on the mountain
    With high output and quality.

That was no more evident than in the products I unveiled.
    My swords, shields, axes, maces and daggers
    Were high quality artifacts
    That had been tested in battle and held by kings.

I did not produce the same product twice as
    I believed that each weapon should stand alone;
    That led to its worth.
    To own something that had no comparison
    Was a respect that I offered my customers.
    Warriors and battle masters from across the land
    Beckoned my services and I was not hard to locate.
    Depending on the item, I liked to meet the owner
    To judge their weight and strength.

A heavy shield for a light-weighted warrior
    Would not help him in battle.
    Same for weapons, as a long blade
    For a shorter fighter would prove useless.

For that reason, I needed to meet the owner
    To properly craft the item for its full potential.
    My customers ranged from the mightiest of barbarians
    To the smallest of princes.

Each weapon was built for only one person.
    I could not guarantee the same results
    For anyone using the weaponry
    That it was not originally designed for.

A few days had gone by and
    I did not hear the familiar sound
    Of the squeaking wheels of the delivery wagon.
    A new delivery of fresh ore was something that I never
missed.
    Finding that high quality ore
    Buried deep in a case of dirt was something
    I looked forward to when delivery day approached.

It was getting late of the fourth day
    Without an approaching wagon.
    Usually, I received my ore on the third day
    After my striker left for the mountain.
    Being a day behind was rare, but not too unusual,
    So I closed down the fire pit and retired for the night.

I began work the next day as I usually did,
    But the level of my current ore
    Would not allow me to make it through the day.
    I had never had that long of a pause
    In the process before.
    I was beginning to worry about the welfare of my striker as
    I had not seen him in four days.

I quickly finished up a current project
    I had been working on and prior to beginning another one,
    I decided to travel to the mine and inquire about his status.
    With a sword attached to my back
    To aide in my protection from natural predators,
    I walked along the path that the striker had taken so many
times before.
    I rarely traveled to the mountain,
    Mostly due to the amount of work I received.
    I remember my first trip to the mine,
    When I blazed that very trail
    In order to make it through the thickened woods.

The path was just wide enough to allow
For a wagon to advance through.
The constant leveling of the land
From the large wooden wheels
Had proven to make my current travels easier.

I had three separate mines that I had acquired,
But I first went to the largest one where
I believed my striker was currently mining the ore.
The blacksmiths who owned several mines
Had rituals for the strikers that were meant for safety.
The main one involved a red flag
That was placed at the entrance to the mine.
It allowed for anyone at the beginning
To know that a striker was currently working.
With no flag, it was impossible to know
Which mine they were in.
The flags were usually battered and torn
From the constant staking and
Spending half of the time lying on the ground.

I came to the entrance of my largest mine and
Upon further exploration, I saw the red flag upon the
ground.
Knowing he was not in there,
I traveled to my second mine.

After arrival, the evidence was the same
With the red flag lying on the ground.
Becoming frustrated from my travels,
I journeyed towards my third and final mine
Where I would soon discover a red flag flapping in the
wind.
Another ritual that the strikers had
Was to light torches to mark the depth
That they were going within the mine.
Every few corners of the mine had a torch attached to the
wall.

As the striker passed them,
They would light it to remind themselves
Regarding the depth they had achieved.
Not only did the light provide them with the ability to see,
But also offered safety from roaming animals that often
entered.
The mine had changed since I had been in it last.
My striker had done a great job excavating
A properly laid out path that spiraled downward
According to mining standards.

The path was a good size
With mining burrows equally spaced out
On either side in order to avoid the potential of collapse.
The structure of the mine required expertise and precision
When burrowing new paths.
The mountain was still under the ownership of Mother
Nature
And if angered, she could deny us of her resources.
She could deny us of her resources.
The respect for her was always high
As it was told that a few strikers
Had fallen victim to her and were never seen again.
Some say they were consumed by the mountain
Others claim they had become her personal servants.
Either way, it was always beneficial
To give proper admiration to the mountain and its resources.

I proceeded down the mine path and
Passed several torches before coming to an abandoned
wagon.
I ruled out the option of thievery
As the wagon was almost completely full with fresh ore.

I found the scene very odd.
It appeared that my striker had plenty of cargo for a delivery
and
The position of the wagon led me to believe

That he was making the journey back.

I continued further deeper into the mine
  Passing more torches along my way.
  My concern for my striker increased the further I went.
  The confusion of seeing the abandoned wagon puzzled me,
but
  Provided me with a mental companion for my trip.

After passing the eighth torch,
  I came across a pick axe and shovel.
  There was absolutely no reason
  Why tools should have been that far away from the wagon.
  It did not make sense to mine the ore
  Then carry it further away to the wagon.
  That second round of evidence
  Prompted me to unleash my sword
  As I believed something had gone awry.
  My striker was more diligent than that.
  His work pattern was predictable and timely.
  With sword in hand, I passed more torches.
  The flames danced off of the perfectly etched steel blade.
  I found myself admiring the artwork of the sword.
  It was not one of my more extravagant creations,
  But it was still beautiful to gaze upon,
  Especially in the random light pattern of the torches.

From around the next corner
  I could hear the faint voice of a person.
  I was still too far away to fully understand the words,
  But every step I took offered me more clarity.

I came across a lone man huddled to the ground near the far
wall
  Who was obviously distraught.
  His mannerisms showed evidence that by his body
shivering.
  At first I thought he was my striker, but

I would soon learn of my own mistake when he turned
around.

I had never met him before,
    But he had the personal attributes of a striker
    With his small stature and pale complexion.
    I told him I was the owner of the mine and
    Asked him what he was doing there.

He stated that he was a striker of a nearby mine
    And shared the journey into town with my striker.
    He said that he stopped by the entrance of the mine when he
    Noticed the red flag was still up.
    His concern for his friend
    Prompted him inside
    As he had heard rumors of rabid bears
    Roaming the mines around the mountain.

I asked him about the whereabouts of my striker.
    He pointed further down the mine with a twitching finger.
    I gripped my blade tighter and
    Told him to stay where he was.
    As I walked away from him,
    I noticed that he stood underneath the last lit torch.
    Through the faded light,
    I saw what appeared to be small trenches in the dirt floor
    As if something had been dragged.

I followed the mysterious path,
    Which lead me further into the darkness.
    I saw the hazy outline of the first unlit torch
    And a large mass lying beneath it.

The lack of light severely blocked my rational judgment,
    It intensified my curiosity as I reached to the pile.
    My horrid predictions came true as
    I rolled over the lifeless body of my striker.
    Evidently the darkness was not as black

As I had imagined since
I saw every feature of his mutilated body
In such detail that I leaped back in disgust.

The vision churned my insides and
    Struck me in the stomach so hard that
    I vomited against the mine wall.
    Then the smell assaulted my senses
    As I did not experience it when I first arrived.

The shock soon wore off as visions
    Of a rabid bear still lurking in the mine
    Took control of my mind and guided me
    To follow the path of torches back.

The other striker was still there where I left him.
    I grabbed his arm and said that we had to leave.
    I had a fear that the bear would return to the mine.
    The striker did not hesitate to accompany me
    And was also eager to be outside again.

We came to the abandoned wagon full of ore.
    The striker immediately grabbed the handles and began to
pull.
    The sounds of the squeaking wheels carrying the full cargo
    Echoed through the mine.
    The gesture from the striker was very unselfish
    Considering the latest events and was welcomed
    As I had not received a fresh batch of ore in several days.
    We reached the threshold of the mine entrance and
    Exited into the conjuring moonlight.

I told the striker that he could return to his home, but
    He insisted that he would help me
    By pulling the wagon to my shop.
    He said it was the least he could do.

I accepted his gracious gift

As we journeyed down the base of the mountain.
The moonlight highlighted the woods in an eerie haze.
My early rise for work prompted me to be asleep
Normally during that time frame.
I was a bit uneasy especially with
The large amount of shifting shadows.

The army of bark warriors toyed with my emotions and
Surrounded us on either side of the path.
They moved with the motion of the wind
Allowing their numbers to double in size.

I kept my eyes on the path and
My power fully focused within the grip of my sword.
The striker was a few paces behind me,
But that did not stop him from offering conversation.

He said his name was Leviathan,
But his friends called him Levi.
He said he had not always been a striker,
That he was once an artist.
I did not prompt any conversation as
My attention was fully consumed
By the army of trees that could attack us
At any given moment.

Levi continued his random speaking
By saying that he was not a full-time striker,
That he filled in for other strikers
When something minor or drastic happened.
I had heard of that and used a loan striker
Once when my striker grew ill.
My current situation had prompted me to be in need of
another.

The journey back gave me time to reflect
Upon what I discovered in the mine.
I did have remorse and sorrow for my striker,

But it was not the same level I would have shown
For a friend or loved one.
I was more friends with
His consistency and timeliness
Than I was as a person.
I blamed the lack of time spent with him
For that as I only saw him while he
Unloaded the ore every few days.
I was not alone in my personality as
Most blacksmiths abided by the same concept.
Our work was our first love,
It overshadowed any type of friendships
We may have encountered.

We never stopped to realize how important
A striker was to us until the wagons stopped.
I was not the worst of the bunch and
Tried to make my striker feel at home,
But I never intentionally befriended him.

It was more like a courtesy friendship
With no backbone to support it.
Unlike the current striker
Who was pulling the wagon,
Who had talked the whole journey back to the shop.

His words describing his life
Drained my energy and made the travel appear endless at
times.
At one point, it was almost worth it for me
To pull the wagon myself and leave him behind.

I never underestimated the sound of silence until that day.
I only offered him my attention
During the beginning leg of our journey.
Unfortunately, he took that small portion of acceptance
And bled it like a trapped boar.
I heard every problem that he had in his life.

How he planned on overturning them.
My mind became numb and it was a blessing as
It allowed me to ignore a few of his stories.
He had single handily ruined
The lovely sound of the squeaking wheels that I adored.
The association between the wheels
And his mouth united together
Along the path that night and proved devastating for me.

My next thought was presented to me
Either by my tired body or vacant mind.
I asked him who he was currently working for.
After pushing me off of the conversation cliff
With tangent stories of devastating fates and fortunes,
He arrived at the answer that I desired in the beginning.

He claimed he currently was on loan
For my neighboring blacksmith and
That he had delivered his final load today.
He was the complete opposite from my previous striker and
Everything that I did not want in one,
But I was desperate to return my
Ore delivery back to a more consistent schedule.
The missing loads of the substance had put me in a bind
Regarding certain projects that I was working on.

When he took a moment to pause for breath,
Which rarely happened,
I inserted my own question very quickly and
Asked him if he wanted to work for me.

He responded by asking if I meant on loan or permanently.
I answered him saying that it would be a permanent position
and
The pay would be competitive.
Before I could say any more,
He jumped at the opportunity
Like a wolf devouring a sheep after stalking it all night.

He said as a good sign of faith
    He would take care of the body in the mine
    So that I would not have to travel again.
    That offered me some relief
    As the puddle of flesh I witnessed would cause me
    To lose my appetite for a few days.
    I retired for the night while he unloaded the wagon
    With the understanding that he would
    Journey back to the mine early in the morning.

Work continued as usual over the next few days.
    My excitement even returned from the sound
    Of the squeaking wagon wheels.
    I had yet to receive a full delivery
    From the hands of Levi and his visit today would be the
first.

I was desperate last night and wanted
    To reduce the downtime between deliveries.
    My initial plan was to have Levi work for a few days
    While I searched for a striker who was more my taste.

That concept got washed away as
    I witnessed the first load that Levi had mined.
    The amount was breathtaking to see.
    There was so much ore in the wagon
    With all of the excess dirt almost all removed.

The entire wagon was overflowing with ore.
    My old striker had never brought that much
    For the mere fact that he could not pull the weight.
    Not to mention that he mined that entire load
    Within two days instead of three.
    I was excited about the delivery
    That I even helped him unload it, which was a first.
    I wanted to know how he managed that,
    But I did not want to give off the perception

That the amount was unusual.

As soon as we unloaded the last piece of ore,
    Levi picked up the cart,
    Headed back towards the mountain and
    Left me behind with astonishment blistered upon my face.

Two days later, I heard the squeak
    Coming from the wagon wheels.
    That high crank when the axle
    Grinded with the wooden wheel was the same level
    As it was for his first delivery.

I halted my work and looked down the path.
    I saw the wagon with the same mound of coal
    Extending above Levi's head.
    That amount of ore was unheard of
    Within that short of time period.

No striker cleaned the ore prior to delivery
    As it took too much time.
    Levi was mining faster than any other striker
    I had met and dusting the ore during the process.

I thought maybe that he was trying to impress me,
    That it would not last through the season,
    But once again I was wrong.
    Ten deliveries into his work for me and
    All ten had been with the same quality and quantity.

I started projects that I had only dreamed of,
    But were unable to create due to the amount of ore required.
    The everyday creations benefited greatly
    From the increase in ore and
    I was able to hand pick certain qualities for particular
projects.
    That type of ore freedom was scarce.

Levi had personally increased my
    Productivity and quality of my work,
    However, I kept my excitement to myself.
    I did show my gratitude in other ways
    By providing him with food and a bed when he made a
delivery.
    With so much ore at my disposal,
    I often allowed him to rest the night of his arrival
    Since my demand was at a comfortable level.
    The next morning prior to heading to the mountain,
    Levi was not his usual talkative self.
    I hesitated asking him about it
    As his answers were always long winded.

I took a deep breath and
    Asked him what was troubling him.
    He stopped preparing the wagon and
    I braced for an onslaught of verbal abuse.

I often times thought how useful
    He would be as a diplomat in battle.
    A kingdom could send him to their opposing enemy
    To dampen their spirits with his stories.

The enemy would have no choice
    But to surrender to the terms constructed by the opposition.
    Then I imagined that his own kingdom
    Would not request for his safe return.
    I usually felt remorse after reliving the idea,
    But I could foresee it happening.

I was so used to blocking him out and
    Daydreaming about something else as he spoke
    That I did not hear the first few sentences he had to say.
    I was nodding uncontrollably at regular intervals and
    Had no idea as to what I was agreeing to.

He ended his one-sided conversation and

Must have felt that I understood him
As he loaded up his wagon and headed towards the
mountain
To retrieve another batch of ore.
I honestly could not recite one word
That exited his mouth if my life depended on it.
I was never the one to feel pity
Regarding the problems of other people.
I always lived by the concept
That I should not have to hear your issues
If I was not going to share mine.

Two days went by and Levi returned
With the sound of the brilliant, heavy squeaking wheels.
Anxious to see the quality of the ore,
I met him in front of the shop.
After a few of his standard solo conversations,
We began to unload the cargo.
I was eager to sort the ore
As I was beginning a massive battleaxe
For a local warrior prior to him heading into battle.

The design required a large amount of high quality ore
And carbon if I was going to complete it in time.
As I sifted through the ore,
I noticed that there was not a lot of high grade in the wagon.

The ore was light in weight and slightly dull in color.
I asked Levi about the cargo.
He explained that he had told me
During his last stay that the mine was running low.

He said he asked if he should mine the common ore and
That I nodded in agreement.
I immediately felt that vomiting feeling once again,
Instead of a mine wall, I was about to spew on
The batch of low grade ore.

I persuaded him to tell me his story again
    Without him thinking that I ignored him the first time.
    I listened to him intently
    As he told me that the mine was emptying of high ore,
    All that was left was the low quality.

My sigh at his words
    Translated as frustration to him.
    He followed up with an idea that I quickly took offense to.
    He stated that the previous mine
    He worked in prior to starting with me
    Was filled to capacity with high grade ore of
    Even better quality.

I knew what he was thinking,
    I wanted no part of thievery against a fellow blacksmith.
    He continued to say that he was aware
    Of the new striker's schedule,
    That he could easily acquire the ore if requested.

I gave no such order and sent him back
    To my mines to gather ore as usual.
    To be honest, I did contemplate the special ore
    Later that night as I looked to the useless pile I had
acquired,
    But the thought of stealing did not rest well with me.

Levi arrived earlier than usual for the next delivery.
    The sounds of the wheels were a little lower than normal,
    But the amount was of no concern to me
    I was more interested to see if the quality of the cargo
    Had improved from our previous encounter.

As always, Levi immediately started in mid-conversation
    As if I had been traveling alongside him.
    Lately, I had been trying to pay more attention
    To what he was saying, but it was challenging
    And I entered into the fold the fourth sentence in.

He never restated anything he said,
    So I did not bother to ask.
    His thoughts and topics were so rapid,
    So random that I doubted he could remember
    Any of his previous remarks.

I could tell he was excited about something
    Through his mannerisms.
    I was sure that he was explaining it to me,
    But he had lost me the moment he approached.
    It was very difficult for me to pay attention
    To such long-winded stories,
    Let alone several combined into one.

I sifted through the coal and was somewhat disappointed
    In the quality as I was hoping that it would have improved.
    I needed better ore in order to finish the barbarian's axe.
    I was never going to get it done in time with cargo like that.
    Levi saw my frustration and assured me
    That he had something that would challenge
    My current emotional state.
    From the back corner of the wagon,
    Buried deep beneath the ore,
    He extracted a bundle of black cloth.

He slowly revealed a piece of ore
    That was perfect in all aspects
    From underneath the cloth.

It was as if the relic had come
    From Mother Nature's secret haven.
    I had seen many variations of ore in my lifetime, but
    None matched the perfection of what I saw that day.

Levi walked over and handed me the piece of ore.
    I carefully grabbed it like it was a fragile child in need of
shelter.

The ore felt at home in my hands.
My hardened fingertips felt around the edges and
I found no imperfections.

I am sure that Levi told me where he found it,
    But I did not hear him.
    Holding the ore allowed my creativity to soar like a black
bird
    Over a snow-capped mountain range.
    Visions of new creations and possibilities
    Tattooed my mind and gifted me with inspiration.
    I soon came down from my cloud when I
    Realized that I was only holding one piece of it.

I would only be able to make a fine goblet
    From such a small portion.
    My dreams of exquisite shields and swords
    Vanished as quickly as they appeared.

Levi lifted up my spirits again
    By stating that there was more.
    I knew what he was talking about,
    At that time I was only concerned
    With rejuvenating my creative visions again.
    I wanted my mind to flow freely like
    A flooded stream seeking a new path.

My silence and lack of denial prompted him to continue.
    He said the very piece I was holding
    Came from the neighboring mine where
    The abundance of it were not like anything
    He had experienced in his striker existence.
    He spoke of burrows with walls
    That were speckled with the ore
    Like a blossoming apple tree.

He said that the soil in the walls
    Was so loose that the ore

Could easily be extracted from its core.
I felt my mind salivating over his description
As if he spoke of roasted boar ribs over an open fire.

I knew what he wanted me to say.
    I knew he wanted my blessing to retrieve the ore,
    But I did not have claim to the mine.

He continued to say that the owner of the mine
    Was a trinket creator in the next town.
    I flinched at the comment.
    I was disgusted that such high quality ore
    Was being used for trinkets.

It was a waste of earth's most perfect resources.
    Levi paused in his words to allow me to speak,
    I offered him nothing in return.
    My mind was tunneling through emotions
    Both positive and negative.
    The pressure to make a choice
    In such an elegant situation was overwhelming.
    His last words regarding trinket creation
    Weighed heavy on my thoughts and
    Brought about jealously towards the other blacksmith.

My envy was strong towards someone I had never met,
    However, knowing that he was receiving
    Large cargo of that precious ore clouded my judgment.
    I could do wonders with the ore;
    I could create weapons the world had never seen before.

The element deserved better than to be made into useless
goblets.
    The other blacksmith did not deserve the ore
    As he did nothing to preserve its greatness.
    I deserved it more than him,
    I would respect it more than him.
    Does that not make it right?

I wanted what he had.
Levi had given me the opportunity to acquire it.

I offered no words to justify my answer,
    We communicated with only a smile.
    I did not want to know the details
    Of how he would obtain the ore;
    I just wanted him to bring it to me.

We unloaded the lesser ore in the wagon.
    Once completed, Levi took off towards the mountain.
    I knew that once he was down the path,
    I could not change my mind,
    My desire for the substance was too intense to stop him.

The idea of his return with a full wagon
    Interrupted my sleep that night.
    My thoughts were comprised of perfectly created shields
    That would defend their owners
    From the most savage attacks and
    Swords that could slice through solid stone.
    The visions that raced within my mind
    Tired me as if I was physically running the race myself.

The next day proved long and tedious
    As I awaited the arrival of my striker.
    I was unsure as to when to expect him back
    Since he needed to mine the ore
    Around the schedule of the other striker.

I caught myself staring down the path
    In hopes to see the wagon approaching.
    At times I even forged the sound of the wind
    To reflect the squeaking of the wheels.
    The excitement always prompted me to go outside
    Where I was delivered the cruelty of denial.
    I was growing impatient and
    Had thoughts of Levi not being able to mine the ore.

Knowing that the other blacksmith
    Would be the only one to have access to the ore
    Churned my anger and brought it to the surface.
    I pounded the molten metal hard that night
    To release my frustrations
    Until the faint whistling sound of the wagon penetrated my
ears.

I was hesitant at first as
    I was unsure whether or not the wind was playing with me
again.
    The whistling continued and pulled me outside
    Where I saw the distant vision of a striker and wagon
    Approaching from the path.
    All my hatred for the blacksmith subsided as
    I was about to receive my first delivery of his ore.

The wagon came to a halt.
    Levi had a large smile on his face.
    He knew I was excited about the cargo,
    He could see it in my eyes as I stared at the mound.

The ore was beautiful sitting in the wagon
    With the moonlight glistening on the smooth surfaces.
    That was not high quality,
    Rather excellence that Levi had delivered to me.

My mouth salivated
    Prompting me to swallow excessively
    As we began to unload the wagon.
    The ore was treated with the utmost respect
    And not dumped to the ground like other deliveries.
    Instead, we hand placed each piece on the ground
    Like they would leak the plague if dropped.
    After the wagon was empty,
    Levi looked to me and asked if I desired more.

I laughed under my breath and said that I wanted it all.
    My response pleased him as
    He was anxious to return to the mountain.
    I wanted that mine emptied of the ore
    So that the other blacksmith did not have access to it.
    I could not handle knowing that the blacksmith
    Was creating trinkets from it.
    The resource deserved better and
    I was going to unleash its inner greatness.

Over the next few days,
    Levi continued to deliver the high quality ore and
    I smelted it as fast as it came in.
    The new ore allowed me to finish
    The barbarian's axe prior to his arrival.

The axe was my first creation with the new ingredient.
    The power that I was able to harness
    Within the core illuminated the blade to perfection.
    I imagined that nothing would stop that blade
    In battle as it would easily cut through
    All in its way including wood, stone, bone and other blades.

My next conquest was a large circular shield
    With a serpent dragon etched on the front.
    Any other time, I would not have been able to bend
    The metal in such a way,
    But the creative juices that seeped from me now
    Easily processed the product.

Levi continued to deliver loaded wagons
    Of the ore on a regular basis,
    It allowed me to create some of the most wonderful items
    My mind had ever conjured.

My increased creativity spread throughout the lands.
    I envisioned every battle that was taken place
    Involved at least one of my creations.

I often desired to watch my relics in action
Whether it was seeing an arrow
Bouncing off of my shields or
Observing the steel forged blades of my swords and axes
Crushing an enemy skull with a mighty swing.

The experience had to be beautiful to behold.
I imagined a successful warrior holding up my sword
As a sign of triumph on the battlefield
Prompting his army to follow suit.
I knew I would never witness those spectacles,
Regardless the visions were soothing to my creative soul.

With my stock running low,
I was on the lookout for the arrival of Levi.
My ears were always on attention
For the wagon wheels during that time and
The anticipation often forced me into a realm of panic.

My stress about cargo always subsided
With the first initial encounter of
The faint squeaking sound of the wagon.
I stopped working on my current project and
Headed outside to greet my striker.

By the time I exited the shop,
Levi had already traveled up the path.
His characteristics were different than usual as
He rushed around the cart nervously looking down the path.

He was not his talkative self and offered
None of his long-winded stories.
Instead he frantically paced about
While rubbing his hands together.

I asked him what had happened.
He mumbled a few words, but I could not understand.
I asked him to speak again,

He began to stutter and slur his speech.
Something had frightened him.
Deciphering it proved to be a challenging feat.
I decided to let him calm down first before
I pried him for information.

It seemed to work as he started to speak clearer.
    He kept saying that they knew over and over.
    I asked him who he was talking about.
    His response rattled my emotions like a trapped snake.

He replied that the other striker knew;
    That they had crossed paths as Levi was exiting the mine.
    The fear and hesitation that I originally felt
    When Levi offered the first piece of ore
    All came back to me at that moment.

Any normal person would have felt
    Remorse at the situation,
    But I only felt envy towards the other blacksmith.
    I took control of the situation and
    Told Levi that he should alter his mining schedule
    To avoid the other striker.

Up to this point, no other striker was utilizing the mine.
    We had to be more cautious in our timing.
    I reassured him that we could continue mining the ore and
    He agreed with only a smile.
    My words calmed his nerves and I could read from his face
    That he was pleased with my reaction.
    He said that he could mine at night if I allowed it.
    At that point,
    All I wanted was to deny the other blacksmith of the ore.

The new scheduling worked for quite a few days as
    My stock continued to increase
    Allowing me to construct more weapons.
    However, my perfect blacksmith life

Would soon be devastated and reduced
To the dirt that encased the ore.

A messenger approached my shop and handed me a letter.
    I peeled away the wax seal and unraveled the scroll.
    As I read the words that etched their way deep into my
brain,
    I had no one to blame but myself.

The words were my banishment
    From the blacksmith community in the region.
    The signature of all my colleagues on the mountain
    Sealed my fate in the area.

I was no longer recognized as a blacksmith
    By the surrounding kingdoms.
    The stamps of each king made it official.
    I kept reading the letter again and again
    With the hopes that it would have a different outcome.
    With paper in hand, I walked outside and
    Looked up to the stars for any type of forgiveness,
    But found none.
    I felt as if my entire self-being imploded.
    I had nothing left.
    I had no desire to finish any of my projects
    As no one would be there to claim them.

As I sat accompanied by my friend of misery,
    I heard the faint sound of the wagon wheels coming up the
path.
    Along with the squeaking
    Was the howling of the wind in a rhythmic pattern.
    I looked down the path and saw Levi pulling the wagon
    Being followed by several wild wolves.

The scene somehow coincided with the letter and
    Offered me a vision of death with Levi being the grim
reaper.

I stared at him slowly coming up the path
With the wheels and wolves providing him support.

I could not help, but think about my life without him.
I go back to the moment I met him.
More specifically when I asked him to work for me.
I would have never known of the special ore
If it were not for him.

The cart still approached, but unlike the other times
I was not eager for it to arrive.
I offered the wheels no excitement.
I felt it whistling around my head desiring attention,
Trying to penetrate my skull like a claw to ice.
The sound only reminded me of what I had done so
I forcefully blocked my ears to protect my thoughts,
But it was useless as still it crept closer.

Levi approached me with a demeanor
As if he already was aware of the situation.
He told me that I had done well in the task,
That the outcome was to his liking.

I looked up from the letter
With a bewildered expression for clarity.
His smile offered me nothing in return.
He continued with his mysterious praise of me
By adding that I made his chore easy for him.
He proclaimed that I had chosen the path
Of envy over humility when tempted by the ore.
I wish I could have blocked out his words
As I had done so many times before,
But there was nothing to offer me that solitary.

I did not know who he was anymore.
With disgust written on my face, I asked him.
He restated his name as Leviathan.
He said that his friends did not call him Levi

Because he had no friends.

His task was to expose my weakness with the ore.
    That he had succeeded.
    I ask him if he killed my striker and
    He responded with only a smile.

The question prompted him
    To approach the wagon and tilt it upright
    So that it would unload the cargo.
    Instead of a pile of ore,
    The rotted corpse of my previous striker
    Rolled to the ground before me.

The stench of the decayed flesh
    Assaulted my senses as I vomited.
    The flesh was crawling with insects and caked with dirt.
    Levi said the striker was easy prey
    Within the darkened mine.
    He said without care that he simply stalked him and
    Drove a pick axe into his chest.
    He went on to say that he did not die right away,
    But no one would hear his call that far down in the mine.
    It all came clear to me
    As I recalled his body dragged
    Beyond the torches.
    The fact that Levi had no wagon of his own
    At the mine entrance.
    I was furious with him,
    Not only for bringing that fate to me,
    But his lack of respect towards me.
    The anger built up within me so much
    That I lunged at him.

I did not know what I was going to do to him,
    But my pulsating heart required action.
    He anticipated my attack and swiftly blocked my arm.
    He struck me once in the head, blurring my vision,

And once in the ribs that sent me back to the ground.

He told me that I should not have done that.
    His arrogance only infuriated me more
    As I reached for a nearby pick axe.
    I wanted him dead and he knew it.
    Anything less would be unsatisfactory for me.
    I tried my luck again, this time backed by a weapon.

Before my swing could connect with him,
    He grabbed the handle and twisted it.
    His strength spun my wrist in an unusual manner
    Forcing me to release the axe.

I looked up in time to see the axe coming down upon me.
    The blade funneled deep into my upper chest above my
heart.
    The force was so strong that I felt the blade exit my back.

Levi followed closely to me as
    I was trying to retreat on the ground.
    He picked up a shovel from the ground and
    Jabbed my stomach, just enough to make a point.

He said he could easily kill me, but he would not.
    He added that he would receive more enjoyment
    Out of seeing me dwell in my choice and
    The fact that I could no longer have my precious ore.

Instead of killing me
    He swung the shovel into the axe handle.
    The vibration rattled my wound and
    Sent tremors deep into my chest.

The pain was intense and
    Made it difficult to breathe at times.
    He stood above me staring into my eyes and said nothing.
    I felt his vision piercing my mind

As if trying to read it.

If he was looking for pain and suffering,
    Then he would find a great deal of it
    As they were the only feelings I had left.
    He owned all of my other emotions already
    And added them to his sadistic collection of grief.
    He leaned back from me and grinned.

With the wagon empty and me no longer a threat,
    Levi began to load up my remaining stockpile of ore.
    He paused for a moment and said
    That he was going to deliver the ore to its rightful owner.
    My mind fell away from the pain.
    It was replaced with jealously over the idea,
    But there was nothing I could do.
    I asked him why he betrayed me.
    His response was that he did nothing but offer me a choice.

He said his task was simply,
    Provide me an alternative way
    That I eagerly accepted.
    Everything he said was true, but
    It did not make the reality any easier to comprehend.
    I was lost in my emotions and
    Did not know what to think.

My entire life and credibility had vanished.
    I could have easily continued down my original path
    With ore from my own mines,
    But the idea of someone else
    Using that special ore for trinkets cut at my heart.

The utter disgust that I felt for that blacksmith
    Was real and justified in my eyes.
    I should have been the one
    Who owned that resource, not him.

He did not deserve that quality and
    It did not deserve him.
    I saw the potential in it.
    I released its inner power, not him.

Levi sensed my continued frustration
    Even under the worst conditions.
    He offered me more praise and
    Said that dwelling on my feelings
    Only made me stronger and that one day
    I would be glad that I did.

He added that the weak minded
    Often times toss aside their true feelings
    Before they are able to fully revitalize them;
    Therefore they are buried into the subconscious and
    Can never fulfill their potential.
    He added that I would be successful and
    That he looked forward to seeing me again.
    I had no idea what he was referring to, but
    The vision of seeing him again was not something
    That I wanted, as my first encounter with him
    Had not ended to my advantage.

Levi loaded up the last of the ore
    And offered one piece of advice.
    He said that I should have thought about the outcome.
    The words caught me off guard
    As he said them in an evil demeanor.
    The outcome was something that never occurred to me
    When he first held up that lone piece of ore.

My mind portrayed no other option, but desire.
    I initially wanted the ore for personal use,
    But the notion of the other blacksmith
    Twisted my desire into envy.

Once I released that emotion, I was lost at sea.

I found it odd that the only time
I dwelled on the outcome was in the outcome itself.
It made me think that my mind did not allow me
To choose, as it had already chosen for me.
It persuaded me with many positives and no negatives.

The wheels of the wagon squeaked
    Along the path for the last time.
    I saw Levi delivering my quality ore to the other blacksmith.
    I laid at the entrance of my shop
    With a pick axe protruding from my chest, a dead striker,
    A destroyed career and lasting envy
    Towards something that I could no longer have.

~

The silence is growing.
    I feel that when each of my
    Shadowy friends leaves
    That they take a piece of my soul with them.

Each departure adds to my misery and solitude.
    The compounded pressure of sadness
    On my mind is reaching its apex.
    I am afraid that I may not venture
    Out of my situation alive.

My mind has become an enemy and depicts my death.
    I try to battle it, but it is too strong and overwhelming
    With vivid images of my demise.
    It is apparent that my mind can no longer
    Relate to the confinement and
    Is exploring other options for escape.

The visions of my own passing are so vivid
    That they leave an aftermath of
    Disgust and denial within me.
    I feel my hatred for my mind increasing

As I reside in vengeance.

Does my mind hate me so,
    That it has resorted to cursing
    My thoughts with death?
    It torments me in my wake and
    Infects my dreams in my sleep.

I choose not to become its prey
    Even though it stalks me always.
    I have no choice but to battle and
    Defend myself from its onslaught.

If not, I fear that it will entrap me and
    Poison me for eternity.
    If that were to occur,
    I dread that I would no longer
    Have a free mind and
    The ability to think on my own.

If it were in full control,
    I worry for my safety and for those around me.
    Regardless of how much I fight,
    The harsh realism is that I am losing the battle,
    For it is much too strong for me to deny.

The struggle weakens my body and
    Slowly consumes my muscles.
    Why does my mind do this to me?
    Why does it choose suffering over satisfaction?

The images of my death
    Do not stop and grow more rapid
    If I try to avoid them.
    Each vision depicts my suffering
    In various forms of torture.

My mind is very creative in this aspect,

But the sorrow that dwells within me
Does not allow me to respect the talent.
I have come to know death so well
That I am close to befriending the concept.

Death comes to me and fills my thoughts.
　It is the only logical exit from life.
　When the mind becomes so torturous and
　Offers only pure resentment to the soul;
　Death offers a solution.
　I will not coward to my mind;
　I will not allow it to conquer me
　As I believe that I would be gifted
　An eternity of evilness if I were to take my own life.

My mind wants me to die
　So that it would rule in the afterlife,
　But I will not allow this.
　I will defeat it and overcome its sadistic visions
　As I do not wish to encounter the alternative.

Only two of my friends remain
　In the shadows and I sense that
　They are eager to follow their comrades.
　Somehow my transcriptions relate to them and set them
free.

This is only one of my many questions
　That I have about my situation.
　I only hope that I will have a few of them
　Answered upon reaching the apex.
　If not, I will not dwell on them.
　I imagine that having my own life back will suffice me.

I try to think positively about
　What will occur after my task is completed,
　But my mind distorts the thoughts and suffocates them.
　I begin thinking about my farm and livestock

Then the idea is morphed into a life of flame.

Not to give my mind any satisfaction,
    I often cease my thoughts
    Trying to think of nothing in particular.
    If it is thoughts that feed it, then I will starve it.

This process does provide anger
    As when a vision does travel through my blockade,
    It is intense in detail and devastating in its results.
    I am determined to not have a thought within my head,
    Not as an insult to God,
    Rather an infliction to my mind.

I cannot continue on like this and
    Allow the visions to consume me.
    I have done nothing to deserve this.
    I have only desired freedom for my dreams and
    Cannot achieve it as long as my mind is in control.

I often times find myself rubbing my skull
    In an ill attempt to soothe my mind,
    But it spits on me in return
    By supplying me with rapid thoughts of dismay.

It is trying to break my spirit and
    I am afraid that it is achieving its goal with each passing
period.
    What does it want from me?
    To surrender? To kneel before it?
    To recognize it as a God when I know that it is not?

I will not give it death.
    I will not sacrifice myself for its cause.
    If it is my death that it desires
    Then it will not be happy with the judgment.
    I have little control left, but the small portion I
    Do have will hold onto life with a slippery grip.

My mind may be pulling at my conscious,
    But I will resist as my final act of defiance.
    I feel my mind is listening to me and
    It is rattled within its skull.
    It is desperate for a new vision,
    To subdue my increase in self-righteousness, but
    It will not succeed.

The confusion that it is experiencing
    Is empowering me.
    It gives me a brief calmness that is much appreciated.
    I am enjoying this peace
    As I know it will not last.

The determination of my mind is much too strong
    To allow me with victory.
    I dwell in this period before the storm
    For I know that it is conjuring something
    More destructive and so explicitly detailed
    That it will devastate me.

Until then, I am at peace and all is right.
    I do not worry about what is to come
    Or when it will occur.
    To do that would be an insult to the small victory
    That I have achieved.

Instead I offer my mind a simple smile
    As it contemplates its next move,
    Not as a gesture of revulsion or insult,
    Rather as a way to inform it that I am here to play.
    I would be lying
    If I were to deny that the small triumph
    Did not give me some satisfaction and increase my ego,
    But I realize that it will be short lived,
    As I soon will be wallowing in my river of self-pity once
again.

To God, I apologize for halting my transcriptions,
    But I must provide energy to my body
    So that I may defend myself from the visions
    As they are intensifying.

VIII

We called it Reflection Point,
    A place where the prophets could go to reflect
    Upon all aspects of life.
    It was a beautiful and inspiring place
    In every detail of its existence.

Sitting high on a hilltop in the northern valley,
    It was not an easy place to venture to.
    One had to endure long distance and treacherous encounters
    With land and animals in order to reap its benefits.

All those who traveled to seek guidance
    Respected the foundation and its surroundings
    As it was the basis of which existence
    Became understandable.

Fellow prophets would travel
    From far lands to envision the ancient relic.
    It was told that the creation of enlightenment
    Was conjured from its presence.

The structure was simple in design
    With an open courtyard that was surrounded
    By marble pillars and statues of God.
    Being atop of the hill gave the visitor an opportunity
    To view the surrounding world in a full spectrum.
    The clarity of the horizons was breathtaking to behold
    And provided much inspiration to those

Who took the time to contemplate it.
There was no denial that God himself
Constructed the monument
As a way to thank the prophets for their service.

No human hand could ever recreate
The wonderful etchings within the statues
Or the expanding columns that protruded into the heavens.
It was considered an entry point to the glorious blessings of
God,
Where one could pray and worship
Knowing that their words would be heard by the clouds.

The weather around the monument
Was always perfect and ripe
Regardless of what hardships
Were endured during the journey there.
The tranquility of the scenery was unmatched
By any other portion of the world;
As if God withheld the ultimate peace from the planet
In order to make the monument atmosphere
That much more unique.

The hill that supported the monument
Was dense with forests and
Provided no assistance to reaching the top.
The terrain was not for the physically weak or undetermined
As the lack of a man-made path
Served as a righteous passage
That blocked most visitors who were deemed unworthy.

Only the strong willed would see the treasure and
Reap the benefits of achieving their goal.
Their determination would receive the visions
And riches of the hilltop
Through enlightenment and creativity.

Most prophets believed that one

Could grasp the same gifts
By remaining at the base of the hill
Instead of venturing to the top.

It was untrue as God strategically
Placed dangers that lurked around the base
In the form of predators and poisonous vegetation
To distract those who lingered beyond their welcome.

At the bottom, prophets only had two options.
One was to ascend the hill
While the other was to turn and leave.
God did allow for a brief period
Of thought gathering in order to make a proper decision.

When rushed, the mind would often
Make immoral decisions
Without the full consent of the body.
Therefore, to enable the mind to fully absorb
The greatness of the task at hand,
God granted for an interlude of deep thought.
However, if the prophet overstayed
Or chose to selfishly extend the time,
He would be promptly escorted from the area
Either by an invasion of fearful thought
Or pushed out by a pack of wild dogs.

Either option was demoralizing to the prophet and
Would last in their memories for quite some time.
It was meant as a punishment for their confusion.
It was believed that all misunderstandings should be
depleted
During the journey prior to reaching the threshold of the
hill.

The long duration of the voyage served
As a means to drain the rational thought of the prophet.
One had to relinquish all personal goals and dreams

So that the mind was capable to receive more.

It was believed that one could not fully focus
    His attentions on the visions of God
    If he was concerned about his current salvation or
    Burdened by worrisome acts.

A true prophet bled for the opportunity
    To sacrifice his will in order to ascend the hill.
    The greatness that he would gather once atop
    Would return his passion in a more prosperous state.

It was accustomed to relinquish your soul
    In the security of God
    Prior to climbing as a sign of respect and faithfulness.
    Only then would a prophet fully justify his reasoning for
being.
    Only then would he truly understand the greatness that
awaited.

The monument was a place of worship and enlightenment.
    Some believed that they would hear the words of God
    While others utilized the scenery for prosperity.
    Regardless of why they came,
    Each prophet would leave with a greater purpose
    And a well-driven soul.

No one spoke of what gifts they received during their stay
    As each translation was different per person.
    Every vision or sign was meant for one prophet
    And one prophet only.

It was considered disrespectful for the prophets
    To share their experiences amongst one another.
    If God intended for his visions to be shared among many,
    He would have showed them the same visions himself.
    That was not the case
    As no two prophets received the same experience.

A normal stay on the hilltop for a traveling prophet
    Lasted no more than two days.
    Staying longer deciphered into greediness,
    An overabundance of God's word.
    Those who greedily stayed passed their welcome
    Would have the vengeance of God
    Forced upon them and
    Stricken of their enlightenment.

There were no comforts of a town or city
    To grant a decent night sleep.
    It was believed that one did not need these materials
    As the dreams provided everything one would desire.

When you slept, you were allowed to envision the heavens.
    You were allowed to walk amongst its long-grained fields.
    You were allowed to taste the sweet nectar of its fruits and
    Feel the warm breeze of its meadows.
    Only sleeping upon the hill,
    Were you allowed to dream in God's garden
    That many would not have the opportunity to experience.
    It was considered a blessing to rest amongst the clouds
    As it was the most peaceful slumber imaginable
    Due to the protection that one felt.

There were no bad dreams,
    Only visions of purity and contentment.
    It served as a way to cleanse the soul and
    Heal the wounds that often scar the mind.

The replenishment allowed for a complete recovery
    From the hardships endured during life.
    All emotional constraints and shackles of fear
    Were broken so that the soul would be released.
    That was why I traveled the distance from my homeland.
    That was why I longed for the monument.
    For the opportunity to cleanse myself

Of the grime of life,
The utter filth that one collects along the way
While trying to worship God.

The infestation of normal people
Haunted my sleep as I feared of becoming one.
I felt that those who did not share my beliefs
Endangered my existence with God.

Those who did not worship or
Pray were not worthy of my touch.
I kept my thoughts sacred from others and
Used my talents to preach the word of God.

Those who allowed for the opportunity
To hear my words were greeted with respect and friendship.
Those who denied my words
Were shunned from me and deemed a lost soul.
I had no energy to lend to lost souls as
I believed they would be dealt with
By the hand of God and
I was not going to trespass on the eternal punishment.

Conformity was not an easy task
In a human society with different opinions and views
Towards worship,
But I continued my lectures
In hopes to free more minds.
I tried to venture to the monument
At random intervals
Especially when I felt that my faith was lessening
Or if I felt overwhelmed by the number
Of lost souls engulfing me.

I would often feel besieged by the lost souls
As they tempted me to plummet into their
Sea of misery or tease me with their
Acts of evilness, but my faith for God

Always remained strong in the battle and
Allowed me to overpower their temptations.
The monument gave me a sense of purpose in my life.
It reassured me that I was not alone in my struggles.
I was never unsatisfied when leaving the hill,
I always had thoughts of inspiration to sustain me
Until the next visit.
It was comforting to see other prophets
With the same idealism as me,
Trying to spread the word of God
To those who desired it.

When returning to my town,
    I would preach to the citizens
    About my discoveries in hopes to better their lives.
    Not all would listen to my words,
    But I believed that those who did would benefit greatly.
    I felt I had to at least provide them
    With an opportunity to understand worship and
    How it could increase their happiness.

At that moment, I found myself at the base of the hill
    With others surrounding me and seeking the same visions.
    The pause before the uphill journey began was always
somber.
    The hesitation in thought would determine
    Whether the person would proceed or not.
    If fear was allowed to intervene
    Then their journey would be halted.
    It was a stress endued task
    To enter the demanding dense woods that aligned the
bottom.
    Many dangers awaited those who trespassed within it and
    Once entangled there was no altering the course.
    Changing direction midstream was considered disrespectful.
    It was looked upon better if one were to not start
    As opposed to shifting course
    Once one was decided upon.

All prophets knew of that.
    That was why many hesitated at the base.
    Even I paused, though I had previously
    Made the journey several times before.

It allowed for an opportunity
    To reflect upon myself,
    For my doubt to be subdued.
    Some prophets reach the base and never ascend the hill.
    They allowed their anxiety to conquer them.
    Their punishment would be that they would never
    Envision God and hear his words.
    After a small hiatus of thought,
    I left behind several others at the base.
    I squeezed through two trees and
    Decided that my destiny involved reaching the heavens.
    The journey often times called
    For creative foot placements and
    Sturdy tree limbs in order to succeed.
    All aspects of survival were to be tested.
    All aspects of humanity were to be tested.
    While climbing, a prophet would never see another.
    The sensation of being alone
    In the labyrinth of trees
    Could be upsetting if one dwelled within it.

The most caustic onslaught on the mind
    Was when a prophet became lost and twisted in their
direction.
    Panic and fear was not a companion
    That was preferred during the journey.

Being able to focus with faith
    Was the greatest asset
    That would lead to success and the summit.
    If lost, it was not easy to find the way
    As God would tease the weak by contorting the landscape.

Turning around did not always mean
    That one was returning to where they began.
    An endless loop of trees was given to those
    Who became flustered and tormented by their surroundings.
    Being lost in the woods was not
    A situation that any prophet beloved.

My first journey proved to be the worst as
    I had indeed gotten lost where my patience and soul was
tested.
    Misery became my only ally and even he could not be
trusted.
    My mind battled with my body
    Regarding which way to proceed.

The thought patterns were draining as my energy faded.
    Being so weak minded, I even questioned my faith
    As to why I was allowed to be lost
    When all I desired was to worship.

I had failed.
    Up became down and right became left.
    I found myself spinning around
    Trying to understand my direction, but
    The identical trees that surrounded me made it difficult.
    I had nothing left to give,
    No energy and no commitment.
    My heart had spilled more of its livelihood
    With every tree I touched until it was empty.

I was completely beaten and betrayed by my mind.
    I had no other option but to kneel and pray.
    When all was lost and my faith was being questioned,
    A single sun ray penetrated the thick trees and illuminated
me.

The warmth of the sun pierced my skin and renewed my faith.

The sign pulled me from my coffin of despair and
Gave me the courage to continue.
I rose to my feet and singled out one path
Through the trees and kept to my thoughts.

I no longer randomly ventured with different directions;
    I stayed to my path with purpose and faith in my decision.
    For that, I was thankful to God.

My current journey offered the same difficulty as the past ones.
    One never gets accustomed to the battered conditions
    Of the lower hill area as they become altered
    With every change of season.

Being that I had already previously been to the monument,
    The visions of the reward aided me and
    Gave me the necessary energy that I needed.
    I had seen the glory that the journey led to.
    I had experienced the peaceful slumber of the heavens
    And required nothing else to persuade me further.
    I doubted that I would see many of the visitors
    That I bypassed at the top
    As a few of them would not make it beyond the first
challenge.

Choosing the unknown was never an easy task,
    Especially for prophets who pride themselves in realization.
    It was difficult for me at first to forego
    My prior knowledge of the heavens
    So that I would receive the new visions.

I had to realize that my previous
    Understanding of God was incorrect.
    Only then could I discard
    My original thoughts and accept new ones.

Those who are unable to complete the task
    Would be bombarded by both old and new concepts.

That internal struggle never ended well as
It would often break the spirit of the weak minded.
It was said that God used the process
As a means to exhaust the person and
Reduce it to a mere mindless being.
In order to succeed, a prophet must lose himself
In the situation and absorb the chaos of confusion
Before they were able to find themselves and
Truly rejoice in the glory.

The mind could only hold so many concepts
Before it blocked new ones from entering.
When filled to capacity, the mind would deny thoughts
Regardless of how beneficial they would be to the person.
It was common practice to reduce the capacity of the mind
So that the prophet could receive new visions.
The more vacant space there was
Meant that more of God's ideas could enter and be held.

Those types of ideas kept me company
As I ascended the hill.
Occasionally, I lost my footing or became overwhelmed
With the dense trees,
But I always kept my mind focused on reaching the summit,
For it was there that my appreciation would be reinvented.

Each trip proved easier than before
As the key to success resided in the idea
That one never questioned their decisions.
A single path always led to the top
Regardless of the direction that was initially taken.
Prophets entered into a realm of dismay
When they doubted their choice and
Altered their route.

My tired body and drained mind
Were replenished as I stepped out of the trees
Onto the flattened terrain at the apex of the hill.

The burn within my legs subsided
As I looked upon the monument.

Several other prophets exited the trees and
Were caught up in the vision as well.
All the traveling, climbing and mental exhaustion
Led each of us here and
We respected the vision by not appearing too eager.
I took a brief moment to collect
My thoughts and adjust my clothing.
The surrounding radius of the hilltop
Was etched with hedges and vines from the greenest
pastures.

The monument itself consisted of a squared
Outlay of high marble columns
That pierced the low lying clouds.
The structure rendered into the minds
Of those who were lucky enough to ponder upon it,
That the monument supported the heavens;
Therefore, those that stepped foot within its perimeter
Would also be sustaining the heavens.

One path supplied travelers
With the only option of entry
Where large circular pools of water resided.
These served as a cleansing ritual
For the hands and face of the weary travelers.

It was understood that the dirt and grime
That often found its way upon the prophets
During traveling would contradict the words of God.

After grabbing the rough bark of the trees for support,
The cool water felt refreshing on my splintered hands.
The cleansing ritual also allowed me
To rid my body of what I perceived as human waste
material

From those who clung to me or did not believe my words.

Normal water could not penetrate like the holy water.
    The human contamination that I endured in my homeland
    Would all be released and destroyed
    There in the pool at God's garden.

The monument had no ceiling or other structure
    That would shield the views of heaven.
    The architecture was simple,
    But the concept and understanding was complicated.

Several prophets were merely staring up into the clouds
    While others transcribed their surroundings.
    Each one would receive their own unique vision
    That would not be duplicated.

For me, I usually tried to find a vacant place
    On the inner floor that sunk down with steps.
    The area provided me with a great opportunity
    To witness the heavens
    As well as the ability to feel the compassion of my
colleagues.
    I enjoyed watching others receive
    The word of God and the transformation
    In their mannerisms that would occur shortly thereafter.

No conversations between prophets ever occurred atop the hill
    Since the notion that the presence of God was always felt.
    However, on that particular day, something odd happened.
    As I was looking to the heavens for answers,
    My attention was captured across the monument floor
    Where I noticed a lone prophet walking towards me.
    He was dressed in a fine robe that was etched in red fabric.
    His long, yellow hair matched his beard.
    His eyes were fixated on me as he approached.

At first I did not know what to think about the situation,

As I dared not greet or converse with the man
Out of respect for God and the surroundings.
However, he did not to share the same belief
As he continued towards me.

He greeted me with a smile and I returned the gesture,
    But then I turned away as a means
    To avoid any further encounters.
    My denial did not alter his notions as he began to speak.

He said his name was Lucifer and
    That he had been admiring my work for quite some time.
    I did not understand his words and
    Thought that he had possibly
    Heard one of my sermons within the town,
    But that was not the situation.

I felt uncomfortable carrying on a conversation with him
    Especially in such a holy sanctuary,
    But then realized that we were the only prophets there.
    The steps and inner area of the monument were completely
bare.

He halted my confused stare at the emptiness
    By stating that I had done well in my tasks,
    That God was pleased with me.
    I offered no response
    As I was still concentrating on the idea
    That everyone had suddenly left the vicinity.

He continued with his praise of me
    Stating that I had exceeded his expectations,
    That it was natural for me to be confused and
    It was his task to rid my mind of the uncertainty
    So that I would truly see the reality of my situation,
    Of which I currently believed was that my worshipping
    Was being interrupted by another prophet.
    I did not realize that my current belief

Would be butchered and replaced with a notion
That even the most talented mind would question.
His next statement seemed to awaken my inner spirit, but
It provided me with nothing more than additional questions.

He stated that my recent endeavors
    Were deemed successful in the eyes of the Lord.
    I asked him to clarify what he meant
    By endeavors and he offered more insight into the
statement.

He claimed that too much information
    At once would cloud my judgment and damage my mind.
    To avoid that, he would start at the beginning.

He claimed that I had been chosen by God
    To live through sin.
    He then mentioned the confinement of a cave.
    The thought jarred my mind as if I were struck by a solid
object.

My mind immediately went into battle mode as
    I tried desperately to counteract the visions of such a cave.
    The harder I struggled,
    The more difficult it was to believe.

The reality of the hilltop monument
    Was clashing with those of a darkened cave.
    The battle carved at my soul and
    Slaughtered my belief system
    To the point where I could not determine
    Which vision was real.

Lucifer placed a hand on my shoulder
    As I continued to focus on the assault occurring on my
memory.
    I could not decipher his next concept.
    He stated that the monument and surrounding areas

Were mere thought patterns
Much like the ore mine, wheat farm, and blizzard.

I was losing my grip on my mind the more he spoke.
    I felt that he was pulling me into
    A downward coil of resentment and
    I was unable to find a sturdy platform to sustain myself.
    I needed to defend myself,
    But I had no method of acquiring it.
    The whole situation was too much for me to handle and
    I had no idea who Lucifer was.
    My body reacted as I held up my hands and
    Requested for him to stop talking to me.
    The encounter was unlike any other
    That I had experienced on the hill.

I could not get passed the idea
    That he approached me during my personal worshipping.
    I became fearful as to what God would think.
    Had he ruined me in God's eyes
    Due to his selfish need for conversation?

I viewed his words as a disease to my beliefs and
    I was not going to allow my mind to be infected
    Any more than it already had.
    To avoid the situation,
    I walked to the other side of the monument,
    But was met instantly by him once again.

He said that my confused state was justified,
    That it would subside in time.
    My body reacted again by holding up my hands
    As if to push him away from me.
    My mind was more concerned with God and
    His reaction to the disrespectful demeanor of my actions.

I looked to the clouds for some sort of reassurance, but found
none.

Lucifer had doomed both of us
Through his outburst of words and lack of respect
For the tranquility of the monument,
But he appeared not to share the same concern
As he continued to talk.

He stated that he was not there
    To offend or disrupt me;
    He was only there to provide me with realism.
    My mind began to hurt with every word
    That spewed from his mouth and I wanted him to be quiet.

I covered my ears as I looked for any type of safe haven
    That I could escape to and hide within.
    The openness of the monument made that idea useless.
    Instead I opted to close my eyes and
    Pray to God for his understanding.
    The back of my eye lids only provided me
    With visions of an ore mine
    Where I vaguely remembered red flags.
    Next was a wheat field with a farm that felt familiar at first
    Before it was swept away and replaced
    With images of a village surrounded by a large wall.

I grabbed my head to stop the rotation,
    But the action was unsuccessful.
    My mind had succumbed to a whirlwind of rapid visions,
    None of which I could relate to.

They were embedded within my skull.
    They were separate from my original past.
    I would briefly contemplate the additions,
    But would always fall back on my travels to the hill
    Along with the painstaking journey up through the dense
woods.
    Those ideas seemed natural to me
    In an almost comforting manner.
    They had more purpose than the words of a prophet

That I had never met before.

I opened my eyes and the vision went away,
    But Lucifer remained in front of me.

He said he was there to offer me understanding and
    The opportunity to believe again.
    I knew of what he was trying to accomplish and
    I would fight him down every path that he took.
    He was a lost soul and he was trying to sway me from God.
    I had battled with his type in my homeland before and
    I would defend my beliefs in the name God.
    Was he resentful of my worship
    Or was he my vision from God?
    The one that I traveled so long to achieve?

It did not seem fair that I journeyed
    Across the land only to acquire confusion and visions
    That I did not remember.
    For a moment, I assumed that the whole situation was a test.
    In order to receive my true vision,
    I would have to pass the judgment of God.
    I intended to do so and repositioned myself
    On the marble steps near Lucifer
    As a sign of good intention.

He understood my frustration and
    Offered me kindness as I remained in a confused state.
    He said that it was astonishing how well
    I consumed the sin in each one of my tasks.

I told him that I had never sinned
    As I was a prophet of God.
    I had dedicated my life to serving God and
    Preaching his words to those who chose to believe.

He paused in his speech momentarily,
    Then asked me to let go of reality.

My mind began to spiral once again with the visions,
With more detail than before.

Images of being a poor peasant and
 A blacksmith raced through me and appeared so real.
 I began to relate to the visions and
 Even offered a continuation of them
 With understanding and acknowledgment.
 I was remembering items that were not portrayed
 Such as an irrigation system and daggers.
 The visions still offered me no reasoning
 Or justification as to why they were there.

Again, Lucifer said that he was there to help me remember.
 He was there to guide me through the last process of my
task.
 His voice was soothing and relaxed the dreams.
 It brought them down to a reasonable pace.
 He rose up his hand and prompted
 Another prophet to enter into the monument.
 A very seductive woman holding two daggers
 Strolled across the center of the monument.
 I knew instantly who it was,
 However, I could not remember her name.
 Lucifer welcomed Amon to our meeting.
 I soon felt the harshness of society crashing upon me.
 The hatred for the wealthy and
 The disrespectful nature that they unleashed
 On the peasants funneled through my veins.

Her smile was so beautiful and desirable,
 And yet it was the evilness that embodied her
 That made her irresistible.

Her smell triggered my vengeful demeanor.
 I remembered looking into the eyes of my prey
 Moments before their death.
 I felt the power of stalking the wealthy,

Defending the weak all over again.

Society needed the fear that I provided.
    The wealthy needed to fear the rise of the shadows.
    They needed to realize that their level in society
    Meant nothing once the streets were filled with blackness.

Lucifer raised his hand again and summoned another.
    I immediately recognized the man
    Who was dressed very similar to my guide.
    I could not recall his name,
    But Lucifer announced that his name was Mammon.

The encounter assaulted me with visions
    Of both fear and pain as my arm became numb.
    I looked to Lucifer with a worried expression,
    All he told me was to remember.

As Mammon got closer, the blackness in my arm grew
stronger.
    My mind displayed a showcase of visions
    Involving carpentry, the plague, and a village of death.
    I remembered my dog and my shop, but more importantly
    I remembered the hatred that I had towards Mammon
    Who stole my arm and life.

Visions of the mass graves that I created
    Churned in my stomach and siphoned my spirit.
    I offered two words to Lucifer,
    Which prompted the pain in my arm to subside.
    I remember.
    I remembered consuming the greed and
    Keeping the cure to myself.
    I remembered forcing all of those innocent people towards
death.
    I felt their pity, but denied them remorse
    As I watched them die before me.
    They were not like me

As I deserved to live.
Lucifer asked about remorse of the sin.
I felt sadness that I was not allowed
To watch more of the creative effects of the plague take
place.
That was my only remorse.

Mammon smirked at my words.
I could smell the stench
From the massive piles of the dead and
Could feel the undesirable touches
Of the mindless people as they reached out for me.
Their disgusting bony, fleshless hands
Clawed at me for help as I pushed them away.

I had offered them peace and a place to die.
If I had told them of my disease,
They would have banished me from the village.
My choice was less selfish,
As I provided them with a coffin,
Which proved to be quite an undertaking.

Lucifer smiled as he gestured to Mammon to sit.
I felt stronger after the encounter with him
As if I had completed an obstacle of sorts.
Lucifer was satisfied with my comments
As he summoned for another visitor to appear.
I was instantly bombarded with visions of wheat,
Farmland and large oak trees.
Lucifer announced the arrival of Belphegor.

I felt that he was already my friend,
It was somewhat odd at the time.
As I studied his persona,
I felt the warm breeze of the fields and
Envisioned the humble abode of a farm.
I remembered his creativity with the oak irrigation
Felt the agony of laziness all at the same time.

Lucifer prompted me to express my feelings.
    I accepted by saying that I should have
    Cut down the trees earlier when I was in the valley,
    My rational thought would not allow it.
    The earlier construction of the system
    Would have allowed me to avoid work sooner.
    Belphegor was so talented in his work ethic
    That it was an easy choice to become lazy.

I rotated both of my wrists
    As I remembered seeing one of my hands residing on a
table.
    I saw nothing wrong with living
    Off of the strong values of others and
    Would have continued reaping the rewards from the farm
    If it were not for Belphegor leaving.

My work ethic was once strong,
    But I was allowed to see the benefits of a restful mind and
spirit.
    I was gifted the opportunity to rely on others.
    Over time the gift became a desire.
    I reaped the benefits of others
    While they reaped the wheat from the fields.

My only regret was that the farm
    Was not established to prosper by itself.
    With that process in place, I would have had the potential
    Of stealing the profits for a longer period of time.

Lucifer interrupted my thoughts
    By asking me how I felt.
    I answered him honestly
    That I felt great.
    It was such a joy to be able to remember
    As if a section of my mind had been reopened.

I still had confusion regarding the relation
    Between the memories and
    How they coincided with my life as a prophet.
    Lucifer added that I was not a prophet,
    But a prophecy was being written for me.
    The statement confused me more, but
    Before I was able to clarify,
    He signaled for another person to come.
    My memory was much stronger now.
    I even was able to remember the name of the new visitor.
    Beelzebub walked from between the columns.
    A burst of freezing air barreled through the monument and
    Provided me with vision of a blizzard.

A feeling of hoarding swelled within me as
    I remembered stockpiling the food.
    The people of city did not listen to the prophets' warnings.
    I should not have been blamed for their deaths as
    They had the same opportunity for survival as I did.
    I felt no pity on those who chose the path of death.

My storage of food was meant for my survival
    Through the storm;
    Through the duration of the aftermath.

Lucifer and Beelzebub smiled at my comments.
    I wanted more memories as
    I became anxious for my mind to be filled.
    I felt as if I was reborn again.

The new thoughts that were being uncovered
    Within my mind became addictive.
    I even caught myself trying to remember memories
    That were not even there
    So that I could continue the feeling of recollection.

The wind carried with it
    An aroma of my beloved maiden.

The essence that I inhaled
While being in her quarters carried me back
To the day that I treaded within the palace.

Asmodeus appeared from behind a marble pillar.
    She greeted me with a warm smile.
    Her friendly appearance and
    Her eagerness to listen was a welcomed addition.

My maiden would never know how deep my love for her went.
    She betrayed me by loving another while she loved me.
    She kept her marriage secret from me
    In order to not hurt me, but it was her lack of remembrance
    For the love we had for one another that led to her death.
    Her denial destroyed our prosperous relationship and
    Allowed her to drift from me.
    I could not forgive her and I could not allow her to live.
    Maybe in her afterlife she would remember me and
    What I had sacrificed for her.

She was an aura that surrounded me wherever I went.
    She was my companion when I needed her,
    My creativeness when I requested ideas.
    She flowed within my veins and was
    The source of life within my heart.
    She was also the blackness within my soul and
    The scars upon my flesh.
    She was the cracks in my bones and
    The torment within my mind.

She twisted my life and controlled my desires
    When I offered them to her, she shunned away.
    She did not love me as much as I loved her,
    But I have her heart now and no one else would ever claim
it.
    Her love and heart will always remain mine and mine only.
    She was my one true desire of which I will cherish forever.

From outside the vicinity of the monument,
    I heard the faint sound of wooden wheels.
    The sound pierced my ears and soothed my racing nerves.
    It was so beautiful in its high pitch tone that
    I could not help but think of a blacksmith shop.

The smell of ore with the heat of the flames
    Seduced my emotions and calmed my soul.
    My senses were overloaded and I did not want it to end.
    The squeal of the wheels got louder as Leviathan
    Entered into the middle of the monument pulling a wagon.

The sight brought me back to my shop where
    I eagerly waited for him to deliver the next batch of ore.
    The exhilaration I endured when seeing
    A full cargo of the high quality ore was too much for words.

My resentful spirit did not want
    The other blacksmith to obtain the ore
    Even though it was his.
    I wanted to cleanse his mine and
    Claim it as my own.
    Knowing that he had the ore
    After my banishment set my blood on fire.
    The idea guided me down a path of corruption and revenge.
    I sat there in the center of the monument
    With Lucifer and six other friends from my past.
    With everyone gathered and no one else to summon,
    Lucifer stood and walked around the circular marbled
structure.

He once again spoke of how my interactions
    With sin were successful and that
    God himself was pleased with me.
    He said that my transcriptions were accurate
    And related closely to my emotions.

With my memories reborn,

He believed that I was ready to receive my past life as well.
My confusion grew slightly
Until a memory deep within my mind
Crept forward to reveal a farm in a small valley.
The vision was beautiful to behold.
At first I did not recall the image,
But as I dwelled deeper into the concept,
I began to remember.

The vision was of my farm.
My emotions immediately prompted me to weep.
It was not sin.
It was not someone else's wheat field,
Blacksmith shop, cottage, city underground
Or vendor shop; it was simply real.

It was the first memory that did not confuse me
Nor offer me a stomach churning outcome.
It was merely my memory.
I saw the goats and other livestock roaming the nearby
fields.

The comfort that I felt soothed me beyond belief.
It saved me from the horrible ideology
That Lucifer was portraying.
At that moment,
Nothing else mattered to me,
But the return of my one true memory.
I held tight to it and observed every little aspect.
From the colors of the trees
To the temperature of the warm breeze.
I did not know what Lucifer had planned for me next,
But I was not going to let go of my farm.
A sensation of happiness came over me
That I had obviously not felt in a long period of time.
It was overwhelming and I did not care
What I must have looked like to the others who were there.

All of the previous visions Lucifer provided for me
    Brought about negative intentions,
    But the revelation of my farm was different.
    It gifted me with simple pleasure and contentment.

While I still swam in my sea of joy,
    Lucifer announced that he had gifted me
    With my life's memory so that
    I could truly interpret the path in which I intend to take.
    At that point, my mind was contemplating
    Everything that had recently bombarded it.
    I sat back down amid the group and
    Did not know what to think
    As my mind became a blank canvas with thoughts and
ideas.

Lucifer stated that I had been given
    A great task from God.
    I had met his expectations,
    But the Lord required one more choice from me.

My nerves began to twitch
    As I looked to each of the party members and
    The pain that they had caused me.
    What more did God want from me?
    My life had already been stolen and replaced with sinful
thoughts.
    Lucifer continued by saying
    That he was also like the others and
    That he too represented sin.
    He tightened his arms as massive
    Darkened wings extended from his back.
    His posture changed to be more comfortable
    As if he had broken from a confined molding.

He said that he too was a demon serving God.
    That he too was sent to me with a task in mind.
    I looked to him with caution in my eyes as

I was able to understand that sin was once again
approaching.

The others tempted me into sin and
    I was not aware until the deed was completed.
    Lucifer, on the other hand, foretold his intentions and
    Allowed me to properly think on my own
    Without the influence of riches or power.
    He did not try to overpower me
    With twisted words or demented beliefs.
    He made me believe that he and I were equal.
    I wanted to relieve him of his task
    As he had been so kind to me.

He said that it was time
    To make my final choice in the eyes of God.
    The clouds began to swirl overhead.
    I believed that God was watching me.

Any other person would have been intimidated,
    But I was not.
    I was confident in my past decisions.
    I was even more confident that I would serve God
    In Lucifer's task as well.

The final demon stated that my choice
    Would seal my fate and forge my destiny.
    He continued to say that there are now two paths
    Leading from the monument.
    One would take me to my farmland,
    The other would send me back to my cavernous cell
    To complete my journey with God.

The decision instantly infested
    My rational thought and devoured my dreams.
    He added that one path would deny
    My past sinful decisions and
    Allow me to live a common life

That would end in a common death.
The other path would allow me to take pride
In my sins and allow me to become immortal
While continuing to serve God.
I quickly became intimidated
By both Lucifer and God
As they awaited my choice.
By far, that was the most difficult decision I had to make.

All of the others failed in comparison
To the pressure being provided by the heavens.
I thought about each option.
My farm gifted me with the most comfort,
But the reality of life that would end in death
Did not appease me.
Whereas the trait of immortality
Was associated with the other choice.
One would allow me to live my own life
While the other had me be a servant to God.

I reflected upon my acts of sin
While I gazed to each of the associated participants.
They were each unique and highly skillful
In their tasks that my respect for them was abundant.

I looked deep into their eyes.
They did not try to persuade me anymore or tempt me.
They merely offered me a smile now.
I took that gesture as a sign of faith that they had in me.
A faith that I would make the right decision.

Each one of my encounters with them
Ended with betrayal, but it was not betrayal by them
That I experienced.
I had betrayed myself by accepting their temptations.
They merely provided me with an alternate path.
Not one of them forced me into a decision.
Not one of them made the choice for me.

I was disloyal to myself in each scenario and
Realized my weakness for sin.
I had made the choice of sin,
Most without hesitation.
It was my destiny.
To not sin was never an option for me.
My mind sought out the notion and allowed my body
To postpone through confusion and disagreement.
My mind would always conquer in the end.
I must follow my mind in my new task as well.
It was useless of me to deny my fate
As it was already written for me.
I just needed to accept it.

I stood proud for the first time in my life
    As I looked up the heavens.
    The clouds continued to twirl and dance around beautifully.
    God had already known what choice I was going to make.

The others stood and joined Lucifer
    With each of their eyes fixated on me.
    They knew my answer
    Before I even took the first step on one of the paths.

They could see it in my eyes.
    They could see it in my mannerisms.
    They all welcomed me to my new destiny
    With an appreciation of what I had accomplished.

I now felt a part of them with every breath that I took.
    I had the wrath from Amon,
    The greed from Mammon,
    The sloth from Belphegor,
    The gluttony from Beelzebub,
    The lust from Asmodeus,
    The envy from Leviathan
    And the pride from Lucifer
    All flowing freely through my veins.

They were my shadowy friends within my cave
Who protected me and guided me along my journey.
They kept me company when I was lonely.
They kept me forward thinking on my task when I retreated.

They never let me stray from the course.
    Their task was to deliver their respective sin,
    Display it before my eyes and they did so admirably.

They each broke my will
    In order for me to truly understand myself and
    Consider freedom in the eyes of God.
    Each provided me with necessary pain
    That weakened me to the point of death.

I know now that it had to occur.
    How else would I embrace my power
    If I did not lose all ambitions and strength?
    Only then would I be able to appreciate
    What was now bestowed upon me from the heavens above.
    My veins were pulsating with energy.
    I could hear the thoughts of my fellow comrades.
    They were pleased with me as their leader.
    Lucifer kneeled and bowed to me.
    Prompting the others to follow closely behind him.

I felt the power of God running through my veins,
    Draining me of my mortal life.
    The visions of my farmland
    Were overshadowed by the feeling of being reborn.

Lightning from the heaviest of clouds
    Streamed through the skies
    As if they were wild horses released from a cage.
    I had completed the six tasks portrayed to me and
    Gained God's acceptance.
    The only chore left was to walk the path
    That I had chosen and complete the seventh duty.

Empowered and full of life,
I walked slowly from the center of the monument
Between the marble columns where the two paths resided.
My comrades stood and watched me leave.
Each of them in their thoughts
Offered me a swift return and precise judgment.

I walked away from the monument
  Until I came to a split in the path.
  The crossroads served as my last chance
  Before my destiny took hold of me.

The seven demons had put so much faith into me that
  I could not live with myself if I let them down.
  God alone believed in me even
  Through the toughest of trials,
  He never altered his opinion of me.

I looked down the path to the right and
  Saw the faint vision of my farmland
  Complete with full livestock and vegetation.
  The image was serene and gifted me with a comfort
  That none could compare with.

I imagined the peace that would come
  With my farm and the tranquility
  The surrounding environment would provide,
  But I realized that the farm was not truly mine.
  Its sole purpose was to grant me with a safe haven
  Until God requested my service.

I did not own the farm or the animals in which I cared for.
  They were all depictions supplied by God.
  They neither enhanced my mind
  Nor benefited my character.
  The farm was more of a prison than the cave
  And offered me less satisfaction over time.

The vegetation and animals all belonged to God.
    I had no claim to them;
    They only served to distract my judgment
    As I awaited my destiny.
    I required everything from the farm.
    It gave me nothing but shallow memories of a past life
    That I did not understand.
    It was merely a play and I was the actor portraying God's
script.

I could not return to my slumbering life
    Of false ideas and unknowing thoughts.
    How would I live?
    With my friend of misery and partner of denial?
    I had traveled too far with a mind
    That was inflicted and altered against the shape of sin.

Sin was my only guide now.
    It took many encounters and choices in order to realize that.
    Peace was not something that I felt within my experience.
    To view the restful scene of the farm
    Was as if I was looking through a dense forest
    To find a wandering deer.

I could not understand serenity now;
    I could not understand a life of tranquility.
    To live in peace was to deny sin.
    To deny sin was everything against who I now was.
    I had embraced temptation with every demon.

My grip on sin was tight now and
    I could not let it fall
    Even for the most precious vision of my past life.
    It was a part of me now and I was a part of it.

I could not entrap sin within my soul and deny its exit.
    Doing so would destroy it.
    Sin was now my burden to carry; my burden to protect.

Denying it would not benefit either of us.
It feeds from me like a child to a mother and
I will provide for it like a father to a son.

It was the one true relic that I possess now.
    I will cherish it always and never leave its side
    As it was a personal token from God.
    I imagined my wisdom and courage would be tested.
    When that occurs I would rely on my friend
    To pull me from depression and
    Guide me through the storms of confusion.
    I will feed it my emotions and
    Allow it to devour my soul in order for it to grow and
prosper.

My farm served as my past life,
    One that helped me through my darkest hours
    Within the cave and for that I am always thankful.
    I disregarded the path with respect and
    Grasped the creativity of the landscape to enhance my fate.

I looked down the left path and saw my dirt infested cave
    Along with my trusty quill, stack of papers
    And the lone candle that provided me with protection.

The cave served as my alteration,
    My draining of the old to create room for the new.
    The cave broke me as a man,
    But developed me as something much more.

The torment was often too much for me to handle,
    I know now why it had to occur.
    The paths were completely different in their outcomes.
    As I stood at the threshold of the crossroads,
    I felt sin conjuring within me.

All of the desires that I needed pulled at my temptations.
    I could not resist them as they were a part of me now.

The rebellion that occurred within me
While standing at the gate of decision
Surpassed my capability of thought.
My comrades were calling me.
God was calling me; sin was calling me.
My past life was not.
I looked down the right path once more.
I saw that the vision of my farmland was fading.
It was growing weak both in imagery and within my mind.
Before it disappeared, I captured a small portion
That I would secure in my soul.

The goats that I so loved and admired
 Would be carried with me always.
 With that in place, I let my farm slip away
 As the path sealed up and was no longer an option.

The left path with its unpredictable
 Attitude and rotating vision lured me.
 What awaited me at the end of the path was unknown,
 But that was what I admired about it.

I grew accustomed to the confusion and
 Chaotic nature of my sinful world.
 The continuation of such a place would be a blessing.

While looking down the lone road,
 I saw my cavernous dwelling in the horizon.
 The place that I hated had become a visionary feast for my
eyes;
 A blessing in disguise.
 I longed to feel the warmth of the candle and
 The security of the quill within my hands.

With one foot I chose my destiny.
 It served as my first step towards my immortality;
 The continuation of my service to God.
 I no longer was a lone farmer.

I no longer had a home to call my own.
My home was with God; my life was with God.

I walked down the path
    With full confidence in my choice as
    I believed it was the only outcome.
    After all that I had experienced and seen
    In my trials of sin, I could not justify living a regular life
again.

My mind was damaged and beyond correction.
    I envisioned trying to live a normal life,
    The ideology of sin always showed the darker side of me.
    I would have died a man with a heart full of sin and
    God would not have been pleased with me.
    In order to control the sin, I had to live a life
    Where I could focus all of my attention towards it.
    I would feed the sin as if it were my pet and
    Allow it to run free in my surroundings.

The path proved to be longer
    Than I had imagined with plenty of twists and turns.
    The slow process of the journey
    Provided me an opportunity to reflect upon myself and
    All that I had recently remembered.

The reality that Lucifer had granted me
    Released my soul and I had finally felt content.
    I did not recall ever feeling so alive
    In either of my life situations.
    I believed God required more reassurance
    Of my choice as the path soon entered
    A valley where my farm resided.
    I stopped and looked to my farm not with sorrow,
    But with happiness
    That it would always be a part of my memories;
    That I could travel to it whenever I so desired.

The rolling fields would always
    Be lush and green in my vision,
    The trees would always sway in the wind.
    I had captured the scenery deep within my mind
    Where no one but me would be able to retrieve it.

Regardless of what my destiny had for me,
    I would always remember
    Where I had come from and the tragedies
    I endured along the way.
    I know God allowed me to cherish my farm
    As a gift for my good deeds.
    For that I would always be thankful.

A single goat roamed the nearby field.
    It ran to me when I caught her eye.
    She was not afraid of me or my touch.
    Her presence humbled me and pulled
    At the small amount of emotions that I had left.

I turned from her and continued to walk.
    God wanted me to remain modest and
    Keep a few sentiments as he allowed
    The goat to break free from my vision and become real.
    Followed closely by my new friend,
    I walked further down the path.

I soon encountered a wealthy man
    Dressed in extravagant clothing.
    His lifeless body was butchered by two blades
    Protruding from his chest as he lied upon a pile of gold
coins.
    With no hesitation, I pulled at the daggers.
    I believed that his cadaver was no home for such artifacts.
    I cleansed the blades with his silk robe and took them.

Traveling further, I arrived at a large wooden wall
    Littered with skeletons of the dead.

The vision did not startle me
Although the goat was a little intimidated.
I felt the wall that I had constructed and
Offered it no sorrow as to why it was erected.
Upon the ground was the empty vial
I grabbed the vial and left the vision behind.

My journey led me through two wheat fields
Being replenished with the oak irrigation system.
While walking, I ran my hand along
The grains of the wood and dipped my fingers
Into the cool stream of water.
I paused for a moment to allow for the goat to drink
And noticed a small slither of wood lying upon the ground.
I turned over the relic and saw the etching of a lion.
The artifact was to come with me,
I gathered it up and continued to walk.

The weather turned snowy and windy,
However, I did not feel the effects.
The path was covered with snow, and ice
Crystallized the trees on either side.
I came to several frozen corpses
Who were desperately trying to retrieve apples from a tree.
Their extended arms were frost bitten and a deep hue of
blue.
Their painful expressions and starvation
Were sealed perfectly upon their faces.
Only one frozen apple resided on the tree.
I easily plucked it from its limb and continued on my way.
I followed the path as it led me around a bend
Towards two bloody, beating hearts lying on a bed of roses.
The scene conjured up a heavy dosage of love within my
veins.
My heart pounded with emotion
As butterflies soared within my stomach.
I picked up a single red rose and continued on my way.

The path soon wrapped around the base of a large mountain.
The smell of fresh ore filled the air and carried me further.
I came across a barren wagon on the side of the path.
The back was all but empty except for a small piece of ore.
The symbol was beautiful in my hand and even made me smile.
Up a hill I traveled and at the summit was the marble monument.
I weaved in and out of the marble columns
Allowing my hands to glide over their smooth surfaces.
I halted when I felt an alteration in one of the columns.
A small portion of one of the columns was cracked.
Upon further investigation,
A chip of marble fell from its abode and into my hand.
I looked up to the clouds and offered a smile to God.

Armed with a relic from each of my memories,
I proceeded further into the unknown and
Edged along deep trenches and vast underground caverns
Led only by the hazy light of torches that aligned my path.
The dusty environment offered very little visibility,
But the closeness of the rocky walls
Allowed for me to funnel along.
The small tunnel exited
Into a wide cavern where a river resided.
The path took me onto a wooden bridge
That spanned the width of the river
And allowed me safe travel to the other side.

The turbulent current of the water was unpredictable.
It often violently shifted without warning.
The crests of the waves appeared to battle
One another for dominance of the current.

With no wind or environmental powers controlling the waves,
The river was just mystically upset.
The brutal shifting water followed me
With every step that I took upon the bridge.

Every sounding creak that the wooden planks
Made awoke more of the waves
Until I found myself dodging their onslaught.
I was concerned about the sturdiness of the bridge
As it began to get bullied by the river.
The splintered construction offered no resistance;
The rope handles provided no support.
I had to rely on the uneasy balance of my legs
To avoid being swallowed by the blackened water.

I was very content to be off of the bridge and
   Away from the shoreline of the river.
   The howls of the bloody current
   Echoed through the cavern and followed me
   For quite some time before finally fading
   Into the shifting sounds of the rocky walls.

I continued on through a few well lit tunnels
   And soon came to a small crevice.
   The darkness of the crack prompted me
   To seek out a torch, but I could not retrieve any.
   I tried several of them, but either my strength was not
enough
   Or I was simply not given permission to carry them.

I was not excited about entering into the crevice
   Without a light source as the sheer darkness
   Inside was tormenting and belittling me.
   I felt it laughing at me and testing my courage.
   Much like a wild animal observing its prey
   For a sign of weakness that could be used against it,
   The split in the wall was studying me.

In a sign of fear, the crevice spilled
   Its darkness upon me as if it was vomiting on me.
   I gave no physical reaction in return
   So that I would not appear afraid.

Apparently, I passed the test as
    The darkness gradually crept back inside.
    A moan of dissatisfaction exited as I shielded my eyes.
    I smiled at the challenge in an almost conquering demeanor.
    It was important for me to show the confidence in myself,
    Which had been building throughout my journey.

I touched the outer wall of the crevice
    To calm its nerves and reassure it that
    I was just passing through.
    My foot disappeared as I took a step into the darkness.
    The blackness was unlike anything I had seen before.
    My vision was useless and forced me
    To rely on my sense of awareness.
    Instead of wandering around aimlessly
    With my arms extended outwards,
    I closed my eyes and inhaled the darkness.

I felt it flowing through my body and filtering through my
heart.
    I did not resist it;
    I allowed it to become one with me.
    I allowed it to befriend me no matter
    What physical cost it wanted from me.
    The darkness left no portion of me untouched
    Both externally and internally.
    Every organ, every vein and every bone
    Was observed and devoured.
    After I felt the darkness exit me,
    I opened my eyes and could see.

My vision was improved.
    I held up my hand to touch the entity of dark.
    My act of kindness was well perceived
    As a howling breeze surrounded me.
    Exiting out of the crevice
    I found myself in a narrow cavern
    With a dirt path winding between two rivers of fire.

The rivers spit flames high up into the air.
As I walked along the path,
I réalized that the fire was celebrating.
Sparks flew within the air in a joyful spirit of happiness.
At a certain height, the sparks fizzled out
Leaving behind a cloud of smoke.
The illuminations ignited the cavern walls and
Bled the rocks with a red haze.
The scene was inspiring and beautiful to behold.
I had gained the respect of the water,
The darkness and now the flame.
Each one I offered my full respect in return.
I treated them as if they were each my offspring.

I held up my palms and allowed sparks to dance upon my skin.
They leaped back and forth from each hand
In a playful pattern that formed a smile upon my face.
I did not force their departure from me;
Instead I allowed them to decide how long
They wished to accompany me as I walked.
They soon leaped from me and rejoined the others in the
fire.

The next cavern I came to was a circular land mass
That rose up in the middle to create a small hill.
Atop was a plateau with seven marble-lined pits
That dove deep into the middle of the environment.
I knew what the hill wanted me to do.
I knew what it desired;
The sacrifice of my relics that I had collected.
One by one I dropped the artifacts into a respected pit.

I showed no hesitation, no remorse and
No self-doubt when unleashing my grip.
I banished the memories into the belly of the beast and
Unburdened myself from their clutches.
They no longer tempted me with sorrow;
They no longer entrapped me with unwanted desires.

They were simply gone.

With all of my possessions spent,
    One remaining empty pit remained.
    It was time for me to leap from the edge of sanity
    And return to my prison.
    I stood at the threshold of commitment and stopped.
    Another test, I imagined, to voluntarily enter the unknown.

My first encounter was out of my control,
    I now felt the power of the dirt filled sanctuary.
    I inhaled its essence as a wind pushed me
    From behind prompting me to enter.

The cave needed me as much as I needed it and
    I was not going to disappoint it.
    I stepped off of the ledge and fell
    Inside the darkness as it flowed over my body.
    It embraced me like a new child.

I landed graciously upon the familiar dirt floor
    In the safe radius ring of candlelight.
    The dust cloud from my landing encircled me
    And was joined by the blackness of the shadows
    That swirled around me and lifted me from the ground.

I closed my eyes and enjoyed the welcoming
    The cave was politely providing me.
    I witnessed myself being carried by the darkness
    Towards the candle that had lighted my journey for so long.
    I stepped down from my carrier and felt the dirt floor once
again.
    I was home.

IX

realization

I awoke from a splendid, restful sleep.
    The aches in my bones told me
    That I was on the ground for quite some time.
    They cracked and moved back into place as I stretched.

Normally, when I would awake,
    My mind had already been penetrated
    With various scenarios and visions,
    This time I had woke up merely in the cave
    Without a story to transcribe.

It was quite pleasant to have the understanding
    That I had arose within reality and not
    A predetermined scenario that would
    Most likely end drastically for me.

It was comforting to view my quill and paper
    As if I was being reunited with a long lost friend.
    They resided in the dirt like they had always done,
    Patiently awaiting my interaction.

I no longer have the sensation of boredom within the cave,
    Mainly due to my altered outlook on my life.
    I treasure the remaining time with my dirt room now
    As I know it will not last.
    I look to the shadows with kindness instead of worry.
    I look to the rocks as padding instead of bars.
    I cherish everything that the cave presents to me.

It had given birth to me, nourished me and
Fostered me when I needed protection.

I look at my abode in a unique way now as
I am finally able to understand it.
I appreciate it more than I did in the past.
It is my sanctuary;
My own piece of heaven provided by God himself.
It has everything that I desire.
The darkness, the dirt, the shadows, and the flame
Are my personal relics now and
I treat each with the fullest respect that I can conjure.
I am at peace with my surroundings and
Comfortable being alone in my dwelling of solitude.
My mind no longer races with thoughts and
Bombards me with confusion.
I am able to see clearly and conceptualize
My relationship with the cave.
Every crack in its stone wall is a scar on my body;
Every dust cloud is a breath of air within my lungs.

The cave is a reflection of me and I represent it.
It was not meant to entrap me and torture me.
It was meant to increase my understanding of who I truly
am.
It allowed me to free my mind and contemplate my inner
demon.
It was not meant to rob me of my past life and destroy
memories.
It was meant to awaken me.

With the candle illuminating the paper,
I am determined to finish the task that God has given me.
I have no new memory of which to transcribe so
I will entrust in my mind and within the quill
That they will work together to meet the demands.

God has only given me the memories

In which he wishes for me to remember.
For that I am grateful.
If I am not meant to know the whole tale,
I will take the small portion that I have received and be
content.

The balance between good and evil is a structure so
    Complicated that only he can truly understand it.
    He alone controls the scales and
    Never allows one side to tip too far
    As to plunge civilization into an endless trench.
    The humans will never
    Have the full wealth of the heavens.

They merely are balanced in their lives.
    I have been given an opportunity
    To test their behavior and tip the scales ever so slightly.
    I will not pull them to either side;
    I will merely offer suggestions and
    An alternate path that strays from God.

He will use my research for judgment and
    Decide their fate accordingly.
    I will not entrap the humans or seek to destroy them.
    I will simply lure them to me with my offerings of sin.

They will neither understand sin nor
    Realize what shape it is capable of portraying.
    They will have many questions as to what sin is.
    Some will seek guidance,
    But they will truly not comprehend the core of sin.
    I will misshape it and twist its meaning.
    I will feed off of the natural curiosity of the humans and
    Tease them with deception.
    When they want less, I will give them more.
    When they want more, I will take it away.
    When they lock me out of their mind, I will turn the key.
    When they push me away, I will pull them closer.

When they toss me aside, I will cling to them tighter.
When they ignore me, I will make myself more available.

I will be as much or as little in order to tempt them.
Some will require more of me than others.
Those that require less will be easy prey.

I will strike them first and infect their minds.
I will coil their concepts of the world and
Employ them to spread my disease.
I will harness their bodies and capitalize
On their social abilities to bring others to me.

I will be addictive and undeniable in my actions.
Once I have them, they will not stray far from me.
Some will repent against me, but I cannot be discarded.

Once inside, I cannot be cleansed; I cannot be destroyed.
Once inside, I will own them;
I will own their thoughts and control their minds.
Once inside, I will turn their minds against their bodies and
Decay their bones with methods of betrayal and hatred.
My darkness will slowly devour
Their soul and plague their beliefs.
They will question God's authority and existence;
At which point they will be lost.
I will deliver the lost souls to God
Where they will experience his sheer power of judgment.
The more souls I deliver, the more I prosper.

Those who stay true to the faith of God
Will do so with my respect.
Let it be known that I will
Attack faith with severe hardship and suffering.
Only a dedicated mind will be able to outlast my battle.
Only a true soul will be able to deny all of me.
That soul will be free of sin and
Allowed into the heavens after death.

It will not be an easy task
    As I will know every desire,
    Every need that tempts man.
    I will surround myself with a cloud of confusion and
    Use the darkness to promote fear.

I will concentrate on those
    Who have a strong belief system and
    Unleash my entire arsenal to alter their path.
    If required, I will revisit to fulfill my needs.

I will not stop until I obtain what I seek.
    The souls of the humans will be shattered
    Under my clutches and splattered
    With my diseased notions and ideas of betrayal.

Some will admire my work and accept it as their own.
    Those who follow me will be spared
    The full span of my evil, but they will do
    As I say and aide me in spreading the shadows.
    They will convince others and lure them to me.
    They will speak of me as a God,
    But I am no God.
    My servants will carry on my evilness
    Even when I am not there.
    I will rule over the other demons and
    Work with them to alter their sins
    To best suit the human population.

Not every human will see
    All of the demons as I predict
    That their weak minded souls will only desire
    One sin before my name passes through their lips.
    Those who prove to be stronger willed
    Will be visited by more until they kneel before me.
    There will come a time when my sin
    Will blanket the planet and all who dwell upon it.

At that time, all will question themselves
And reflect upon their lives to decide whether they have
sinned.
The answer will be yes.
Everyone will sin regardless of their age, sex and beliefs.
I will make sure that sin is a common practice
In the daily rituals of the humans.
Avoiding it will be an impossible task that many will fail
To see and few will understand.

Those who sin will know.
They will try to deny their actions
In order to please God.
They will try to repent of their sin
Even as they face death, but God will not hear you.

He will not be the one hearing your prayers.
He will not be the one to decide your salvation.
I will be the one who hears your prayers.
I will be the one to decide your salvation.

Once you sin, your soul belongs to me.
The path that I will create and gift to you
Will not lead to the heavens.
You will not find everlasting peace and tranquility
Within my gardens of devastation.

If a human denies all aspect of my sin
And all of my temptations,
I will leave them alone and
Allow them to journey their path towards God.

If in my observation I find one small glimmer of doubt,
I will feed it and grow it like a seed
In a freshly plowed field.
I will be there to water it and nurture it
So that it will blossom into an aura of full potential.

I will not ignore any thought of doubt
    Regardless of its size, scope or intention.
    I view doubt as an unlatched door and
    I will enter through it every time I see it within a human.
    I go forth into the world with the idea
    That all humans can be tempted and
    I will test my concept accordingly.

God works in unforeseen ways.
    It is useless to try to understand his meaning
    As even in my position I cannot comprehend.
    I was chosen for a simple task
    That proved difficult for me to complete.

The tortures that punished my mind
    Still reside inside me, but I do not fear them.
    I do not fear my past, my present or my future,
    For it is what creates me as a being.

During my encounters, I believed
    That I was a carpenter, a blacksmith,
    A farmer, a peasant and even a prophet.
    My life was complete in every detail and
    Portrayed equally through my mind.

In reality, I was none of them.
    That was not what God intended for me to be.
    I now realize that I was born into sin.
    My farm provided me contentment so I would not leave.
    I was bred for sin and although at first I discarded it,
    I now know that it is a part of me.
    My life did not begin on the farm,
    It began within this cave.
    God believed in me even when I doubted him,
    Even when I angered him.
    I will serve him now as I had done throughout my journey.
    I will see to it that his demands are met.

I have much to thank God for.
    He released me from a life of lies and
    Opened my eyes to see my true self.
    Much like he has done for the other demons,
    He has also done for me.

He halted my life dream
    Allowing for my inner demon to step forward.
    He allowed me an understanding
    Taught by Lucifer so that my mind
    Would not suffer between what was real and what was
portrayed.

Although I dreaded most of my demon friends
    During my encounters with them,
    They each now have my full respect
    For succeeding in their given tasks.
    I learned patience, understanding
    And the art of luring from each of them.
    I learned to balance my frustration, denial
    And self-pity through their evil methods.
    I also learned what my mental and physical limits are.

They guided me to near death
    And pushed me to the edge of insanity.
    They invaded my mind with their sin
    Allowing me to use it to develop my own outcome.

They each showed me an alternate path that
    I willingly walked down.
    They never accompanied me
    As they allowed me to live through the results of my
choices.
    They never responded to my questions,
    Never tried to make me realize
    Why I opted to choose the sin.
    They merely told me that I had done well,
    That they were proud of my actions.

After that, they simply left and
Provided me with the opportunity to be alone
With my decisions and encounter the fate of my actions.

The cave is pleased with me
As my shadowy friends have all returned.
I no longer try to protect myself from them
As they are now my comrades.
There is one question that I do have.
Why are there eight shadows that lurk around me?
Have I not met one of the demons?
As with everything, I am positive that God
Will enlighten me when the time is appropriate,
But that does not stop me from pondering.

The shadows are relaxed and are not so frigid around me now.
They seem to dance and play
Within the cave in a celebrative fashion.
I try to read who was who amongst them,
But they move so fast in and out of the darkness
That it makes it quite difficult.

Regardless, the shadows seem very content
To be in my presence and I with them.
I had always admired them when they were here.
They provided me with a sense of belonging
During my periods of severe mental isolation.

They served as my visions of hope
When I doubted myself,
As my sounds of inspiration when the cave was silent.
Most importantly, I had always seen them as my friends.
I do not believe I would have survived my task
If I were truly alone.
The solitary confinement would have been
Too much of a burden on me in my already fragile state.
For that, I owe them each my gratitude for appearing
Within the cave when they did.

From the darkness, Amon appeared and
    Greeted me with only a smile.
    No words were spoken;
    Instead she merely collected her shadow,
    Bowed before me and entered back into the darkness.
    Mammon soon appeared and gathered up his shadow.
    To be honest, I wanted to tear the flesh from his bones,
    In a respectful manner of course
    For the pain he put my body through.
    Yet I withheld my powers as he was now my friend.

Belphegor appeared next and took his shadow as well.
    The spirits of the demons that looked over me
    Were going back with their owners
    As their duties have been completed.

Beelzebub arrived next followed by
    Asmodeus and Leviathan.
    Finally, one of the masterminds
    Behind the creation of the different scenarios
    Strolled out of the darkness.

Lucifer showed himself and
    Nodded his head to me out of respect.
    I predicted working closely with him
    As his collective creative imagination
    Would be quite useful to me.
    One of the last two shadows absorbed into him.
    He told me that we will do well in our new tasks.
    He bowed before me and backed into the darkness.
    One shadow remained and I was to claim it.
    God had broken my spirit prior to me entering the cave.
    I understood that aspect of my tenure here
    As an intact spirit would be more difficult to control.

I could not have had the success
    I obtained with my spirit in control of my mind and body.

I stood with my quill in hand and approached the shadow.
I could tell it was eager to rejoin with me,
But it was also hesitant as I had undergone changes.

I held out my hand as it accepted me back as its host.
    The spirit was too weak to tempt me with goodness.
    Instead, my mind lured it towards the sin and entrapped it.
    The only option I offered it was to join me in my quest.
    It graciously accepted without concern.

It proved to be my first successful temptation to sin and
    It would not serve as my last.
    With my shadow consumed, I felt whole.
    With the concepts of a false livelihood and portrayed
encounters,
    I felt hollow inside.
    My own shadow has illuminated me and
    Refilled my lungs with the breath of fulfillment.

As I write this, the cave walls and ceiling are trembling.
    Dust is filling the area making it difficult to see.
    I am not sure as to what is behind this,
    But something demands my attention.

I am struggling to write as the ground
    Is no longer supportive.
    I have collected the paper, quill and candle
    And have huddled against the far wall of the cave
    To avoid getting hit by falling rocks.

There is no calmness in the cave
    As every grain of dirt is being dislodged and
    Shifted to another destination.
    My balance is being tested;
    However I am holding my stance strong.
    The movement of the ground shifts my feet
    Making it difficult to dig my toes within the dirt for support.

I dare not move as I do not wish
  To get struck from the tumbling rocks.
  Instead, I opt to stay within the comfort zone of the candle
and
  Take my chances with my body becoming unstable.
  The random fluctuation of the intensity is unpredictable.
  At certain moments the trembling is but a low growl.
  Other times it is much too intense to describe.
  It pushes my papers and makes my writing barely legible.
  I do not know what God is doing to the cave,
  I assure myself that much like everything else,
  There is a reason behind the madness.

The destroyed walls of the cave have lost many rocks
  In the process and have changed
  The characteristics of my abode greatly.
  I now sit inside a rattled cave that is completely
  Filled with loose dirt and dust.

The atmosphere has ridden my eyes and mouth
  Of any moisture and makes it somewhat hard to see and
breath.
  The trembling has now subsided,
  But something more extraordinary had taken its place.

A few moments after the dust settled,
  A large crack appeared in one of the cave walls.
  The crack began in the middle and etched
  Its way downward then upward.

Large portions of the wall were loosened
  Allowing them to fall to the ground.
  A bright light leaks into the darkened cave
  With every piece of rock that was removed.

Right now, the wall is being split
  As if someone is prying apart the solid rock structure.

The power of the shifting rock walls is quite a remarkable
feat.
    The light that is filling the cave is violently
    Blinding me to the point where I
    Can only open them for a short period of time.

When the light was no longer my enemy,
    I peered through the new open crevice and
    Saw the lush landscape of the outside environment.
    The rolling green valleys meeting
    With the snowy mountain ranges
    Against the blue sky was an energizing vision.

It served as my first taste of freedom
    Within my new life and
    No one would take this memory away.
    I took my time observing the world
    Through my altered eyes and saw the horizon in a different
way.

With no more crossroads in front of me and
    A clear path leading to my destiny,
    I stood at the verge of the cave and my eternal life.
    Of all the tasks that were handed to me,
    The one that stands before me now
    Proves to be the most difficult.

The unknowing about the real world
    Offers me a heavy burden and
    A conscience that is riddled with questions.
    Am I truly capable of unleashing sin?
    How will the human population react to my demoralization?

These are but a few questions that hide within my mind.
    The fact that I will never know the answers to them
    Does not destroy the words, but rather allows them to grow.
    I do not wish to take on the persona of a weak minded
servant

In the eyes of the Lord.

However, I cannot deny my concerns.
    They are real and justified.
    I only wish to gain more knowledge
    In order to succeed at my task.

I realize through my past situations that
    I will answer my own questions with my own actions.
    That process only frustrates my eagerness to know,
    But it is logical in its message.
    The darkness of the cave has all but vanished.
    My own shadow remains and is strong in appearance
    Against the entering sunlight.
    The candle that once provided me with protection
    Against the shadows offers no additional light source
    And is weakened against the sun.

The once strong relic of light that inspired me
    Through my journey has been reduced
    To a mere flameless smoke stream
    That snakes upward to the ceiling of the cave.
    My new light source and inspiration
    Has been replaced by the sun.
    I will seek my courage from it and
    My evilness from the moon.
    They will guide me and provide me light
    Within the vast darkness of the planet.

My time within the cave is nearing its end.
    The light from the sun has wrapped around me and
    I sense that it is pulling me towards the outside.
    My candle is no longer lit;
    My quill barely allows me to write.

My stay within the very place
    Where I have been reborn
    Will soon end and my journey

Through life will begin.

I feel sorrow about leaving my abode
    As I view it as my true home,
    But I shall find a different dwelling amongst the humans.
    I will live as they live and survive as they survive
    In order to truly understand my prey.
    I am eager to start, but hesitant to begin.

Before I venture outside and begin my quest,
    I will write one last passage out of respect for God,
    The cave, the quill and the paper.
    Let it be known to all who read this,
    That after I complete my next entry,
    I will have stepped out into the light of the sun
    With a full understanding as to what God has asked of me.
    I will fulfill my destiny with him.
    Please him with my resounding commitment to serve him.
    I do not know how I will begin
    As I am exiting the cave with simply my clothes.
    I have no tools to assist me,
    Only my memories of past events.

I will summon my fellow demons and
    We shall unleash our sins upon the world
    As we have been instructed to do.
    We shall not disgrace the name of the Lord.
    We shall not shame the name of the Lord
    By avoiding his demands and failing in our obligations.
    We shall not ignore the name of the Lord
    By settling when we should be increasing our outcome.
    We shall not deny the name of the Lord
    By overlooking those who are capable of sin.

Instead, we shall carry the name of the Lord
    Within every torment, every hardship, every disaster,
    Every catastrophe and every sin that we hand deliver.
    We will work fluently and precise in our actions

In order to increase our efforts.
We will prove to you that we are fully
Capable of carrying out your task
That you have demanded of us.
We will meet your expectations and venture beyond them.
My comrades and I will do all of this
Within your name and will not stop until we
Have met your ultimate demands as we are all your
servants.
    With all that I have written and all that I have experienced,
    I grip my friend and will begin my last passage within the
cave:

Lord, provide me with guidance so that I may
    Fulfill your vision of me.
    Please do not hide from me when I seek you
    As I only wish to serve your needs.

I will use my immortality to serve you for eternity.
    My only wish is that I do not disappoint you.
    Give me the strength and courage to greet my destiny
    With a welcoming, gentle hand.

Give me the wisdom to guide my fist of judgment in a swift
manner.
    Subdue my inner remorse and deplete my pity
    So that I may focus on the task at hand.
    Unleash my inner demons so that they may steer my ship
    Through the approaching storms.
    Guide my sails so that I may reach my destination.
    Give me the creativity to conjure the hardships,
    Disasters and catastrophes to use at my disposal.
    Provide me with strict discipline
    So that I may stay true to the path that you have blazed for
me.

Allow me to transfer my pain to the humans with accuracy.
    Allow me the patience to never stray from your words and

To never question your authority.
Provide me with humbleness so that my power
Never overshadows my work.

Let my eyes see the inner spirits of the humans
So that I may seek the proper execution of my sins.
Give me the intelligence to focus and
The stealth to stalk so that I may blend with the population
And corrode the wheels of their structure.

Give me the ability to rule over my fellow demons
And demand their excellence as you have done by me.
I will empower them and utilize their individual abilities
To sweep darkness across the land.

Allow me to feed from the night;
To inhale the chill of evilness that lurks within.
Give me the jurisdiction to rule all those
Who will follow me and unite those who will know my
name.

Allow me the ideology to torment
Those who banish me and
Safe passage through any barrier
They may establish around their souls.

The Lord has challenged me once more.
This time my task will coincide with my chosen destiny.
All of my relationships with sin will be put to use
As I venture out of the cave and into the human society.

I will seek the weak minded and infect them.
I will lure them into my darkened cave and twist their
thoughts.
I will appear to them in their dreams and embrace them.

I will destroy their patience with wrath,
Their charity with greed,

Their diligence with sloth,
Their temperance with gluttony,
Their chastity with lust,
Their kindness with envy and
Their humility with pride.

I will visit you within your darkest hour,
    I will visit you when you believe that God does not hear
you.
    I will visit you when you are depressed and confused.
    I will visit you when your life is in question.
    I will visit you when your faith has failed you.
    I will provide the comfort for which you so desire,
    As I was once like you.

I know that life suffocates and drains your energy;
    I will be there to replenish your soul.
    I will be the thorn in your heel and the cane
    That supports you as you walk along your path towards
God.
    Many will not see the heavens
    As their temptations will not allow it.
    You will not walk alone through the valley of darkness
    As I will answer your questions along the way.
    I will open your eyes and allow the shadows to consume
you.
    Your society is eager for my arrival.
    Your society craves an alternative
    To the glorious acceptance of God.

By allowing me entrance,
    You unconditionally relinquish your soul to me.
    I will collect and discard them as I please
    For I will be your judge and jury.
    Your fate will be sealed without the possibility of release.
    I cannot promise a salvation of peace and prosperity
    For I am not the keeper of the heavens.
    My ruling will be one of hardship and insecurity

So that all who come to me will know
The consequences of their actions.

Some will beg for forgiveness,
But I am incapable to hearing prayers.
I cannot hear the self-pity and remorse
That will spill from the mouths of the weak.

I will seek out the fragile and reduce the strong.
There is no human mind that I will not touch.
The equality of my disease will infect the old and young,
Male and female without transparency.

Society will begin to judge you
On how much of a relationship you will have with me.
They will banish you, but their actions
Will only bring you closer to me
As I will listen and understand your frustrations and
concerns.

My kingdom of sorrow will have no walls.
It will have no limitations to access.
My kingdom will be an open, ever changing
Environment that will embrace the abnormal
And provide shelter for the discouraged.

It will not have gates leading to tranquility and peace.
Instead, it will have an open tunnel leading to
Your endless turmoil and everlasting hate.
It will be the curiosity of the unknown
That will bring them to me, not the teachings of prophets.
It will be their lack of understanding
That will tempt them to take the first step upon my path.
It will be their resentment towards society
That will have them progress further.
Their destination will frighten them
As they get closer to me and some will try to escape,
But I will always be there to herd them back into my palms.

Their fleeing tactics will amuse me
As I will provide them with a vision of freedom.

As their minds contemplate a victorious
    Return to the path of God, I will punish them greatly
    With my arm hammer of vengeance
    So that doubt in my power no longer exists.
    I will cherish watching them
    Scurry away from me and will enjoy
    Crushing their hopes and dreams upon their return.

Everyone will have a choice as I did.
    Your fate will be determined by how
    You perceive the choice and what option you select.
    You will have many encounters with me and
    My demons will offer you several choices.
    Choose wisely, as it only takes one temptation
    To place you within my grasp.

One slip upon the steep, icy path to God
    Will have you plummeting down
    Where I will catch you as you fall.
    Within the confines of my acquaintance,
    You will believe everything that I portray to you;
    Everything that I fill your dreams with.

You are mine and exist
    For the sole purpose of meeting my demands.
    Only God can save you from my clutches.
    It will be unlikely as your initial denial of him
    Is what sent you to me in the first place.
    My pit of despair will be filled
    With those who cling to the edge;
    Those who try desperately to scale its walls
    In hopes to prove their faith to God,
    But I will be there to deny their escape and
    Drag them further down into the abyss.

The walls will tell stories of those who try to return
    To the heavens, but they will all end
    In torment and ignorance.

    I will entrap them so that all who pass
    Will hear their moans of agony and
    Their pleas for forgiveness.

Whereas those who walk the path of God
    Focus on acceptance, the travelers on my path
    Will dwell in defiance.
    It is a simple choice that all will have,
    But the question will be hidden
    Around every corner and invisible to the eye.

You will not see sin, but it will always watch you.
    You will not seek out sin, but it will always find you.
    You will not want sin, but it will always desire you.

Some will worship me, while others may not.
    Some will believe in my existence, while others will deny it.
    Some will summon me, while others will be sought after.
    Some will sacrifice themselves, while others will avoid me.

Regardless of the individual outcomes,
    All will live in sin; all will know me.
    All will know my name.
    I am evil. I am demon. I am sin.
    My name is Satan.

K. Trap Jones is an award winning horror author of literary horror novels and short stories. With a strong inspiration from Dante Alighieri and Edgar Allan Poe, his passion for folklore, classic literary fiction and obscure segments within society lead to his creative writing style of "filling in the gaps" and walking the line between reality and fiction. He is also a member of the Horror Writer's Association. More information can be found at www.ktrapjones.com.

www.ingramcontent.com/pod-product-compliance
Lightning Source LLC
Chambersburg PA
CBHW022139170626
46807CB00005B/1993